Holy. Sl
Non
could h:
Novak

releasing all of his violence d
me in the doorway, but Novak ɪɪᴀu.

And he'd held my gaze with each swallow. Each pump of his hand. Each spurt of pleasure.

I shivered.

He still watched me now, his startling eyes radiating satisfaction and amusement. He'd held me captive with those icy irises, forcing me to watch every sensual reaction of his climax.

Auric finally found me in the doorway, his expression shifting from violent pleasure to just plain violence as he released a curse under his breath.

Novak merely grinned, then drew the back of his thumb along his bottom lip before effortlessly rising to his feet. He started to shower as Auric grabbed our cell's only towel.

My throat went dry as Novak began lathering the soap along his torso, his irises seeming to freeze me in place.

I couldn't stop staring.

I *needed* to stop staring.

But, golden gates, that'd been unlike anything I'd ever experienced. It had my thighs clenching with inexplicable need, something I knew Novak could smell because he made a show of inhaling deeply.

Auric cursed again, stepping in front of me. "Turn. Around."

Two words.

Snapped under his breath.

And underlined in a fury that made my blood run cold.

Noir Reformatory

FIRST OFFENSE

USA TODAY BESTSELLING AUTHORS
LEXI C. FOSS   J.R. THORN
WRITING AS JENNIFER THORN

Noir Reformatory: First Offense

Editing by: Outthink Editing, LLC

Proofreading by: Jean Bachen

Cover Photography: Wander Aguiar

Cover Models: Jacob Cooley, Sam, and Kerry Smart

Cover Design: Covers by Juan

Title Page Design: FrostAlexis Arts

Published by: Ninja Newt Publishing, LLC

Print Edition

ISBN: 978-1-954183-09-4

To Alexis, for bringing two cover addicts together. We're forever grateful for you <3

Noir Reformatory

FIRST OFFENSE

Trapped in a world of sin and sexy alpha angels.
Forever defined by my black wings.

My father, King of the Nora, sent me to Noir Reformatory to atone for crimes I didn't commit.

So what's a girl to do? Escape, obviously.

Except I need allies to accomplish that feat and no one wants anything to do with King Sefid's daughter. If anything, my claim to the throne has only made running that much harder, and worse, I'm stuck with two hot angels standing in my way.

Auric is my supposed guardian, his white wings marking him as my superior in this deadly playground. Only, I'm his princess and I refuse to bow to a warrior like him.

And Novak, the notorious *Prison King*, is hell-bent on teaching me my place. Which he seems to think is beneath him. In his bed.

This prison resembles a training camp for soldiers more

than a reformatory for the Fallen. I suspect something nefarious is at play here, but of course, no one believes me. I'm the guilty princess with black wings. Well, I'll prove them all wrong. I just hope it isn't too late.

My name is Princess Layla.
I'm innocent.
And I do not accept this fate.

Note: Noir Reformatory is a dark fantasy ménage romance spanning six novels. There will be cliffhangers, adult situations, violence, and MM/MF/MMF content.

Suggested Reading Order:

Noir Reformatory: The Beginning — A standalone prequel to the Noir Reformatory universe
Noir Reformatory: First Offense
Noir Reformatory: Second Offense
Noir Reformatory: Third Offense
Noir Reformatory: Fourth Offense
Noir Reformatory: Fifth Offense
Noir Reformatory: Final Offense

PROLOGUE

AURIC

"LAYLA HAS FALLEN."

Three words. A statement. One I'd refused to believe until I saw the proof in her black feathers.

I stood in her doorway, stunned by the sight of all those ebony plumes.

King Sefid was right. His daughter had Fallen.

Oh, Lay, what have you done? I wanted to ask her, but I was too stunned to speak. Too furious to move. Too enraged to trust my own voice.

I knew something was wrong when the king requested a midnight meeting. But this was worse than wrong. It was catastrophic. Life-destroying. Lethal.

The future queen of my kind had sinned so horribly that her wings had turned black, marking her as an infamous Noir. And it was now my job to help her reform. To guard her. To ensure no one harmed her while she underwent reformation.

A task I wouldn't wish upon my worst enemy.

But the king had requested it as a personal favor.

"You're the only one I can trust to guard her."

A bold statement, considering our history. However, I wasn't one to refuse my liege. Nora Warriors always bowed.

So I accepted my new assignment. Which was what brought me to her door now.

"Auric!" Her blue eyes sparkled with excitement, her cherry blossom scent circling me in a claiming stroke that nearly undid my resolve. It served as a pungent reminder that she'd entered her courtship season to find a mate.

Then she hugged me.

Like her wings weren't a shade of startling black.

Like she'd done nothing wrong.

It sickened me that she could be so oblivious to the pain she'd caused everyone around her. She'd defied us all. Threatened her royal placement. And for what?

I refused to ask.

I refused to listen.

I refused to *hug*.

"Let go," I snapped.

She stilled against me, her slender shoulders curving ever so slightly. "S-sorry," she whispered, releasing me far too slowly. "It's just been a while since—"

"Do you think I'm here to chat?" I demanded, arching a brow. "I don't want to talk to you. I don't want to see you. I don't even want to be near you. But you've made that impossible, *Princess*. Now pull your wings into your back. These men are here to strap those ugly feathers down. Then we'll be on our way."

"I..." She frowned. "On our way?" She blinked at the two Nora Guards behind me, their bulky size similar to my own. "Auric, I don't understand."

"You don't need to understand," I replied. "Prep her."

I stepped aside, allowing them entry.

Layla stumbled backward. "Auric, what's going on? I don't... I—"

"Snap your despicable wings in, or they will do it for

you," I informed her, already bored by her crude act. As if I would ever consider her an innocent again.

"M-my wings?" she repeated, then flared the plumes wide instead of doing as I instructed. Her lips parted as the ebony tips came into view, and just for a moment, I wanted to believe her shock.

But I knew better.

Nothing she could say would save her from this fate. Her father had forgone the trial to keep this out of the public eye. As far as everyone else would know, she'd gone on a long vacation somewhere to continue her training for the crown in private.

"Oh gods," she breathed. "Oh, Auric, you have to—"

"I don't have to do anything," I corrected. "Now tuck in your wings. Last warning."

"I haven't done anything wrong!" she exclaimed, backing up to the wall beside her bed. "I'm innocent!"

Like I hadn't heard that from other Noir before.

Despicable angels.

And now Layla was one of them.

Fucking perfect, I thought, stalking toward her to grab hold of one wing and shove it into place. I was done playing nice. She would submit. She would behave. She would reform. And then, I would be done with her once and for all.

CHAPTER ONE

LAYLA

WHITE WINGS.

Everywhere.

In the cockpit. The aisles. Next to me.

But not behind me. No, my wings were black. Something everyone else on this plane had made abundantly clear when they strapped me into this damn chair.

No trial.

No questions.

No chance to ask for remorse.

Just an old guard—whom I once considered a friend—showing up to deliver a sentence.

Noir Reformatory.

My fate.

The plane's engines thrummed in time with my pulse. Fast. Hard. Terrifyingly *loud.* I couldn't control it, my heart fluttering inside my chest with the fury of a thousand wings.

Every part of me shook from head to toe.

Including my legs, something I realized when Auric's hot palm landed on my bare skin.

He shoved my thigh down, ceasing the nervous motion, and glared at me from behind a curtain of long blond strands. "Deal with your emotions, Princess. Or I'll deal with them for you."

Electricity danced along my limbs.

I used to crave Auric's touch.

Not anymore. Not since he was assigned as my personal warrior guard on this mission to *reform*.

I jerked my leg free from his hard fingers and scooted as far away from him as I could. Which wasn't far, thanks to the strap securing me and my black wings to my seat.

How is this my life? I wondered for the millionth time. *What have I done to deserve this?*

Auric blew out a long-suffering breath, his flinty, turquoise gaze leveled at the armed guards near the front of the plane. I could feel his irritation as plainly as I could smell his evergreen scent. It wrapped around me like a warm blanket.

A complete contradiction.

He was harsh, cold, and dismissive.

Yet he reminded me of home.

The duality was maddening.

"I've done nothing wrong, Auric," I said for probably the hundredth time. "Come on. You *know* me. This is all some sort of mistake."

He rolled his head on the seat rest to look at me. So beautiful with his smooth, unblemished skin, those delicate blond strands of hair, and an angular face that looked as if the gods themselves had sculpted every valley. But his expression remained remote. As distant as if the entire ocean beneath the plane separated us rather than six inches of battered vinyl seat.

He said nothing and looked away again. Dismissing me. Ignoring me. Not believing me. Just like everyone else.

My throat tightened.

6

Auric and I had been close, once upon a time. But playing the role of my Royal Guard had possessed an entirely different meaning back then. His absence had changed me, had changed us both.

To see him again like this... I bit my lip. This wasn't *my* Auric—the one I'd fantasized about for years—but a stranger.

When I'd hugged him earlier, there'd been no familiarity. No kindness. No emotion.

He wasn't my guard anymore but a warden assigned to fix the broken princess.

And now he hates me, I thought, my stomach twisting as I gazed out the tiny porthole window.

My reflection didn't match my new role as prisoner— aside from the black wings strangled by the leather straps that cut into my feathers. The secured ends wrapped around my shoulders, digging into my exposed skin in a pointless effort to keep me flightless.

Like I had anywhere to go inside this tin can.

The plane heaved as we took a turn, mocking me as the motion sent Auric's intoxicating wintergreen scent rolling over me. I inhaled, finding a sliver of comfort in what his presence used to mean to me. If I didn't look at his stoic, perfect face, I could pretend he still respected me. I could imagine we were back home in the castle, talking and laughing like we used to.

This was all a dream. A nightmare.

A guard shoved his way to the cockpit, conversing through the plume of white feathers with the pilots, then straightened. His gaze landed on me as he ambled up the aisle, stopping right next to Auric.

"Yeah?" Auric sounded bored, his eyes having fallen

closed at some point in the last few minutes. Maybe he didn't want to look at me either.

"Ten minutes 'til we reach the reformatory," the guard said gruffly. His gray gaze slid to me. "We're a thousand miles from the nearest landmass. I'd suggest you follow orders once we remove your bindings, Princess Layla."

I glowered, then fought off a shiver as his eyes drifted down to my cleavage. Because yeah, I wasn't dressed in prisoner garb like the others. Instead, I wore an outfit meant for the court—a gauzy white top, gold shorts, and high-heeled sandals with bands that laced all the way up my calves. I'd selected that outfit before realizing today's itinerary included a plane full of male Nora Guards.

Including the one in front of me, who still hadn't removed his gaze from my breasts.

Great. Just flippin' great.

"Message received and understood." Auric didn't open his eyes, but he slid his dagger half an inch from its sheath, causing the steel to glint in the low light beaming down from overhead. "Now move it along, Hawk. Don't make me draw blood before we even land."

I envied his ability to be so in command like that. All muscular grace with not a hint that he felt threatened or incapable, even while seated with his feathers up against a wall.

I wasn't sure I'd ever be able to close my eyes again.

The guard grunted and stalked off with a sour look on his face, presumably to bark orders at the rest of the cabin to overcompensate for his insignificant status. No matter the color of my wings, I still outranked his sorry ass.

I wrapped my arms around my middle and slouched in my seat. "You'd think they'd never seen a woman before."

"Many of them haven't," Auric replied, though he still

didn't open his eyes. "At least not for a very long time. It's incredibly rare for one of the female Nora to *Fall*." He uttered that last part with a sneer, making me flinch.

"Don't talk to me like that," I said, my voice strained. "I didn't do anything wrong, Auric. I swear. There's been some sort of mistake."

He snorted and said nothing else.

A tear threatened my eye, but I forced it away with a blink.

Feeling sorry for myself wasn't going to fix this. And obviously, talking to Auric wouldn't either.

Because no one believed me, not even my childhood friend.

After years of being the perfect princess, of doing everything I was told, learning all my royal duties, and spending endless time indulging the suitors my father had chosen for me, my parents tossed me away like trash. They hadn't even given me the courtesy of a goodbye. No, they'd sent my former guard to my quarters to whisk me away like some dismissed servant.

Huffing a breath, I glanced out the window and frowned as we began our descent at a rather sharp angle. "Um, Auric? Are we supposed to—"

The plane shuddered, cutting me off. Then our world began to turn... turn... *turn*...

I grabbed the armrests on either side of me, tensing at the wrongness of being trapped inside a flying tin can with my wings handicapped behind me.

"It's called turbulence," Auric remarked dryly. "Chill."

"Easy for you to say," I managed to reply through gritted teeth. My knuckles turned white from my death grip on the armrests.

Wrong.

Wrong.

Wrong.

After a few more minor shudders, the plane steadied at its new, lower altitude, but the uneasy sensation in my stomach remained. I preferred control, especially when in flight. I had wings for a reason. And this metal death trap didn't even have feathers.

"Inmates!"

I jerked at the sudden shout, and my palm slipped off the armrest onto Auric's thigh. Heat caressed my cheeks as I yanked my hand back to my lap, then shifted my attention to the guards at the front of the plane.

A red-haired Nora Guard with piercing green eyes and shining white wings surveyed the cabin. He gripped a rifle to his chest, his finger resting dangerously close to the trigger.

"On your feet," the guard barked. His tone indicated that if anyone failed to comply, he wouldn't hesitate to shoot them.

Lovely.

Auric clicked the buckle on my seat belt, granting me partial freedom. Then he slid smoothly from his seat to stand in the aisle and stared back at me without offering any additional assistance. With my wings so tightly bound at my back, my center of balance had vanished. I placed my hands on the armrests and shoved against them to leverage my body upright.

Just as the plane pitched forward again.

My knees buckled, and I fell forward, stumbling into Auric's chest. He caught me by my elbows, but not fast enough to keep my chin from slamming into his collarbone. He grunted and shoved me upright, barely giving me a second to stabilize myself before letting me go.

"Sorry," I muttered and tried to rub the tingling sensation from my skin. His touch always made me feel jittery, even more so now in this confined space.

A guard appeared in the aisle behind Auric and motioned for me to follow him. "You first, Princess."

I glanced at Auric, but if I was hoping for some kind of reassurance, it was clear by his blank expression that none would be coming.

Fine. I'll do this myself. I lifted my aching chin and sidestepped him.

CHAPTER TWO

LAYLA

THE GUARD LED US TO THE BAY DOOR, SEVERAL FEET FROM THE cockpit, where two other men waited. As we approached, one of them grabbed a bolting mechanism on the steel door and unlatched it. I braced myself when he tugged the heavy metal open on sliding hinges, sending a blast of air into the cabin as my ears popped.

"Are we not... landing?" I asked, side-eyeing the guards with their fluttering *free* wings.

"Nope," Auric replied, sounding bored, but I knew him better than that. His gaze flicked to each of the other guards, cataloging their weapons, their stances, and their demeanors.

I knew, because he'd taught me to do the same.

The first guard reached for my shoulder and guided me toward the opening. Wind whipped my hair wildly into streaks of brilliant fuchsia across my vision.

"Um, I—"

"You'll jump and fly straight for the island," the guard interjected as he worked at the straps binding my wings. "Don't get any ideas about escaping unless you have a burning need to drown. You'd have nowhere to land before your wings gave out."

While he tugged at the straps to free my wings, I looked out the open door at the ocean. Night had nearly fallen, but I could see flickering lights in the distance emerging from the vast darkness of the sea.

Fire, I realized. *Towers of fire.*

Yeah, maybe drowning was the better option here.

"Auric," I started, only to cry out as the guard yanked the strap off my shoulder with a handful of feathers. "Ow!" My wings were still bound and, if possible, even more tangled up than they were before.

"Apologies, Princess," the guard said, his voice gruff. "The straps are too tight."

No, kidding, I nearly snapped, wincing.

Auric unsheathed his dagger. "I'll cut them off."

"You're not damaging Reformatory property," the guard retorted. His fingers dug into the sensitive skin beneath my feathers again.

Auric shoved the guard away from me. "And you're not damaging royal property."

Great, I thought, holding back a sigh. I was property of the crown *and* property of the prison. That didn't make things complicated at all. *How about I just be property of myself?*

As if to answer that unspoken suggestion, the plane pitched forward again.

My knees buckled, and I fell forward, my arms flailing for anything to stop my fall. For an interminable moment, I hung suspended against gravity.

Oh, sh—

My arms pinwheeled, my hands seeking purpose, but all I met was air as I tumbled out through the open hatch with my wings still bound.

"Aur—"

13

I didn't even have a chance to finish my scream before the free fall took my breath away. I tumbled head over heels three times, then barrel-rolled, my arms waving uselessly. My wings strained against the leather straps, trying desperately to beat at the open air and stop my descent.

Think, Layla. Think!

Arms spread.

Legs spread.

Balance.

I managed to stop spinning, but the wind hummed around me in a dangerous welcome. The last of the day's sunset gleamed orange on the dark water below as it rose up to meet me.

Guess I'm gonna drown after all.

Something slammed into me, and I spiraled again. This time, I did scream as the world rotated in a disorienting blur of color. Then fingers wrapped around my arm, and I felt the bite of a blade against the edge of my wings. One leather strap sprang open, and then with a second slice, the other strap fell away.

Strong hands gripped my arms, and we rotated until I was facing the ocean again. Those hands moved from my arms to my waist as Auric's voice drifted to me like a ghost over the roar of the wind. "On three, open your wings."

I balked at the idea. We were in a total free fall! If we opened our wings to stop now, the pain would be devastating. Not to mention the fading glitter of the water beneath us looked way too close. Even if we did try to put on the brakes, we were about to slam right into the water.

From such a height, we'd break on impact. And the minute our feathers became waterlogged, we'd sink to the bottom of the ocean like stones.

He must have sensed my hesitation, because Auric's fingers tightened on my waist. "Trust me, Layla!"

Layla. No sarcastic "Princess"? He hadn't called me by name once since showing up at my chambers to escort me out today. I had glowed like an idiot, ecstatic to see him. At least until he'd revealed our fate.

"Layla!" Auric shouted, repeating my name. It didn't warm me the way it should. Instead, it left me feeling cold and alone.

I didn't want to have black wings that I didn't earn. I didn't want to go to prison.

"... right now!"

But I didn't want to die, either.

So I spread my feathers.

The force of my tumble slammed into the underside of my plumes, yanking me upward in a harsh gust of flight. Agony shredded through my bones, causing stars to burst in my vision and ripping a scream from my throat.

This is going to break my back!

Auric grunted as his wings blew open, his grip on my waist bruising. His lips parted on a curse, his strength and agility overpowering mine and taking the brunt of the burden.

Our momentum slowed exponentially.

Then the updraft leveled us out, and Auric guided us into a horizontal glide. My wings throbbed in time with my heartbeat, feeling weak and overextended. *Except not broken,* I thought. *Not entirely.*

Thanks to Auric.

His turquoise gaze caught mine, a hint of concern lurking in his depths. But it was gone in a blink, and then his focus fell on the fiery lights looming menacingly ahead of us.

I shivered, my muscles aching from the impact of our bodies and the recorrected flight. However, despite all that, I sensed the air whirling around my feathers, teasing my senses to life.

My wings began to beat at my back, helping to carry us to shore.

Auric released me just before we landed. The unexpected disappearance of his strength and my abnormal forward momentum sent me stumbling forward to my knees against the cement landing platform.

Sharp pain lanced up my thighs and into my hips, joining the agony in my back.

My heart cracked as my world was miraculously reborn.

No one would help me here.

Not even Auric.

And he made that perfectly clear as he stood beside me without a word. The only reason he cut me loose in that free fall was to ensure I survived. Nothing more.

Message received, I thought at him. Not that he could hear me. Nor would he care.

Placing my hands on the concrete, I gasped and let my wings fall forward to wrap around my body. My head still swam from the way I'd tumbled on the way down, and my wings ached as if someone had set them on fire. I clung to the ground, to the way the concrete still held the sun's warmth.

I'd never been so happy to be on the surface.

That happiness was shattered when two thick black boots scuffed against the concrete in front of me and a man snarled, "On your feet, inmate."

Still breathing hard, I sat back on my heels and blinked blearily up at the armed guard. He gave me a cold look that rivaled Auric's stare. Everything about the guard screamed *warrior*—his shorn, dark hair, his bulging muscles, the lack of *any* emotion on his rugged face.

Somewhere, wires were crossed inside my head, and I couldn't quite process what he'd said. I heard it, but my legs and arms didn't seem to want to cooperate. I quivered, my limbs jelly and my lungs burning from a lack of proper breaths.

The guard snatched at my arm and yanked me to my feet. "I said *on your feet*. Are you deaf?"

"No, but you're about to be," I grumbled, looking for a way to shove a dagger into the idiot's ear for talking to his princess that way.

Except, I had no weapons. No chance to overpower the male Nora who caught me in a bruising grip.

And right now, I didn't feel like a princess anymore.

Auric stepped forward and grabbed the guard's wrist, his movements so casual he could have been picking up a napkin to dab his chin. However, the pop that followed wasn't casual at all. And neither was the guard's responding shriek.

He immediately dropped his hold on my bicep, allowing me to wrap my arms around my middle. I backed up several steps, my heart in my throat.

"I'll only say this once. Keep your hands to yourself," Auric said flatly, dropping the guard's wrist.

The dark-haired male cradled his hand against his chest, fury glinting in his gaze. "My apologies. *Sir*."

There was nothing respectful about the man's *sir*, but Auric ignored him. "Let's get the princess off the platform before the rest of the inmates arrive, yeah?"

The guard's lips curled up at one corner, but he nodded and inclined his head, motioning for us to follow.

He pressed his thumb to a nondescript pad outside an

iron door, then twisted the knob after a series of beeps sounded, and led us into a stone corridor.

My feathers bristled, the kiss of cool, murky air unwelcome. The sensation worsened as we reached a stairwell at the end, the rocky steps leading downward into the bowels of the prison.

Flickers of flames illuminated our way, turning the walls and floor a sickly green in the dim lighting.

At the bottom, we emerged into another corridor, this one highlighted by the low din of voices that echoed off the ceilings.

Doors dotted the interior, each laced with heavy iron with little square windows at the top.

Definitely a prison. Not that I'd expected otherwise.

All the entryways were open, allowing me to see and hear the occupants inside.

In one cell, two inmates grappled in the low light, throwing punches and dodging each other's blows. I couldn't tell if they were out to kill each other or just passing the time. In another room, two men screamed at each other, obviously in the midst of an argument. We passed several men lounging in their beds and several more sitting on visible metal toilets.

Ugh. Yuck. I would never be able to unsee any of that.

But more importantly, I really hoped my cell had a solid door. Because I would *not* be doing that in the open.

At the shuffle of our feet on the dusty stone floor, most of the occupants darted forward to see who had arrived. All male, I realized. I didn't see a single female.

"Aren't you pretty," a gruff voice said, drawing my attention to a rough, crazy-eyed male who stood with his pants open and his hand wrapped around his shaft, pumping slowly as his gaze danced over me.

Oh gods...

I averted my eyes, bile rising in my throat. I skipped out of his reach, then froze as another hand stroked my feathers from the cell across the hall. I spun in a circle, then pressed my back to a solid piece of rock and wrapped my wings protectively around myself.

How could my parents have sent me here? To this prison? To this hell? *I don't belong here. I don't belong here. I don't belong here!* I kept repeating the phrase in my head, my eyes squeezing shut as I tried futilely to wake myself up. To abolish this insane nightmare. To be anywhere other than here.

But their voices continued around me.

Purrs that left me weak in the knees.

Grunts that had me longing for the ocean, wishing Auric had just let me fall.

No. I can't think like that. I have to fight this. I have—

"Princess!" the guard yelled. "Keep moving."

I shook my head, unable to breathe properly. "No," I forced out, my voice choking. "I don't belong here."

Auric shoved against my side, his presence providing the oxygen I needed to inhale. "Not now," he bit out warningly. "Let's get out of sight."

Oh, but that voice wasn't right at all.

Filled with hatred and condescending bitterness.

"I don't belong here," I repeated, my eyes opening to reveal the hell around me once more. *Very real. Too real.*

The guard growled irritably and stalked forward to grab my arm and yank me forward. I fell, my feet dragging on the stone and my weight dangling from his hand. His manhandling ignited a spark inside me.

No one treated me this way.

Not ever.

Because I was a royal. Even with my black wings, I was *still a royal.*

"Let go of me!" I demanded, planting my feet against the floor to right myself. "I swear I didn't do anything wrong. I'm not supposed to be here!"

"Your wings say otherwise, Princess," the guard snapped. He dragged me forward again, this time veering off toward an open door in the wall. "Get the fuck in that cage, or I'll toss you inside."

"That won't be necessary," Auric cut in before I could argue. He took hold of my other elbow and glared pointedly at the guard's grip on my arm. The man let go quickly, and then Auric guided me toward the cell.

I trembled, but I didn't fight his touch. I just let his evergreen scent surround me and gulped deep breaths of him as I walked into the cell—anything to mask the lingering vile scents in this place.

Then I froze again, staring at the small, hard bed. The exposed toilet. Four stone walls. One door at my back.

"I'll handle her from here," Auric said in a low growl behind me. "Touch her again and I'll kill you myself."

"Yes, sir," the Nora Guard replied through his teeth.

The door clanked shut.

Welcome to your new life, Princess.

CHAPTER THREE

AURIC

FUCKING CHERRY BLOSSOMS.

I needed a break from that intoxicating scent. From *her*. From the way she made me feel. The way she made me *need*.

Layla was a weakness, a fucking chink in the armor I'd worked so hard to build up. And now I was stuck with her in my own personal hell.

She still stood stunned inside the cell, her expression one of a weeping flower. So delicate and broken. And so not my fucking problem.

"Stay here," I demanded, opening the door less than a minute after that idiot guard had shut it.

"What? Where are you—"

I stepped outside and slammed it shut before she could voice another word. My nose twitched at the putrid stench cluttering the hallway. It was a welcome reprieve from Layla's natural perfume.

I folded my arms and leaned against the stone wall, then studied the prison corridor.

Noir Reformatory was supposed to be new.

Yet this place reeked of rot and age.

Something wasn't right here. It ruffled all my plumes and left a sour taste in my mouth. I also didn't care for the

Nora Guards. They weren't respectful of my far superior position, likely because they were bitter about their lowly station here. Not my problem. They would either learn their place or die by my blade.

I didn't fuck around on a good day.

And today had been the opposite of *good*.

A hiccup sounded through the door, making me grunt.

"Your tears won't fix this, Princess," I muttered, aware that she could likely hear me just as well as I could hear her.

"I hate you," she retorted, sounding furious, not sad.

So maybe they were angry tears. That I could work with.

"You only have yourself to blame," I drawled, glancing up and down the corridor once more, searching for a guard. I needed a phone or some sort of device that would connect me to the king. He'd want a report on our flight, which would likely end in a few guard executions.

Those idiots had nearly killed King Sefid's precious daughter. She might have black wings, but she was still heir to the throne.

Unfortunately, all I found lurking in the hallway were black-winged Noir.

Disgusting peasants. They reeked of sewage.

I rubbed my jaw and shook my head. No way could I leave Layla unguarded at any point, not with the way the Noir kept poking their heads out to sniff the air.

Layla was fresh meat, and all these animals wanted a taste.

Including the icy-eyed Noir standing sentry at his door a few paces down.

Novak.

I met and held his gaze, the former Nora Warrior one I knew very well. He used to be mine. A lethal soldier with razor-sharp feathers—at least when he allowed that part of himself to be displayed. He'd been the elite of the elite.

Until he forgot his place and challenged a direct order.

My order.

And for that, he Fell.

Not by my choice, or even by my sentence.

That wasn't how our world worked.

Sin painted our wings black.

He folded his arms and just watched me, his upper body a wall of carved muscle. I waited for him to speak or to acknowledge me as his superior, but he held my gaze instead—an alpha challenging a fellow alpha.

I knew how to make him kneel, and I reminded him of that by stroking the hilt of my dagger. His gaze followed the movement, his lips quirking up at one side into a dark smirk.

Then he returned to boldly holding my stare.

I see, I thought, narrowing my gaze. *Someone thinks this is the land where he's king.*

Well, I'd have to set the record straight.

I pushed off the door just as it opened behind me. "I'm hungry," Layla said, her blue eyes hard. She'd tied her thick fuchsia hair up into a knot on top of her head. "Can we eat something?"

"I'll give you something to eat, baby," a male voice said from across the hall.

"Fuck off," I snapped at the random Noir, then glanced to where Novak stood, his icy eyes on Layla.

She didn't seem to notice, her arms wrapping around her exposed midriff.

That damn outfit was going to get her hurt. It hid absolutely nothing and showcased every fucking curve. I hadn't thought to make her change, too caught up in the moment of witnessing her Fall from grace.

Damn black wings.

I hated them.

I hated *her*.

"Get your ass back inside," I demanded. "*Now*."

She huffed and took a step back.

"Ah, come on, man. Let the girl eat. I'd love to watch those pretty lips—"

I turned toward the voice and sent my fist into the Noir's jaw. He fell backward on a whoosh of air, out cold from a single punch. "Anyone else want to play?" I asked. "Because I'm dying to draw some Noir blood."

Novak grunted from down the hall, his expression amused. But rather than try my patience, he just slipped back into his room to shut the door behind him.

Normally, I'd call his action cowardly.

Except I knew him.

He wasn't walking away from a fight. He was dismissing it—and me—before we could begin. The closing of that door served as a proverbial *Fuck you, you're not even worth the effort*. And damn if that didn't make me want to charge down the corridor to wring his damn neck.

But the tapping of a foot behind me forced my attention to the impatient *princess,* who apparently wanted some food.

All right.

I'd find *Her Highness* something to eat.

Watching her forcibly swallow the shit they fed inmates here would be a beautiful punishment. Cathartic, even.

"One prison meal, coming right up, *Princess*," I said, unable to hide my cruel grin. "I'm going to thoroughly enjoy watching you choke on it."

CHAPTER FOUR

NOVAK

"I hear that Layla convinced Auric to allow her outside today," my cousin said with a sense of amusement. He nudged me, as to ensure I heard him.

Zian was my flesh and blood. Of course I fucking heard him. I *always* fucking heard him. Just because I chose not to speak didn't mean I was deaf.

"What do you say, Novak?" he pressed. "Curious to meet the princess?"

I yawned. Even if I were curious, I wouldn't admit that out loud.

"Poor Auric," Sorin said with a laugh. "I hear she's been giving him a hard time. You'd think he could handle such a little thing."

I nearly grunted. It'd been the highlight of my week seeing the famous Nora Warrior downgraded to a royal lapdog. The princess sent him out to fetch meals frequently, something I suspected he only agreed to because he wanted to avoid her delicious scent.

Cherry blossoms.

Fuck, she smelled so sweet. I wanted to sink my teeth into her flesh just to see if her blood rivaled her perfume.

"You have a penchant for underestimating females," the

angel beside me mused, her voice low and sultry and oozing sex. Probably because she'd just spent the morning fucking Sorin and Zian.

Imagine my surprise when I'd returned from my stint in solitary to find out my cousin had taken a little raven-haired mate. I'd damn near killed the poor thing, as I'd scented Zian all over her and thought the worst. Then he'd charged into the cell with Sorin at his side and had nearly taken my head off.

"The last bitch Sayir sent here tried to kill me. I learned my lesson the first time," Raven added, her black eyes glinting in the sunlight. She was a feisty little thing. Then again, she would need to be to handle two former Nora Warriors.

Zian and Sorin enjoyed fucking. *Hard*. And fortunately for them, their little minx didn't mind being in the center of all that male aggression.

I closed my eyes as they lost themselves to frivolous conversation of the princess. Something about jealousy. Then Raven added, "I'm pissed that the Reformer thinks he can just do whatever he wants. He brought his own niece to this hellhole, and she's spent the last week pretending like she doesn't belong here."

I nearly pointed out that they were cousins, since Raven was the Reformer's daughter, but I didn't feel like stating the obvious.

"And you think it's all for show?" Sorin asked. "She's the Princess of the Nora. I don't see what she could gain by intentionally Falling and getting herself locked up."

I'd spent the last century bouncing around prisons with Sorin and Zian, so it stood to reason that they often spoke my thoughts for me. Which was why I continued to remain quiet, as I mostly agreed with Sorin's commentary.

"Maybe. But she still did something bad enough to Fall, so if you want to underestimate her, fine. However, I'm not going to be fooled by a pretty face."

Neither are they, sweetheart, I thought at her, aware that my warrior brothers never judged anyone by their looks. We all knew that sometimes the deadliest of beings hid in the smallest of packages.

Sorin and Zian fell silent, putting me at ease. I thrived in the quiet, where I could listen to everyone and everything around me and monitor my surroundings with my instincts more than my senses.

There you are, I thought, picking up on the subtle hint of cherry blossoms. *Mmm, it seems Zian was right. You managed to convince Auric to let you out for some fresh air. Well, welcome to the yard, little blossom.*

I didn't look at her, not right away. Instead, I allowed my senses to roam over every alluring inch of her body, my mind functioning as my hands.

I'd caught her scent the moment she'd stepped into the hallway last week. *Ideal mate* practically wafted off her in waves. That she stood beside Auric only added to her allure.

Because I sure as fuck wanted a piece of him. Preferably a bloody one, or ten, that I could feast upon while his soul slowly withered away to nothing.

I'd wait until he made the first move.

Then I'd show him what a century of prison life had taught me. Because unlike the Nora Warriors, Noir fought dirty. There was no sense of duty or honor here. Just death and survival of the fittest.

"You finally came out to play, Princess," a voice cooed from across the yard.

I peeked at the imbecile, curious to see which Noir had the balls to try to approach the royal. The hairs along the princess's arms danced, her mouth curling down into a frightened frown that seemed to heighten her scent.

Both my eyes opened, my own lips curling down to match hers.

Auric appeared unfazed, his expression one of astute boredom. *Oh, come on, now. You won't really let that dick touch her, will you?* I wondered at him, fully aware that he couldn't actually hear me.

Then I caught the subtle tick in his jaw, and my frown dissolved into a smirk.

That's what I thought.

"Just watch," Raven said, interrupting my concentration. I nearly told her to shut it, but she wasn't done. "You'll see. She's going to show her true colors."

More like Auric is about to show his, I murmured back, but not with my voice. It wasn't my fault she couldn't read my mind.

"Why don't you ditch the shiny toy and get yourself some real protectors? I could show you—" The idiot reached for her, thereby igniting the show.

Auric's blade whistled through the air with an accuracy I begrudgingly admired, slicing the Noir's hand clean from his wrist.

I see you've stayed on your game, I mused. *Nice form.*

"Anyone else want to lose a hand, or worse?" Auric called to the crowd, his blue eyes flashing with aggression.

The female beside him paled, the contrast startling against her gorgeous wings. I almost wanted to take Auric up on the offer, if only to be the one to help massage those frown lines from the beauty's forehead.

I didn't care what she'd done to earn her black plumes. Her scent around my cock was all I needed. And maybe her plump lips.

"Yeah, I see what you mean," my cousin drawled. "The princess is absolutely terrifying."

I ignored him in favor of watching the female wrap her arms around her middle, her shiver visible even from here. Auric sheathed his dagger, then walked up to her side.

"I don't belong here," the female whispered, her scent coming to me on a stiff breeze.

I rubbed at my nose, then narrowed my gaze. The stench of royalty surrounded her, that pungent jasmine and rose enough to make me sneeze. I much preferred the cherry blossoms beneath, which fortunately came next.

Zian bumped my shoulder. I glared at him. *What?*

He studied me.

I studied him.

Then I went back to watching the female. Her eyes caught mine as if she could feel the intensity of my gaze on her.

I didn't move or react, not wanting to frighten her more. But I caught the subtle flare of interest in her pupils.

Then Auric interrupted the moment by placing his hand low on her back.

A growl tore through my chest before I could stop it. I clenched my hands so tightly my nails bit into my skin.

Oh, I'd received that message loud and clear. *Mine.*

We'll see, I said back to him with my eyes. Because I didn't sense a mating bond between them. Just general interest. Because she was compatible with him, too.

Given my past with the Nora Warrior, that wasn't surprising.

"It would be so much easier if I could just kill her," Raven whispered mournfully.

I cut my gaze to the female beside me. "I don't recommend it."

Not only would it create a severe conflict of interest—whereby I would be forced to choose between the life of a potential mate over the life of my cousin's mate—but Auric would destroy her. Raven might be strong for an eighteen-year-old angel, but she wouldn't stand a chance against the practiced Nora Warrior. Neither would Zian or Sorin.

No, if it came down to a fight, it'd be between me and Auric.

Because I was the only one aware of his true weakness.

Raven crossed her arms over her chest with a petulant ruffle of her feathers, then turned her glare on the princess.

She stood at the edge of the field now, her eyes on the labyrinth in the distance. Auric's jaw tensed as he watched, making me curious.

Were you not aware of Sayir's penchant for games, old friend? I thought at him. *Oh, who am I kidding? Of course you were. You're a Nora Warrior. All you live for is death.*

The princess gasped as an inmate fell prey to the spike trap, then she backed away from the fence, bumping into Auric. The Nora Warrior slid an arm around her shoulders and pivoted her until she was no longer facing the labyrinth, his face grim.

Is that for show? I wondered. *Or are you truly bothered by the fate you left so many to?*

His focus shifted suddenly to the side, just a hairsbreadth of a second before I heard the approach of engines in the distance.

Oh? Is it finally time to play?

Sorin and Zian had warned me about the cullings and battles—something that had been a common occurrence throughout my time in solitary—but I hadn't yet been given the privilege of drawing blood. Apart from my initial landing in this hellhole, anyway. Apparently, I'd killed too many inmates. Solitary with a bunch of insane demons had been my punishment.

"How many can I kill?" I asked Zian as black feathers began to rain from the sky above.

Zian whistled long and low. "I don't know. That's quite a crowd."

Sorin grunted. "Noir seem to be Falling like rain lately."

"Or maybe they're all being sent here for a reason," Raven said in a low voice. "For Reformer kind of reasons."

Yes. I suspected she was right, because there were at least twice as many Noir coming down right now, in comparison to the day I'd initially arrived. And they were all angling directly for the courtyard.

Hmm, a quick mental count of cells and beds told me the prison was already almost at capacity. And I doubted the guards intended for anyone to sleep on the floor.

Well, they might.

But they wouldn't want to feed us all.

Looks like I'm about to experience my first real culling. That death duel when I first arrived didn't really count.

I stood to loosen up, ready to play. Beside me, Zian and Sorin did the same and closed in around Raven protectively.

Sorin rolled his neck. "Buckle up, little dove."

Raven flashed a feral grin. "I could use some action."

Zian slid his finger down her back between her wings, a glint in his eye. "Don't we give you more than enough, sweet bird?"

A mental image of doing that to the princess caught my focus, causing me to drag my eyes to the female in question. She stood in the center of the yard, watching the sky as the new Noir dropped gracefully to the ground in the yard, completely unaware of what was about to happen.

And Auric had taken a few steps away to converse with a Nora Guard.

They had no idea what was coming.

I couldn't give a flying fuck what happened to Auric, but I felt an overwhelming need to keep the princess safe.

I reached into the hidden pocket on my jeans to pull out my knife, my fingers already tingling with anticipation.

"How many?" I asked again, my wings flickering, ready for action.

"No beast mode," Zian replied, spoiling all my fun.

I glanced at him, arching a brow. *I like my beast mode.* And I rarely exercised that lethal part of me. Too much blood. But razor-tipped feathers were certainly a useful trait to possess during a culling.

"I'd keep it to less than a dozen this time," Zian suggested. "With a regular knife."

My lips twisted, irritated by the small number and my inability to truly play. But I didn't much fancy another stint in solitary. So I nodded solemnly in agreement. "Eleven it is."

CHAPTER FIVE

AURIC

"What do you mean, there's no phone?" I demanded. "I put in my request a week ago."

"I don't know what to tell you, man," the guard drawled, clearly unaware—or more likely, uncaring—of my title and position of power. "I passed your request on to the Reformer. He manages all the communication in this hellhole."

"King Sefid will be most displeased," I said, unable to hold back the threat in my tone. "He expected an update upon our arrival, something I've been unable to provide."

"The Reformer probably provided it for you." He shrugged. "We'll sort it out."

"Sort it out?" I repeated.

"Uh, Auric?" Layla called, the uncertainty in her tone dragging my focus back to her and our surroundings. Yeah, I'd noticed the incoming Noir. There were a few too many for my comfort, which was part of the reason I wanted a fucking phone. The risk continued to grow in this situation, and it was unacceptable. I also hadn't received any sort of schedule or plan for her redemption.

I ignored her unease and shifted back to the guard. "I want a meeting with Sayir. Today."

This whole situation was starting to smell wrong, and it wasn't just the mangy-dog stench of the Noir or the subtle leather and smoke that Novak seemed to drag around him.

No, there was something different that rubbed my feathers the wrong way, and it made my nostrils flare.

"Yeah, sure, I'll get right on that, *sir*." The guard gave me a mock bow and turned to walk away.

"Hey, I wasn't—"

"Auric!" Layla's shriek had me turning to find her in the middle of the yard sifting sand through her fingers.

Fucking female. Was *stay* really that difficult a command to adhere to? Now was no time to go digging for treasure.

Shaking my head, I stalked off toward her, shoving Noir out of my way as several more dropped from the sky.

My warrior senses kicked into overdrive as I began counting the new sets of wings.

Ten.

Thirteen.

Seventeen.

Twenty-two.

Was there another set of stairs in the reformatory that led to additional cells? I hadn't seen one. And there weren't enough beds for the number of angels falling from the sky.

Unless Sayir meant for us all to bunk up together, which was not bloody happening.

Layla's lower lip trembled as two Noir brushed her wings. I growled at them as I approached, my hand on my blade. "Fuck off," I demanded, reaching for her as the ground rumbled beneath us.

What the fuck?

Heat brushed my senses, sending me sideways as a geyser of flame erupted from the sands where I'd just stood.

My eyes widened, a curse leaving my lips.

A cascade of thunderous roars followed as more flames shot up throughout the courtyard in a matter of seconds. I sought out Layla, and my shoulders sagged at finding her unharmed.

She's okay.

She's alive.

"Lay—"

Shrieks pierced the air at my back. I whirled to find a bluster of chaos as Noir launched into the sky, trying to avoid the spikes of fire below as half of the inmates tried futilely to save their fiery wings.

Feathers weren't meant to burn.

They sizzled to ash, forever gone.

I tucked my plumes tight into my back and yelled at Layla to do the same. I had no idea what was going on, but—

A series of pops sounded, followed by Noir dropping like stones.

Machine guns? "What the fuck is going on?!" I demanded, spinning around.

"Survival of the fittest," a dark voice murmured in my ear.

Novak. I spun to face him. A ghost of a smile flirted with his lips, causing me to narrow my eyes. "What the fuck does that mean?"

"You haven't figured it out yet?" He tsked. "How disappointing."

I opened my mouth to tell him to fuck off, when a warning wave of warmth caressed my senses. I leapt, putting myself farther away from Layla, and far too close to Novak. His scent washed over me, all leather and spice and man, and not at all like the dog stench his fellow Noir wore.

"What are you doing?" I asked him.

He replied by delivering a roundhouse kick to an approaching Noir, sending the poor sod into a nearby flame.

I shook my head. "I don't have time for—"

Layla screamed as a Noir exploded into flames beside her, the inferno eating at his clothes and crawling over his skin with preternatural strength. I took a step forward, only for Novak to grab my wing and yank me backward.

I growled, my dagger falling into my palm, when fire billowed up from the ground, right where I would have stepped.

My eyebrows lifted. "*Shit.*"

"It's a game," he said, his voice low against my ear. "Take flight, earn a bullet. Step out of place, go up in flames. Or worse, meet a razor wire."

A Noir to our left shrieked as he did the latter, some invisible net slicing right through his wings and leaving him in jigsaw pieces on the ground.

Holy gods...

This was fucked up.

Was Sayir aware?

King Sefid?

No. He would *never* endanger his only daughter in this manner. And Sayir was meant to reform these Fallen, not *kill* them.

My hackles rose as fire billowed rhythmically across the yard in an indistinguishable pattern. This wasn't some malfunction or shock of fate. This was organized, methodical, twisted, and cruel.

An extermination.

No. Novak had called it a *game. Survival of the fittest.*

Some Noir deserved to die for their sins.

But some were meant to be reformed.

Like Layla.

My gut twisted. *We're not meant to be here.* No way had she done something worthy of this fate. I looked for the guards, wanting to issue a demand to stop this. But they were all in their towers, shooting at any Noir attempting to fly.

This was madness.

Insanity.

Utter—

Another spurt of fire drew my attention back to Layla. She had fallen into a ball of feathers, her black wings wrapped around her in a useless shield.

She was going to die if I didn't reach her in time.

I tried to take another step, but Novak's grip tightened. "Easy," he said as I growled. Then he rotated me away from Layla just as another burst of heat sprouted from the ground.

"This is insane!" I shouted.

Novak smirked. "Welcome to Noir life."

Then he took my dagger and drove it into the chest of an approaching angel. The male went down with a curse. Novak yanked the blade from his heart and wiped the blood on his pants before returning the knife to my sheath.

"Touch my weapon again, and I'll end you," I threatened.

His lips twitched. "Try."

He wanted to dance? Here? In the middle of this chaos?

Oh, but of course he did.

It was fucking Novak. He lived for the dangerous shit. And it seemed a hundred-plus years of reform hadn't changed that one bit.

If only I had my swo—

Layla's shriek ripped through the air, snapping my focus back to her as the tornadoes of flames danced around her block. My heart froze, my lips parting. Only, the fire didn't touch her. Instead, it formed a blazing wall *around* her.

Well, I'll be... By some happenstance of fate, she'd found what appeared to be a safe zone.

I scanned the yard to see several other areas where Noir were clustering into small groups of two or three, their base seeming to be one of the few that didn't go up in flames.

Unfortunately, I wasn't the only one who seemed to have noticed these little fireproof havens.

Two burly Noir were headed right for Layla.

Novak took off toward them, his lithe form cutting a path I begrudgingly followed. He took down the first behemoth of a male with one solid punch to his throat, sending the angel backward into a sizzling spire of fire.

I winced at the bellow the male released, then threw my dagger into the eye of the second one.

Novak pulled it out in a swift move, then slid the blade across the male's throat just as I arrived at his side.

He handed it to me without a backward glance, his focus already falling on the approaching horde of Noir who all clearly craved death.

I rolled my neck.

All right.

Survival of the fittest.

Yeah, I could do that.

I crouched.

Bring it.

CHAPTER SIX

LAYLA

MY SKIN HEATED AS ANOTHER WALL OF FIRE DANCED AROUND me, threatening to turn my feathers to ash.

I'm going to die here.

In this hell.

With black wings.

And I'll never know what I did to deserve this!

Fury licked through my veins, burning a path right to my thudding heart. I wanted to scream at the unfairness of it all and the complete madness of this situation.

Why would my father allow this?

Noir were *dying*. Screaming. *Going up in flames*.

This didn't match any of the stories I'd been told about the reform process. Nora were kind creatures, our wings the same color as our souls. We were meant to help others, to guide them into the light, not fight each other to the death.

"Layla!" Auric shouted.

I peeked at him through my feathers, then gasped as I saw the razor wire heading right for his beautiful wings. "Duck!" I screamed.

But he couldn't hear me.

And he couldn't seem to see the approaching blades

either, something the other Noir appeared too blind to notice as well.

My eyebrows shot up as he twisted in midair, his wings thrusting at his back to place him horizontal to the ground as he arched backward. The wire hummed across his torso, upward to his chin. His eyes narrowed as it nearly skimmed his nose, and I gulped.

He righted himself as a Noir with black hair handed him a dagger.

I frowned at the familiarity between them and the nod Auric gave the other man. Then they went wing-to-wing and began fighting off each approaching assailant.

They were a sight to behold, cutting down the others with precise punches, slashes, and kicks.

Hope blossomed inside me, only to die at the sight of a shiny net falling from the sky.

"Watch out!" I launched forward, only to be tossed back by the flames bursting up around me again. I let out a strangled cry, dancing away from the heat.

Auric looked up, then crouched as he sliced his blade through the air.

It wasn't enough.

The silvery web whirled around him in a sickening display of madness, entangling with his limbs and molding to his thick combat pants and boots. He fell to the ground as the metallic strands ensnared his arms and wings, degrading him to that of a fly caught in a spider's web.

A sick feeling rose up inside me.

I had to help him. I had to—

Tight fingers closed around my arm and jerked me backward into a circle of virile male Noir.

Oh gods...

A tall, muscular Noir with a scar bisecting his right eye

leered down at me. "Look at you," he hummed, his gaze roaming over my gauzy top—no one had provided me with anything else to wear. "All alone, aren't you now, Princess?"

My stomach twisted as my heart fluttered like a frightened bird.

The man's scent was all Noir—fetid and feral like a dangerous, wild animal.

I hadn't realized that Noir smelled so different from Nora until I came here. In the castle, I'd hardly ever noticed anybody's smell beyond Auric's. Nora had a nice, muted scent that was almost calming in its steadfastness.

However, the Noir's stench choked me. I could taste it in the back of my throat.

I yanked against his hold, but his fingers just tightened on my arm.

"Let go of me," I snapped, going for a haughty, royal tone. Unfortunately, the words came out too shaky to land the way I wanted them to.

Gods, I hated this place. I hated the way it shredded my courage, how it turned my resolve into mush and my brain into that of a helpless female.

I wasn't weak.

I was a *royal*.

He should be bowing to me, not manhandling me.

Three other inmates crowded around us, identical glints in their gazes. They looked just as rough and intimidating, covered in scars and healing wounds, their heads shaved and their skin sallow from so much time locked away.

I dreaded to think what they'd done in their lives to be here for so long that they no longer resembled Nora at all. Their descent into Noir life had gone well beyond their black wings, as if the evil inside them had manifested on the outside.

The one holding my arm sneered. "What do you think, boys? Should I let her go?"

His buddies laughed as though he'd said something uproariously funny.

"*Let her go* down on this cock," one of them said, earning more maniacal laughter from the groupies.

All the hairs on my body stood on end. The low level of panic I'd managed to keep submissive until now threatened to overwhelm me.

Why had my father sent me to this awful place? How could he put me in this position? If Auric didn't survive the razor wire, I'd be at the mercy of every man in this prison. I'd be meat, and they'd all take a bite until there was nothing left of me.

My captor gave a slow nod, his tongue darting out to lick his lips. "Been a long time since I felt the warmth of a cunt."

His crudeness lit a fire of indignation under me. Baring my teeth at him, I hissed. "Release me, or lose your hand like the other Noir in the yard."

He sucked his bottom lip between his teeth and glanced over his shoulder with a smirk. "Your guard dog's a little busy, *Princess*. I don't think he'd notice if I took you for a ride."

Bile rose in the back of my throat. My arm was going numb beneath his bruising grip. And his stench was suffocating me. I longed for wintergreen to banish the stink.

But Auric wasn't coming to my rescue.

So I'd just have to save myself.

"I don't need a guard dog," I said, then stepped forward, scraping my foot down the Noir's bare shin with every bit of force I could muster.

The edges of my high-heeled sandals weren't exactly soft. I tore off a layer of skin and followed through by slamming my three-inch heel right into the top of his foot. Unfortunately for him, he'd decided to wear slip-ons to the courtyard instead of boots. My ropy sandals weren't appropriate for prison, but they were good for putting a two-inch hole in this idiot's foot.

But instead of letting me go, the Noir snarled and threw me up against the stone wall behind me right as a flame shot up beside us.

We were still on the safe base I'd discovered, but barely.

My head bounced off the rock as he shook me violently against the wall, expelling the air from my lungs.

"You fucking royal bitch!" he snarled.

I lost control of my knees, slumping toward the ground, but the Noir grabbed me by the shoulders to shove me harder against the wall. Sharp edges bit into my wings like a dozen tiny blades, his iron-like grasp holding me upright.

"Get off me," I seethed, my voice too hoarse to pack the punch I'd intended to deliver. I sent a knee to his groin, trying to shove his delicate parts up into his lungs, but I hit a wall of thigh muscle instead.

He grinned, and the skin around his red scar puckered. "The more you struggle, the more I like it. And the better you smell."

I growled, lifting both of my legs off the ground in an attempt to front kick his knees, but I didn't have the necessary room to follow through and only managed to scratch his ankles.

His sick smile widened. "Keep fighting, bitch. I'll like it better when you scream."

He jammed a knee between my legs and pressed his hips against mine, anchoring me against the wall, then he leaned forward to sniff my neck.

"No!" I struggled against his hold, sickened by the obvious erection in his prison-issued cotton pants.

If he tried to touch me with it, I'd rip it off with my fucking fingernails, even if he killed me.

He roared with laughter. "She's a feisty one, boys! I'll get the first tur—"

The man's weight disappeared, and I fell to my knees on the concrete, a curse welling up from my throat as pain ricocheted up my spine. A spiral of fire to my right had me yanking in my wings again, my delicate feathers warmed by the flames.

I stood up, my back against the wall once more, quivering at the sudden change. Then wide, stunned eyes met mine a second before my tormentor's body flew off the platform on an arc of blood that glistened like a liquid rainbow in the air.

My eyebrows shot upward at the dark-haired male taking his place—the one who had fought wing-to-wing with Auric.

The angel with the icy blue eyes.

His leathery scent wrapped around me in a calming cloak as he took down two more Noir without blinking. Then he looked at the final male, his fingers curling into fists. "Run," he growled, the word for the other Noir, not for me.

I shivered and wrapped my wings tighter around myself.

The final male rolled his shoulders and ducked into a fighting stance, causing the dark-haired Noir to sigh.

"A dozen it is," he muttered, not making any sense to me as he launched into motion. My lips parted at his sinuous movements, his body reminding me of water with his fluidity and grace.

He fought like Auric.

Precise. Lethal. *Beautiful.*

It was like watching a ballet of destruction, his long, athletic form lithe and proficient against the bulkier competition.

Three hits.

Two kicks.

And the hefty Noir fell like a rock, the ground rumbling beneath his collapse.

The icy-eyed male knelt, his fingers going to the other man's throat. I thought he meant to strangle him, only he pressed two digits into his pulse, then nodded as though satisfied.

Because he was dead?

Or because he lived?

The man stood, his long body unfolding gracefully from where he'd crouched over the fallen inmate. Both his hands were clean, as was his exposed torso.

Not a drop of spilled blood.

How was that even possible? He'd sent that one Noir through the air in a waterfall of gore. Yet he hadn't gotten a speck on him.

His blue gaze captured mine, causing my heart to stop.

Time suspended around us.

Then my pulse kick-started in my chest.

He started forward in a slow prowl like a big cat moving in for the kill. His eyes never left mine as he crossed the few feet between us—stepping over a body in the process—and halted way too close to me.

A new scent washed over me, chasing away the remnants of the other Noir. A delicious, amazing scent that had me inhaling deeply. *Fresh leather and woodsmoke.* Heady and intoxicating.

With an undercurrent of blood.

His gaze slowly lowered to my lips as he took another step forward. My breath caught in my throat, his nearness an exhilarating presence I shouldn't accept. Yet my body reacted to his as though we knew one another. No, as though we were *meant* to know each other.

I swallowed, my thighs clenching as he took a final step toward me, boxing me in against the wall just like the other male. But unlike that Noir, I didn't fear this one.

I frowned at the oddity, my mind quickly working through logical puzzles on an errant quest to find a reason for that difference.

He'd just killed at least three Noir right in front of me. Lethality oozed off him. Danger lurked in his icy irises. But as he lifted those beautiful eyes to mine once more, I felt at peace.

Flames billowed behind him, framing his sharp features in delicate shadows that should have made him all the more terrifying. Yet all they did was intensify his exquisite features.

He lifted a single finger to trail a line down my cheek to my throat and then to my collarbone. Goose bumps followed his touch, my lips parting on a necessary gasp to draw more air into my lungs.

And his scent.

Leather and blood and man.

Oh gods...

My thighs clenched and his nostrils flared.

Then a blade appeared on his wrist, followed by Auric's snarl. "Remove your hand, Novak. Or I'll cut it off."

My throat went dry at the possessiveness in his tone.

The one called Novak glanced at him, his lips curling up at one side into an expression of mild amusement. Then he dropped his hand to his side and took a step backward to survey the yard.

"Game over," he murmured before turning away without a backward glance, his steps sure as he maneuvered with ease around the graveyard of fallen Noir.

I took in the scene with blurry eyes, my heart thudding rapidly in my throat.

There were at least forty dead angels wearing varying shades of blood-red, charcoal, and ash.

It was a massacre.

A monstrosity.

A horrifying, macabre scene of feathers and flesh.

Auric wrapped his arm around me, but I pushed him away, wanting no part of his solace and strength. This was a view worthy of my sorrow and pain.

Noir weren't meant to die like this. They were meant to reform and be reborn, not slaughtered like wild animals or pitted against each other in fights to the death.

"I want to go home," I whispered. Not because I was afraid or upset, but because I was furious. My father needed to know about this. He would never approve. "He'd never be okay with this."

"I know," Auric whispered.

I finally looked at him, noticing his shredded torso covered in scrapes and death. His pants were torn. His shoes scuffed. Even his long wisps of white-blond hair were tainted red. More blood painted his formerly pristine feathers.

He resembled a true Nora Warrior.

And I couldn't stand the sight of him and all that he represented.

It wasn't fair or right. Nor was it all that rational. But a part of me truly hated him and everything he represented. Just for a moment.

Then I caught the concern swimming in his ocean-blue eyes.

"We'll demand an audience with Sayir and find out what the fuck this was," he vowed.

I believed him because I knew it wasn't within his genetic makeup to lie. So I nodded in agreement.

Then I allowed him to escort me back to our cell, all the while wondering if I would ever be able to leave again.

CHAPTER SEVEN

RAVEN

"FIVE," SORIN BOASTED, COLLAPSING ONTO OUR BED. HE clutched a cloth to his nose, his dark sapphire eyes challenging anyone to beat his score.

Zian smirked. "Tie." Which meant he'd killed five as well.

Sorin frowned, then both of my mates looked at me.

I perched on the edge of the mattress and beamed. "Three." It might be less than them, but that was to be expected. They had survived this prison world for over a century, plus they had decades of Nora Warrior experience on top of that.

For eighteen years old, and being on the smaller side as a female, three was impressive.

Sorin released a low whistle. "Three? Well done, little dove." He chuckled, then lowered the cloth to give me a bloody grin. "Perhaps I should start calling you *deadly* dove?"

"Maybe I should start adding marks to your arms like I do to Sorin's," Zian suggested, his black irises igniting with promise. Sorin's gaze matched his, the two of them turned on from all the violence.

Mmm, yes, I wanted nothing more than to forget our afternoon of gore by losing myself in their arms.

But something wasn't right.

"There hasn't been a culling that bad in a while," I thought out loud, ensuring they kept their desires at bay for at least a few more minutes. We had all night to tangle up our wings.

Zian joined us on the bed and leaned against the wall, his new shirt riding up to show off the attractive "V" that disappeared into his low pants. He must have stolen the clothes off the back of one of his victims, as he usually went shirtless. Only Zian would consider that a worthy trophy.

"What did you see today, sweet bird?" He lifted his arm in clear invitation. I crawled toward him to snuggle into his side, content to revel in his soothing scent. Sorin's nearness added a touch of warmth to the air as well, mingling the aroma into a melted caramel that tickled my nose.

Zian ran his fingers up and down my arm, careful to avoid the scratches and cuts I'd sustained.

I bit my lower lip as my mates watched me, patiently waiting to hear my reply regarding what I'd seen today. "It's not about what I saw, so much as felt. It all seemed targeted. Well, almost." I couldn't really explain it, but I'd sensed a pattern to the dancing flames and deadly blades.

It wasn't something my mates would have caught, as we'd learned quickly upon arrival that there were certain things I could see that they couldn't. Such as the razor wires.

"Our section wasn't too bad," Sorin said. "Less lethal than usual, anyway."

"Because we weren't the target," I said, thinking back to that random net that fell from the sky. "I think they were going for the princess. Or maybe her guard." I couldn't say how I knew that; it'd just been an inkling I'd picked up on while observing the patterns in the field. "They seemed to be targeting their steps, but Layla found a platform almost immediately. So it redirected toward him."

"Do you think she could see the shifting in the sand like you did?" Sorin asked, referring to my reaction to the ground changing subtly before the culling began.

"I think that's what drew her into the yard, yeah," I admitted. "I don't think she knew what was going to happen, though."

Which had me wondering if I'd been wrong about her. I'd initially assumed that she would be similar to the last family member the Reformer had placed here—a half-sister Valkyrie who wanted me dead. But now, I wasn't so sure.

"She looked really scared today," I added.

And while she'd defended herself on that platform, her skill hadn't been that of a trained killer.

The Reformer had called her the "key."

"The key to everything just arrived, Raven. I think you'll like her. But she'll need your help to thrive here. Can you do that for me? Can you help guide her?"

He'd said that after I survived a lethal game in his labyrinth.

Which he'd dropped me in after revealing that he was my father.

I refused to call him that. He would always be Sayir or the Reformer to me.

I shook my head. "I don't know what he's doing, but I think today was about testing the princess. Or maybe removing her guard." It was just a guess and the best one I had to offer on the subject.

Silence followed as my mates stared each other down in some sort of silent conversation. They did this sometimes.

Over a century of friendship had given them the uncanny ability to converse with just their eyes.

"You should probably wash up and work on healing yourself," Zian said, releasing me as he gestured to the sink with his chin, all the while continuing his stare-off with Sorin.

Layla had become a divisive element between us, and today obviously hadn't helped.

My mates were clearly having an unspoken disagreement over how to proceed with this information. Which would likely lead to a competition of male dominance.

And then sex.

Hopefully, with me in the middle.

"You two have fun," I said as I rolled off the bed to skip over to the small bathroom in the back corner of the cell. I held my breath and lathered the pungent soap over my arms. It didn't help, the stench infiltrating my nose even without inhaling.

Ugh.

Fortunately, my mates would replace the stink with their sweet scent soon. Because things were heating up between them, their voices low but furious as they debated how to proceed out loud.

They agreed that Auric and Layla were the targets, and Sorin wanted to leave well enough alone. "It's not our job to help him," Sorin said, his tone sharp.

"How do you think Raven will feel if her cousin dies?" Zian retorted.

I frowned, uncertain of how much I would care. I didn't know the princess. Hell, I'd only learned of our familial relation, like, a week or two ago. Why should I be bothered by her fate? If anything, I should feel the opposite. The Reformer wanted me to care. To help *guide* her.

I nearly snorted.

Not. Happening.

"Novak isn't going to let this go," Zian added, his voice low. "And I can't just leave him here, Sorin."

"We have a mate to consider now, Z."

"I am considering her," he snapped back. "She and Layla are technically family."

"Yeah, that worked out well with Bryn."

"I think we can both agree that Layla isn't Bryn," Zian retorted. "She resembled a delicate flower on that platform, not a practiced Valkyrie."

"Which is very much not our problem."

"Try telling that to my cousin," Zian muttered.

I frowned. *Where is Novak?* I wondered. He should have been back by now. He hadn't stayed with us at all on the field, instead choosing to join Auric in battling the Noir.

Unfortunately, that indicated Zian was right.

And while I agreed with Sorin's stance about it not being our problem, Novak was truly family. At least to my dark-haired mate. And to Sorin, just in a friendship sort of way.

I switched off the faucet and dried myself with the old towel that we all shared. Then my healing magic rippled across my skin. It warmed each wound, then the broken skin knitted back together until it itched. I didn't dare scratch it, or else the restoration process would have to start all over again.

Distracting myself, I combed my fingers through my hair, yanking through the worst of the snags, before rejoining my mates, who were now both standing with balled fists.

I sighed. I couldn't believe I was about to suggest this,

but it seemed my mates were at an impasse. And besides, it couldn't hurt anything, right? "Maybe I should try talking to Layla—"

Sorin swiped his long white-blond hair out of his blazing blue eyes. "You're going to stay out of it," he ordered.

My knees locked.

Orders and I? Yeah, we didn't get along well. Something Sorin and Zian very much knew.

"Look, I'm not saying I care if she's culled," I said through gritted teeth. "But if we can expect more cullings like that while she's around, this is everybody's problem. We might have ended up on the easier side of the field today, but what about tomorrow? And what about Novak?"

"Novak can take care of himself," Sorin muttered.

"True," I agreed. "But I'd still like to find out what the princess knows. Maybe we can use it to convince him that she's not worth the effort." Or perhaps she'd provide something useful we could use for ourselves.

Zian hummed in agreement as he crossed his broad arms over his naked chest. Apparently, he'd lost interest in his trophy. Or perhaps he'd wanted to distract Sorin. Which, based on how his heated gaze roamed over Zian's chiseled torso, was working.

My guys were so easy.

Blood continued to drip from Sorin's lip, and his nose had an awkward bump in it that hadn't been there before.

Relaxing, I pushed him onto the bed. He slumped down onto the mattress, causing it to squeak. I knew he was allowing me a moment of dominance, but we both liked it. "Is it broken?" I asked, gently running my fingertip across the ridge.

He hissed with pain. "It'll heal," he grumbled.

"Nonsense," I said, sitting beside him. "Stay still."

He didn't protest as my healing energy ignited between us. I spread it over his face with a tender kiss, his lips soft beneath mine. His tongue quickly consumed mine, his need for control lashing out as he deepened our embrace with his skilled mouth.

A sufficient distraction.

One that worked wonders on the tension in the room.

His forehead touched mine as I finished, the blood from his lips now on mine. He tasted as good as he smelled. "You're a useful female to have around," he murmured.

I rolled my eyes. "Uh-huh. All you want me for is my magic."

His mouth went to my neck. "And your heady scent, which changes when you heal."

Yeah, I knew he liked how I smelled, especially when my healing ability came into play. Which was part of the reason I'd engaged my gift.

"About the princess," Zian began, not ready to let this go even though his eyes smoldered with need. "She's obviously not a threat. Novak had her pinned, and all she did was stare at him."

"He saved her," I pointed out. "Maybe that made her more trusting."

"Yes, more trusting," Sorin drawled. "I mean, when I tried to help you on our first day here, you returned the favor by trying to kill me."

"You're never going to let that go, are you?" It came out less angry and more sultry because of his nearness.

"Never," he vowed, his teeth catching my lip and giving me a nibble.

"He's right," Zian said as he closed the distance between us to run his palm up my thigh. "Saving a female doesn't necessarily equate to trust. I think she didn't fight him because she fears him. Or maybe because she needs him alive for something."

"Let him figure it out," Sorin said, his lips on my neck. "He can take care of himself."

"For now," Zian conceded, his skilled fingers unfastening my jeans and tugging them down my legs.

Sorin tugged at the loop of my halter top, freeing my breasts. "Then we're agreed."

"For now," Zian repeated. "But we're not done with this conversation."

"We are," Sorin whispered, his lips drawing a sinful path up my neck to my ear. "Spread your legs for Zian, little dove. He's going to fuck you first."

"A gift for acquiescing?" Zian asked, already removing his pants. "Or a distraction?"

"Both," Sorin said, his teeth skimming my thundering pulse. "Obey, little dove."

I considered ignoring him, but the heat pooling in my core had me reacting to his words and his command. My thighs parted, unleashing my scent through the room and eliciting a growl from my mates.

Sorin reached around me, spreading me open further. The pressure so close to where I wanted him made me whimper. "Do you want to taste her first?" he asked, his voice low. "Or slide right in?"

"She's certainly wet enough," Zian replied as he knelt on the floor. "Smells amazing, too."

Oh gods...

Sorin palmed my breast, squeezing it just the way I liked, causing me to arch into—

The cell door banged open with a hard crash, making me jolt upright.

Novak stood in the doorway like a looming shadow, his

icy gaze narrowing. Normally, he ignored us completely, even while we had sex. But his intense stare suggested he had something to say—a rarity for the typically mute Noir.

However, rather than speak, he picked up my clothes from the floor and threw them over Zian's head, adding a commanding growl to the mix that made his message clear.

Get. Dressed.

The place between my thighs throbbed in denial, but Zian quickly helped pull up my jeans before refastening his own. Sorin tied up my top, his displeasure radiating from his chest.

"What the fuck, Novak?" he demanded.

My nose twitched, causing me to frown as a familiar scent struck my senses. *Metallic. Old. Blood.* My eyes widened. "Oh..." *The Reformer.* "*He's* here," I mouthed.

Zian's eyebrows drew down, then flew upward as he caught my meaning.

Novak dipped his chin, his jaw tight.

Sorin slid off the bed to prowl toward the doorway, fluffing his feathers as everything fell silent in the hall.

All except one voice—a smooth, cultured male tone that I didn't recognize. "Sayir. I want a word. Right fucking now."

"Who is that?" I asked. Because whoever it was had to possess a death wish to speak to the Reformer like that.

"Auric," Zian muttered.

"The Royal Guard?"

His lips brushed my temple as he whispered, "Yeah." He joined me on the bed, his body protective beside mine while Sorin remained at the door beside Novak.

"Yes, I received your message," Sayir replied, his voice smooth and reassuring. "There's just one matter to clear up first." He stopped in front of our cell and snapped his fingers.

"You," one of the guards said, his focus on Novak. "Come with us."

"Ah, fuck," Zian muttered. "I told you to keep it under a dozen."

"*Now*," the guard snapped.

Novak merely shrugged and stepped up to the doorway with his arms out, awaiting his shackles. Except they didn't handcuff him at all.

Instead, Sayir nodded toward the hallway. "This way."

We all shared a look as Novak left without a backward glance.

Then the door slammed shut, locking us inside. *Again*.

CHAPTER EIGHT

LAYLA

"Sayir. I want a word. Right fucking now." Auric's tone made me cringe as I hid behind his wings. He'd been pacing the hallway, agitation pouring off him in waves as he dared anyone and everyone to fight him with a single glare.

Now he stood just outside our door, arms folded, stance wide, ready for a fight. I tried to peek around him to see my uncle but couldn't find a breach in all the white plumes in front of my face.

"Yes, I received your message," someone replied, his tone smooth and elegant and reminding me of my father. That had to be my uncle, the infamous Reformer. We'd never met, but I knew of him. Sort of. "There's just one matter to clear up first."

My brow furrowed. *Only one?* I repeated to myself. Surely there were at least two dozen more, considering all the dead Noir outside. My father would *never* approve of this.

"You," a deep voice snapped. "Come with us."

I tried again to see around Auric's wings and failed.

"Now," the voice added, sounding impatient and cruel.

I shivered and stepped deeper into my cell, giving up on seeing around Auric.

"This way," my uncle said, his tone layered with a calmness I didn't feel.

I was about to meet the Reformer for the first time. My father's brother. The boogeyman of my childhood nursery rhymes.

What would he think of my black wings? Would he hate me on sight? Demand I repent? Would he believe me if I told him I was innocent?

Auric stepped backward, forcing me to move as well. I went to stand beside the bed while he took up the middle of the room, his arms still folded and his wings unfurled in all their pristine greatness. Minus the blood staining his feathers. He'd refused to clean up in our cell, too agitated by the events outside to do anything other than brood and demand an audience with the Reformer.

Well, it seemed that'd worked wonders.

I swallowed as the male in question stepped through the threshold, his black eyes and dark hair so different from my father's blond strands and crystal-blue eyes. But their facial structures were similar, their cheekbones regal and their chins forming a sharp point.

Only Sayir's white wings were tipped with black, while my father's feathers remained unblemished.

The Reformer's gaze fell to me first, his midnight irises roaming over me in a wave of distaste before settling on the Nora Warrior. "Auric," he greeted.

"You nearly killed your niece today," Auric returned. "Care to explain?"

I swallowed. This was not how I expected to meet my uncle for the first time.

"Hmm" was all he said before gesturing behind him for someone else to enter.

"Go," a deep voice demanded.

My heart stopped as Novak entered the cell, his icy gaze sweeping over me before landing on Auric.

"What the fuck is he doing here?" Auric demanded, taking the question right from my mind and adding his angry twist to the inquiry.

"We'll get to that," Sayir murmured smoothly, glancing over Novak to the guard in the doorway. He gave the man a nod, and the door sealed the four of us inside, causing my pulse to skip several beats.

The sensation crawling over my skin worsened as Sayir met and held my gaze.

Even though he dressed like a royal, donning a tailored black suit with pearlescent cuff links, it didn't do anything to dampen the feeling that a hardened predator stood before me. He studied me like a snake, the perception amplified when his tongue flicked out, tasting the air, ready to strike.

I froze, unable to properly breathe.

Auric didn't seem to notice, but Novak did, his nostrils flaring as he ran his eyes over me again. I wasn't any less pacified by his presence, his lethal edge a cloak of darkness that seemed to settle naturally around his shoulders. He might have helped me in the field, but that didn't mean he intended to be kind to me.

No, I suspected his actions were self-serving. Just like every other Noir in this prison.

"I'm losing my patience," Auric said through clenched teeth. "Explain. Now."

My uncle finally broke his gaze from mine, shifting his attention to the Nora Warrior, who seemed to take up half of the available space with his impressive wings.

Yeah, Auric was pissed.

I should have been angry as well, but I couldn't sense anything beyond the cold spike of adrenaline shooting down my spine. This closed-off cell with male aggression vibrating all around me wasn't helping my nerves, not after what I'd just been through.

"A mistake," Sayir said, his tone dripping with charm as he gave Auric a sideways grin. "I assure you, it won't happen again."

"A mistake," Auric repeated, his wings flaring even wider, filling my nose with his evergreen scent. I inhaled deeply, trying to allow the familiarity to soothe me. Except it was tinged with leather.

Novak.

My gaze flew back to his, only his attention had shifted to the Reformer, his expression giving nothing away. Sayir's expression remained muted as well, his dark eyes calculating and intelligent.

Auric rushed the Reformer, making me squeak as I tried to jump out of the way. Novak caught my hip, pulling me to his side, as Auric slammed his fist against the wall inches from Sayir's head.

"An oversight," the Reformer stated, his tone and expression as unruffled as his feathers. He clearly didn't fear Auric, and given that the guards didn't burst inside, neither did they.

A chill swept through me at the realization that no one here perceived Auric as a threat.

That meant they wouldn't respect his superiority. Sayir not bowing to him, I could understand. He was my father's brother, marking him as a royal. But Auric wasn't a pawn. He managed the Royal Guard, granting him a superior title to all the Nora Guards in this prison, as well as many Nora in general.

Novak's thumb circled my hip, reminding me of his presence. He hadn't stopped touching me, something I'd failed to notice because he felt... *right.*

Which had me taking a careful step away from him as Auric growled at the Reformer. "An *oversight*?" he repeated through his teeth. "She *nearly died.*"

I frowned. I hadn't *nearly died.* I'd... Well, okay, there'd been a few close calls. But I hadn't even bled.

"Yes," Sayir replied coolly. "She was supposed to be in her cell."

Auric growled. "Are you saying this is my fault? I can't just keep the princess locked away forever. Solitary is not part of her reformation." He finally released Sayir, taking a step back. "What *is* the plan for her reformation? Besides being burned alive or sliced into a thousand pieces, I mean. Did you have anything better in mind?"

My frown deepened. While I wanted to know the plan as well, I was more concerned with the fact that several Noir had lost their lives outside. I opened my mouth to speak, but Sayir smoothed a hand down his tie and said, "Of course I have a plan."

I expected him to continue, but he didn't.

"Which is?" Auric prompted.

"I'd like to know about what happened outside," I interjected. "And if that's typical yard behavior."

Novak cocked his head slightly, his gaze sliding to mine. Apparently, my comment intrigued him.

Unlike Auric, who glowered at me for interrupting before refocusing on Sayir. "Yes, I imagine the king will want that explanation as well. Which reminds me, I still need a damn phone."

"There's no explanation needed," Sayir supplied with that infuriating, even tone. "It was a minor glitch that we'll ensure is fixed."

"A minor glitch?" Auric repeated, his eyebrows hitting

his hairline. "That net thing tried to kill me! And do I need to repeat again how your little *glitch* almost murdered your niece? The *heir* to the throne?"

"I didn't almost die," I muttered.

Auric snapped his gaze to me, a threat lingering in his eyes that told me to stop speaking. Considering this whole situation was *about me*, I should be allowed to voice my opinions and questions.

But my guardian obviously didn't agree.

"The king doesn't even know that we've made it here alive," he gritted out, his attention returning to Sayir. "He needs to be made aware—"

Sayir flared his wings, the black tips touching Novak and the wall on the opposite side. It had me taking another step back, pressing my feathers up against the wall.

His wings were as big as Auric's, if not larger, and the show of dominance wasn't lost on me.

"My brother entrusted Princess Layla to our care, to be reformed," he said, his tone not matching the lightning flickering in his dark orbs. "That is what we will do. He did not ask for updates, and given the danger in any communication outside the norm, that is for good reason."

He seemed to grow in height, towering over Auric as an oppressive weight pressed down at my shoulders. I wasn't sure if it was my own imagination or some magical effect the Reformer had at his disposal.

"The princess is safe," he continued, the words measured and slow. "No harm has been done. Sefid is well aware that you arrived, just as I will ensure he's aware later tonight that his daughter is still in good health."

Electricity hummed through the room as Auric flexed his wings once more. "King Sefid and I had an agreement. *I* will be the one providing updates to him. I want a fucking phone."

"*You* do not run this prison," Sayir retorted, his calm façade slipping for just a moment into one of manic rage. My lips parted, my spine straightening.

Novak glanced from me to the Reformer, his gaze narrowing just enough to tell me he'd noticed it, too.

"I do not need to explain my methods to you," Sayir said, his wings lowering as his expression returned to aloof elegance. "You're here to serve as the princess's guardian and nothing more. However, since that charge has proven difficult for you to manage on your own, I have recruited a secondary guard. After all, Novak did save her today, yes?"

Auric balked. "You can't be serious. He's more dangerous than the rest of the inmates combined!"

My throat went dry, my head swaying in the negative. He wanted Novak to *guard* me? Sure, he'd helped me today. However, we all knew he had his own intentions in mind, not mine. I tried to voice my opinion, to say how bad an idea this was, but I suddenly felt choked by the scent of leather and *man*.

Oh, this is bad. Very, very bad.

The Reformer merely grinned. "Oh, I'm well aware of Novak's lethality. Which is why he'll make for an intimidating guard. Assuming he prefers that position over another bout in solitary?"

Novak grunted and slid his hands into the pockets of his jeans before casually leaning against the wall beside me.

"I'll take that as confirmation that you want to stay here," Sayir replied.

The lethal Noir beside me didn't move or react, which was apparently his method of agreeing.

My skin went cold.

Novak.

My guardian...

Which meant being with me at all times.

Sleeping in the same cell.

Being only inches away when I was at my most vulnerable.

My gaze snapped to his, only to find the ruthless Noir studying me. No emotion. No reaction. Just quiet observation.

"Sayir," I whispered, my throat constricting on the name. "I... I..." I couldn't speak beyond that single word. *I, I, what? I wanted him to stay? I wanted him to leave? I was afraid of him? I was afraid of what I might do to him?*

What was the end of that sentence?

"Yes?" my uncle prompted, his tone laced with amusement.

Or at least he sounded amused to me because I swore his dark gaze twinkled.

I cleared my throat and tried again. "I appreciate you trying to help," I began, my throat so dry that my voice resembled sandpaper. But I continued on, not wanting to lose his attention now that I had it. "But I think Auric is entirely capable of protecting me on his own."

Except none of you seem to fear him, so maybe not, I added to myself, frowning.

"My, uh, father charged Auric with this responsibility. Therefore, I don't think it's a good idea to dismantle those orders by installing Novak as my guardian as well." Except, looking at the Noir now, I wondered if it actually was a good idea. Because his expression had darkened into something terrifying.

No inmate in his right mind would want to challenge this version of Novak.

Yet, I'd just done exactly that by suggesting he be taken to solitary instead of being assigned as my guard.

Fluff, I can't win, I thought, aggravated by all the testosterone in the air. "Not that I don't appreciate the offer," I added with a shiver. "I-I'm sure he'd be a fine, uh, guard."

Novak's expression didn't change—and it wasn't even angry so much as intense—but he did redirect it toward the Reformer.

"Well, it's a good thing you're not here to think." Sayir's tone was so saccharine sweet that I thought I'd misheard him. "You're here because you Fell, Princess. That is no small crime, and it's one that will take a great amount of soul-searching to repair. Unfortunately, redemption will require sacrifice, patience, and *obedience.*"

He stepped in closer, making me feel trapped against the wall.

But the tip of Novak's wing touched mine. A subtle show of solidarity. A kiss of feathers.

It sent a shiver down my spine for an entirely different reason.

And further proved how bad this would be with him in my cell.

My body reacted to him in a way it shouldn't. Indulging in him would give me a true cause to Fall and perhaps turn my wings permanently black—a fate I couldn't afford to accept.

"Please," I whispered, more as a plea to remove Novak than anything else. Or maybe a plea for Sayir to back off. I couldn't say. My mind was no longer functioning properly, nor could any of my senses be trusted.

Who even am I? I marveled. *Why has this happened to me?*

Just over a week ago, my biggest concern had been dodging suitors as I entered my courtship season. Now, I had a multitude of items competing for the number one slot on my worry list.

I'm never going to survive this place, I realized. *I can't stay here. I need... I need to escape...*

"Your father entrusted me with your life, sweetheart. So you can leave the thinking to me." He patted me on the head for good measure as if I were just an insolent child who couldn't understand. He fluffed his wings as though satisfied with the conversation. "I trust you all to get acquainted. If you need anything at all, please inform one of the guards, and I'll take all requests under immediate consideration."

Yeah, immediately into one of his flame geyser traps, I thought, not trusting my uncle for a second.

He turned on his heel and exited the room. The lock tumbled into place, leaving me with the vile taste of old metallic blood in the back of my throat.

Until the scents of wintergreen and leather with woodsmoke made my entire body shiver in a whole new way.

Novak and Auric were staring at me again, and this time I cursed all the gods, not just for making me Fall when I'd done nothing wrong, but for putting me between darkness and light.

Auric squared his shoulders, his gaze falling on Novak. "We need to have a talk."

The dangerous Noir leaned against the wall, his amusement glittering in his eyes. He arched a brow as though to say, *Oh yeah?*

And here I was, trapped in the middle.

Yeah, I'm so fucked.

CHAPTER NINE

NOVAK

Layla's feathers tickled mine as she shifted uncomfortably against the wall. I purposefully brushed her wing, offering her a soothing stroke while simultaneously goading Auric.

He knew what my wings could do.

Not that I'd ever shift them into blades while stroking her.

But he didn't know that.

"Rule one." He reached for my wing to forcefully shove it away from the delectable female. "No. Touching."

My lips curled. *Like you're touching me now?* I wondered, glancing pointedly at his palm on my feathers.

He growled, releasing me and stepping between me and Layla. Or trying to, anyway. There wasn't anywhere for her to go other than into the corner, which had her huffing in annoyance. "Not now," he snapped at her.

My amusement began to wane. His treatment of the girl truly did leave a lot to be desired. The Auric I once knew used to dote on females, his charm earning us more than a few bedmates to share. But it seemed that male no longer existed.

Good.

Because I, too, had changed. Something I ensured he knew as I folded my arms and leaned against the wall, bored.

"Nod so I know you understood rule one," he said through his teeth.

I yawned instead. Oh, I'd heard him just fine. But I had no intention of obeying him or anyone else. Besides, he'd given up his right to dictate to me over a century ago. Another point I made by extending one black wing in a lazy stretch—the wing that hadn't touched Layla.

Isn't breaking your command how I Fell? I thought at him, fully aware that he couldn't hear me but could definitely see the taunt in my expression. *I think we both know rules aren't my thing, Auric.*

"*Novak.*"

Mmm, I used to love it when he said my name like that. He always did enjoy my mouth. Too bad I had nothing to say or do with it now.

Well, apart from maybe taste the fuchsia-haired beauty in the corner.

Yeah, I could use my mouth for that.

"Do not look at her," Auric demanded.

Is that rule two? I wondered, smirking. *Sort of hard to do now that we're bunking together.*

Two sets of bunk beds.

Pity the mattresses weren't all pushed together on the floor—similar to Zian's setup with Sorin and Raven. Perhaps I'd do a little redecorating at some point.

Ignoring Auric, I stepped around him to take in my new digs, then lifted my arms to stretch them over my head.

He'd affixed a bar to the corner for pull-ups, something I would absolutely be taking advantage of.

The window in this room boasted a view of the ocean—

something I knew was magic and not real, since we were under the ground. It served as a taunt, or maybe a way to make us feel more isolated. Whatever.

A bathroom was situated in the opposite corner, the shower and toilet open, causing me to glance knowingly at Layla.

Which earned me a growl from Auric. "Stop. Looking."

I finally met his seething blue eyes and arched a brow. *And just what are you going to do about it?* I asked him without speaking.

His knuckles popped as he fisted his hands at his sides.

Sayir didn't put me in here to play nice. All those words about guarding the princess were utter bullshit. He had something maniacal up his sleeve, and the darling princess was the key.

That was what he'd called her to Raven, anyway. It'd initially been my cause of intrigue. Although, now, my interest had grown to a whole new level.

Compatible mate.

I'd never desired a mate for myself, but this one certainly held a viable appeal. Maybe I'd claim her. Maybe I wouldn't. But I would absolutely fuck her. And not just because I wanted her, but because it would piss off Auric.

Double win.

I supposed I could inform Auric of what I knew. That would be the gentlemanly thing to do. The loyal warrior way. Except that part of me had died a long time ago. Right along with his chivalry, apparently.

"You used to obey me once," Auric said. "You will again."

I grunted. *Not going to fucking happen*, I told him with a look.

"Auric," Layla said, her tone gentle and reassuring and

completely at odds with the tension in the room. "It's done. There's nothing we can do about it now."

"Don't *Auric* me," he growled, glancing at me.

Too late, I told him with my gaze. *I'm fully aware of your mutual attraction.*

He wasn't telling me to back off her for protective reasons so much as possessive need. He wanted her. Which was precisely why I would take her from him.

Ah, sweet, sweet revenge. I couldn't fucking wait.

I winked at her, then grinned as she curled her arms around her deliciously bare midriff. Hiding wouldn't disguise her scent, and we both knew she was interested.

Not just in me, though. But in Auric, too.

Poor girl was trapped in a cell with two compatible mates. The same thing had happened to Raven. Sorin and Zian hadn't waited more than a few weeks to claim her.

Auric might just have the strength to avoid the pull.

And while I might as well, that didn't mean I would.

Why resist the sweet cherry in the corner? She might even be a virgin, and how delicious would that feel around my cock?

I deserved a treat.

I'd put up with this asinine political shit for over a century, done everything I could to earn back my white wings while living in perpetual purgatory.

So yeah. If there was no way up, then I might as well keep Falling. And wouldn't it be so much more fun with that stunning female by my side?

I drew in a long, deep breath, enjoying her musk of cherry blossoms and allowing her to see the interest in my gaze.

Which thoroughly pissed off Auric. He pulled out his blade and had it to my throat a second later, his hard body up against mine as he pinned me to the post of one of the bunks.

I smiled at him. "Just like old times," I said, my voice soft with memory.

"Fuck you."

"Already have," I drawled. Then I shoved him away with more strength than he anticipated and ducked out of his hold before he could cut me with his vicious blade. He would have to do a lot better than that if he wanted to best me.

Auric growled, the sound causing Layla to visibly shiver. Yes, she was definitely affected by the Nora Warrior, just as much as she seemed to be affected by me.

Multiple compatible mates was natural among our kind, mostly because males outnumbered females by at least ten to one. Perhaps even more now. I hadn't kept up with population numbers among the Nora.

But it was much rarer for a male to find a female of worth.

Layla was my first.

Given Auric's possessive reaction, I'd say she was his first as well.

He glowered at me but sheathed his blade. "I mean it, Novak. Touch her, and I'll kill you."

Layla sighed. "Can I be in charge of myself, please?"

"You want to be in charge of yourself?" He huffed a laugh. "Yeah, that worked well for you outside after you went gallivanting off into the yard like some sort of untrained fledgling."

Her eyebrows lifted. "*Excuse me?* I walked over there because of the shifting sand. I tried to tell you it was moving, but you were too busy talking to the guard."

"What the hell are you talking about?" he snapped.

"The sand!" She threw her arms wide. "What? Did you think I found that isolated platform by chance?"

He gave her an indulgent look riddled with sarcasm. "Didn't you?"

Now her eyes narrowed, a glimpse of the feisty female beneath coming out to play.

Yes, more fire, please, I thought, leaning against the post with my arms folded. *Give him hell, sweet cherry.*

"You're unbelievable! I'm not some helpless damsel, Auric." She shoved out of her corner, stalking right up to poke him in the chest. "I found the platform because of the texture. It didn't have the tiny holes for fire to sprout from."

Auric gaped at her, clearly shocked that she had a brain.

I didn't share in that shock. Raven's enhanced eyesight had helped Sorin and Zian survive several cullings while I was in solitary. It seemed expected that Layla would possess similar inclinations.

"Well, I'll be damned," he said. "I honestly thought it was pure luck."

Her expression told me that'd been absolutely the wrong thing to say.

But, of course, Auric was oblivious. He just shook his head and huffed out a humorless laugh. "Yet you still almost died, Layla. Because you don't know how to properly fight."

"Yeah, well, after you left, all I had was my old fight master, and he didn't prepare me to take on three aggressive Noir males during our training courses," she returned, the accusation thick in her voice.

"Maybe you should have thought about that before you Fell," he snapped.

"How many times do I have to tell you that I'm not supposed to be here?!" she demanded, causing my eyebrow to arch. "I didn't do anything wrong!"

Hmm. That's interesting. Raven had said something similar. She'd been born with her black wings. But Layla clearly had white ones until recently. Still, it was an intriguing similarity.

"Lying is a sin, *Princess*," Auric bit at her through clenched teeth.

She stared him down.

He glared right back.

"You know what, Auric?" She uttered the words softly, yet each syllable was underlined with venom. "You can go fuck yourself."

Well, now there's a word I enjoy hearing from your delectable mouth, I thought, my lips curling.

Auric seethed, his woodsy scent spilling into the room. I inhaled the refreshing cologne, recalling how it used to swirl around me when we fucked.

His eyes flashed to mine.

Because yeah, if I could smell him, then he could certainly smell me.

You're not going to last in this den with me, old friend, I told him with my eyes. *I know how to bring you to your knees.* And I allowed that knowledge to flourish in my gaze, causing his nostrils to flare in frustration.

He was utterly fucked, and he knew it.

He could hide from the girl all he wanted, and she'd allow it. But me? Yeah, I wouldn't let him hide. Not even for a second.

"You want to take your chances with this psycho?" he asked, glowering at her and then me. "Fine. You two have fun."

He stormed over to the single pull-up bar across from the shower. He lifted himself in an effortless motion, dropped down, and then repeated it again.

Nice form, I thought, taking in his muscular arms and tight ass. *Nice form indeed.*

Layla shifted, drawing my focus to the other nice form in the room. Her gauzy top and gold shorts showcased a body built for my version of sin. And I couldn't wait to seduce her into my dark, cruel world.

However, I'd give her time.

The sweetest desserts were best when savored, after all.

"I'm, uh, I'm going to lie down," she said as if I needed to give her permission.

She eyed the options in the room for a moment before choosing the upper bunk across from me. Maybe she thought the height would give her an advantage.

It wouldn't.

Deciding to play with her—and Auric—I took the bunk beneath her. I couldn't see her from here. That meant I was obeying the rules, right?

I tucked my hands behind my head and closed my eyes, envisioning her in my mind instead. Her pungent cherry scent drifted down to me like an alluring kiss while Auric's growls rumbled through the room.

His pull-ups increased in tempo, and I chuckled, knowing my amusement would only piss him off more.

Because the battlefield had been set. The die had already been cast. And this round's victory went to me.

Welcome to hell, Auric. Allow me to be your guide...

CHAPTER TEN

LAYLA

I'm never going to sleep again. I could hardly blink, let alone rest.

Without a real window, there was no telling how many hours had passed. The scenery never changed. Always a dim sky over the fake ocean. No breeze. No reality. No clock. And no matter how many breaths I counted, time seemed to stand still.

Novak's leather and smoke wrapped around me, mingling with Auric's evergreen until I thought I'd go mad.

My fingers tightened as I pulled the tattered bedsheet up to my chin. My body hummed with growing need, reacting to the compatible call of potential mates.

Fate had a screwed-up sense of direction. Because really?

Auric, a Nora Warrior who hated me.

And Novak, a slice of sin that would ensure my Fall remained permanent.

No, neither was a good choice, and yet my mind tumbled over images of a very erotic nature.

Them pleasuring me. Watching me. Touching me.

Ugh, make it stop!

I flipped onto my side and threw one of my wings over

my head. How long did Sayir expect me to survive this? A few days? Weeks? Months?

Longer?

Auric's unsteady breathing drew me out of my tormenting thoughts. He hadn't slept much either, and even now he was the same as me. Tormented. Awake.

Maybe if I hadn't been so attuned to him, I wouldn't have noticed, but years as my guard posted right outside my door meant I'd fallen asleep to the sound of his light breaths. I'd fallen in love with his presence, his everlasting comfort.

I'd fallen in love with *him*.

At least until he'd left and broken my teenage heart into a thousand pieces.

Last night only further confirmed that Auric didn't care for me in the slightest. He saw me as some broken bird with black wings. A helpless female he had no idea how to help or fix. A damsel with no skill other than to cause trouble for herself.

I hated him for that revelation because it broke my heart all over again.

How could he think so poorly of me after everything we'd been through? All those nights where I'd shared my dreams and aspirations with him. I wasn't a damsel. But I also wasn't prepared for this place.

Unlike Novak.

The dark knight whom Auric clearly shared a history with. I wondered what it might be, how deep it went. The power struggle between them was palpable and frightening, but also enthralling. It seemed to infuriate Auric, yet entertained Novak.

Which explained how the Noir slept soundly while Auric remained awake.

His sleepless night wasn't because of me.

But because of *him*.

The overpowering leather scent was the only reason I knew Novak remained in our cell. He hadn't moved the entire night, but the weight of his overwhelming presence assured me he was there, just waiting for me to make a false move.

Or, more likely, waiting for Auric to try something.

I took another breath. And another. And another. Counting as I went, attuned to every subtle move and sound in the cell. Which was why I nearly fell from my bunk when a metallic clank echoed through the room.

The door, I recognized. I heard it every morning, or afternoon, or whenever the guards unlatched it.

The lights flickered on a moment later.

Novak finally stirred, making my bunk rattle as he sat up. I leaned over the bar and peeked at the males below.

Auric swung his legs over his cot, boots still on. His ocean-blue eyes leveled at me beneath a curtain of white-blond strands. "Breakfast?" he asked.

I shifted onto my elbow and stared. Really? He was going to act like last night didn't happen?

I grabbed the pathetic excuse for a blanket and rolled onto my side, fighting with it to pull it over my wings.

He snorted. "Suit yourself."

I stared at the cut stone wall as he stormed out of the cell, the metal door screeching before slamming behind him.

My heart jumped in my throat. He didn't just leave me alone with a bloodthirsty killer, did he?

A shifting of cloth sounded, causing my eyes to widen.

Is that the sound of a zipper?

Oh gods...

He'd been naked this whole time? No wonder his scent had been so deliciously pungent.

"I'll save you a seat," he offered, his sensual and dangerous voice making me flinch. It didn't match the tone he'd used with Auric last night. No snide amusement. Just a soft hum of masculinity.

I almost looked at him because it was the first time he'd actually spoken to me.

But he disappeared in the next breath, the door closing behind him with a whisper of sound.

I drew in gulps of air until their masculine scents diffused, giving me a slight relief.

Although, now that the heady cologne was gone, all I could scent was faint mildew. Not exactly pleasant, but at least I could stop pressing my thighs together.

Listening to the silence, I tried to reorganize my thoughts. Auric's rage was mostly justified, considering Sayir's laissez-faire attitude regarding the violence yesterday. I also seriously doubted that the Reformer cared about my well-being, given we didn't even know each other. He might be my uncle, but we'd never met, and he hadn't exactly been all that welcoming yesterday. Actually, he'd treated me like a little breakable toy with the head pats and "there, there" approach.

Then pairing us with Novak had been interesting. Definitely not my first choice, given his compatible nature, but he had protected me. Sort of. For reasons unknown.

I grumbled a curse under my breath and dug my palms into my eyes. *This isn't helping.* I'd stayed up all night pondering this, and with no sleep, I wasn't doing any better sorting my thoughts.

Maybe I should have agreed to breakfast.

Sighing, I climbed down from my bunk and used the poor excuse for a toilet and basin. The water was clean enough, and I washed the worst of the grime away from my face.

However, my hair was another matter entirely.

It resembled tangled knots and snarled fuchsia strands. Fortunately, I couldn't see my reflection. Something told me I might scream if I could.

I glanced at the shower and figured now would be my only chance to use it without an audience.

With a nod, I stripped quickly and rinsed myself to completion. It was cold. However, I felt a thousand times better afterward. I towel-dried my hair, which caused my strands to frizz at the end, but it was better than before.

Dry enough, I shook out my torn, blouse-like top and put on the old clothes, twining my sandals up my bruised calves. Feeling less gross improved my mood, and I peeked my head out into the corridor.

Empty.

Good.

It felt a bit exhilarating to be on my own as I hurried to the cafeteria. *Take that, Auric*, I thought, proud of myself as I squared my shoulders and clicked my heels along the stone floors.

My chin lifted, some of my regal flair returning, until I turned a corner into one of the communal areas.

Three inmates involved in their own conversation stopped dead in their tracks when they saw me, making me pause.

With the double doors to the cafeteria just past them, I decided to chance it.

"Hey, beautiful," one of them drawled as I hurried my pace.

Ignoring him, I reached for the door, only to yelp when he shot out a hand and gripped my arm. He pulled me away from the cafeteria and closer to him, providing me with a pungent inhale of his wolfish stench. *Ugh.*

I glanced down, noting that he only had one hand to grip me with. The other one was severed at the wrist.

My feathers stiffened, my gaze flashing to his. This was the male Noir that Auric had punished during our first day outside in the prison's yard. The one who had met the sharp end of Auric's blade for touching me.

Anddddd Auric's not here now. Great.

"It's rude not to greet your neighbors," he said, his tone going low as his friends chuckled and crowded in around us. He waved around his stump. "We weren't properly introduced last time. I'm Horus." He leaned in and drew in a long inhale through his nose. "And you smell fucking amazing."

They want a show? Fine.

I was tired of being helpless. I was a fucking *royal,* dammit.

"Release me," I demanded, my voice reminiscent of my mother's regal tones. "I won't be manhandled by you or anyone else."

He chuckled. "Yeah?" His grip tightened. "Or what?"

"Or there will be consequences," I replied, forcing a confident note into my voice despite my waning resolve. He had at least a foot on me, and his wing mass was nearly twice mine. Not a fair fight. But I could best him if I went for the element of surprise. Maybe.

His eyebrows shot up as he glanced back at his friends. "Oh, consequences? Well, what would that entail, baby? A spanking?" His other hand groped at my shorts, pissing me off.

Slamming my heel on his foot, he let out a bellow as I twisted and reached out for the door.

Just when I brushed my fingers over the knob, he yanked my head back by my hair, making me cry out.

"You shouldn't have done that, bitch." He yanked again, exposing my throat.

The "recently imprisoned for no fucking reason" Layla would have been pissing her pants right about now, but Auric's commentary had flipped a switch somewhere inside of me, igniting the royal blood in my veins that would not tolerate this sort of disrespect.

I. Am. Not. Weak.

I jerked my elbow up beneath his, knocking his arm away. He took a handful of fuchsia hair with him, but his grip slipped enough so that I could right myself.

I took the opportunity and turned, jabbing his nose with a closed fist like my trainer had once taught me. A spurt of blood rewarded my efforts, and his hands predictably went to his face, leaving another vulnerable part of him open.

A glance at his friends said they weren't going to intervene, yet. They jabbed each other and laughed, amused while a princess kicked their friend's ass.

Well then, they were going to love this.

I crouched and thrust one knee forward, going straight for his tiny little balls that probably didn't even exist.

He buckled forward, unable to do anything but double over in pain as I tucked my ankle behind his, sending him crashing in a tangle of musty black wings.

His friends winced with sympathetic groans, and finally one decided to come to the poor bastard's rescue.

"You've had your fun," he said, his lips twisting into a

grin. "Now it's time for us to have ours." He shot out a hand and gripped my hip, pulling me around.

I resisted, so *tired* of being grabbed. My arms. My hands. My waist. Grabbing me everywhere like they had some sort of right to touch me, to invade the personal space of a royal.

Reaching behind me, I circled my fingers around the jagged joints of his wrist. I rotated with my whole body, using my momentum to yank his arm behind his back.

Just the right amount of pressure and...

Pop.

He bellowed.

I grinned.

Auric had taught me that move when I was a kid. I'd never used it on a real person before, but my muscles remembered the movements he'd had me do over and over again.

The last Noir moved to tackle me to the ground but hesitated as an emotion I didn't recognize flashed in his dark eyes.

Oh, yes, I knew that expression.

Respect.

Finally.

He cursed me out, called me a bitch, but gathered up his groaning buddies and crashed through the cafeteria doors, leaving me alone.

My chest heaved, and I couldn't scrape the manic smile off my face.

I'd won.

I reached out to open the cafeteria doors and paused, sensing that something still wasn't quite right.

Glancing over my shoulder, I found the source of my discomfort. One of the only other females in the prison stared back at me. I'd seen her in the courtyard before with

Novak, but now to see her up close made me wonder how in the heavens she'd survived this long.

She's gorgeous.

Long, silky hair and ebony wings framed her like a delicate goddess. Her halter top left little to the imagination, and she tucked her thumbs into her jeans as she equally surveyed me.

The two large Noir at her side gave her a wide berth, but I sensed a companionship between them.

Mates?

Ah, maybe that was how she'd survived this god-awful place.

"See?" she said, throwing up one hand. "I knew she was dangerous."

I narrowed my eyes, abandoning my mission to escape into the cafeteria even as my stomach growled again. "Excuse me? Am I not allowed to defend myself from empty-skulled brutes?"

The female stalked forward, narrowing her dark eyes. "Everyone else buys the sweet little princess act, but not me." She stabbed a finger into my face. "I'm onto you."

Clenching my jaw, I bit back the desire to swat away her hand.

What's her problem?

I glanced at the two Noir who were her mates. One boasted a navy tattoo up both arms, but one side was unfinished. The other had shaggy, dark hair that hung over a gaze full of intrigue and danger. These were two warriors. I'd recognize their type anywhere.

Just like Novak.

Maybe it was just a territorial thing. I had no interest in her mates, if that was her concern.

"I'm not actively courting mates," I informed her.

85

At least not here, I added to myself.

Gods forbid if I brought one of these males home as a suitor. My father would disown me entirely. It'd be much worse than that time I questioned the purpose of having a courting season when the choice was never truly mine to make.

Gods, was that only a month or so ago? Or longer now? Time here had a strange way of altering my view of reality. It seemed like a lifetime ago.

Regardless...

"If you think I'm a threat, you can relax," I added when she continued to frown at me. "I'm here to reform, then I'm going home, where I have plenty of royal suitors waiting." Not that I'd been willing to court any of them. She didn't have to know that.

Her eyes widened as if I'd just insulted her. "*Excuse me?*"

Deciding that I'd probably made enough friends, I huffed and said a quick farewell and turned toward the doors.

Only to run right into Novak's hard chest. He'd somehow stepped behind me. Or maybe he'd been coming out of the cafeteria?

Hmm, no, the doors were still and closed, indicating he hadn't just stepped through them.

Which meant he'd been lurking somewhere.

I rubbed my nose, the appendage smarting from slamming into his collarbone. "Where'd you come from?" I muttered.

He jerked his chin to the hallway and ran his fingers up one of my arms, distracting me with the intimate touch. It was so different from any of the other Noir here.

Natural.

Wanted.

"You're not trying to court a mate?" he asked, his gaze smoldering with wicked intent. "Are you sure about that, sweet cherry? Because your scent says otherwise."

"Whoa," the female exclaimed. I turned to find her and her mates stunned.

Sure, Novak had been entirely rude, but I didn't expect anyone else to care.

"He knows how to use complete sentences?" the female whispered loudly to her mates.

"I'm just glad to see he's here and not in solitary," the dark-haired one replied.

My brow furrowed, but I ignored their commentary. They were all friends. I'd gathered that from seeing them in the yard yesterday. Or was that two days ago? I had no way of knowing without a proper clock or the sun.

Regardless, I needed to set the record straight here.

"I'm not seeking a mate beneath my station," I clarified, holding his gaze and poking him in the chest with my index finger. "So don't get any funny ideas. And don't call me *cherry*." Just because we were cellmates now—and he smelled absolutely amazing—didn't mean I was going to fall for him.

Maybe.

Hopefully.

He grinned and didn't reply. Although, he didn't have to. His expression said enough.

I'd just given him a challenge, which was probably the wrong thing to do.

He glanced down, one eyebrow jerking up. "You have blood on your fingers, *Layla*." His tongue flicked out to dampen his lips.

I frowned down at my hand. *Right. Good-for-nothing brutes.*

Huffing, because this most certainly seemed to please Novak, I reclaimed my hand and maneuvered around him to gather my meal and what was left of my dignity.

Because I found that I enjoyed pleasing him.

Which wouldn't do at all.

CHAPTER ELEVEN

LAYLA

AFTER WORKING MY WAY THROUGH THE CAFETERIA'S labyrinth, I scanned the room, not finding Auric anywhere.

Just as well. I didn't want to see his perfect face anyway.

Unfortunately, there wasn't a single table open. The male Noir with shaggy, dark hair stood up, waving me over.

I had no idea how the female and her mates had managed to procure their food before me, but they'd sectioned off a table of their own and had apparently saved me a spot.

Beggars can't be choosers.

Tucking my chin to my chest, I clutched my tray of indiscernible mush and accepted the invitation. Without Auric, I was truly on my own, and I didn't want to try taking my food back to my cell when I'd probably just run into more sex-starved Noir again.

The girl and the blond male gaped at their mate as he grinned up at me.

"I'm Zian," he said, waving at me to sit down. "I think we got off on the wrong foot earlier. This is Raven and Sorin."

The female crossed her arms, ignoring her food even though she really should be eating something. She was skinnier than me.

"Since when are you so fucking chatty?" Sorin demanded.

"Since my cousin said three full sentences to a complete stranger," Zian returned, glancing me over as if reevaluating me.

"Cousin?" I repeated.

"Novak," he explained just as a looming shadow curled around my feet. The male in question took the available seat beside my still-vacant one, then pulled out my chair and gestured to it for me to sit.

"Now do you see why?" Zian said as though explaining something.

Sorin grunted as Novak's lips curled into a knowing grin.

"Um, thank you," I said, sliding onto the chair while internally debating if starving might be the better alternative to this situation. "I-I'm Layla."

"We know who you are," Raven bit out, glaring again at the one named Zian.

Yeah, so they must not have been in agreement about inviting me over.

But the blond one seemed interested now as his blue eyes were bouncing between me and Novak.

Zian chewed off the end of something long and rubbery that might have once been dried meat. Now it more resembled a piece of leather, but he didn't seem to mind.

"So, cous, glad to see you're not in solitary, but where the fuck did you go last night?"

Cousins, I repeated to myself, examining them both. I supposed I could see the resemblance in their darker features, but Zian had a gaze that resembled midnight, while Novak's eyes reminded me of a glacier—chilly, cold, and *cruel.*

The latter jerked a thumb my way before ripping open his drink with his teeth.

"Sayir put you in her cell?" Sorin asked, his dark blue eyes flashing with amusement. "That must have been interesting. Is it permanent?"

Novak said nothing.

So I followed suit and picked up one of the hard biscuits, wanting an excuse to be as silent as my new cellmate. I unsuccessfully nibbled on the side before shoving half of the thing into my mouth and crunching down. *Ow.*

"So you're cellmates now?" Raven scowled at me, making me blink.

Wait. Novak isn't her mate, too, is he?

That question burned an intense dislike for her under my skin. Except, I couldn't explain where that particular urge had come from. Wouldn't it be a good thing if they were mates? It'd keep him away from me, right?

"That doesn't make any sense," she continued. "Why would the Reformer come all the way down to this hellhole just to relocate you to antagonize a princess?"

Novak simply watched her as he worked on another bite of his food.

She rolled her eyes. "Seriously, Novak. The angel's out of the nest. You've already proven to us that you know how to use full sentences, so the jig is up."

Novak simply smirked in response, making the female turn a dark shade of crimson as she ground her teeth together.

Yeah, Novak knew how to piss people off. Just like Auric.

"He saved my life," I said. Although, I wasn't sure why I found the need to explain on his behalf. "My uncle assigned him as my guardian for the time being."

Sorin released a low whistle. "I bet Auric took that well."

He glanced around the cafeteria. "Speaking of that old asshole, where is he?"

So they all knew Auric? I glanced at Novak. He merely shrugged and went back to his food.

"I'm surprised he let you out of his sight with Novak around," Zian added, chuckling. "Did you incapacitate him, cous?"

Novak ignored him but glanced at me and gave a slight shake of his head as though to tell me that no, he hadn't touched Auric.

For whatever reason, that left me feeling just a little more relaxed. "I guess I'm on my own today."

Novak grunted.

"Sort of," I clarified, giving him some recognition as my supposed guard.

We fell into a companionable silence as we ate, but Raven kept shooting daggers at me every few minutes with her eyes. I'd clearly done something to piss her off.

"Are you two mates?" I finally asked, gesturing between her and Novak.

Zian choked on his food as Sorin released a laugh.

"No," Novak said beside me. "We are not mates."

"Another full sentence!" Raven exclaimed.

Novak just rolled his eyes and went back to his almost completed meal.

I studied them all, frowning. "Then what did I do? I've been hiding for a week. Are you threatened by having another female here? Because I would think you'd prefer to partner up, not hate me on sight."

Raven's eyebrows shot up. "Why would I want to partner with you?"

"Because we're both women?" I suggested.

She glared at me. "Yeah, and what else?"

"Isn't that enough?"

"Maybe Sayir told you to partner with me," she countered.

My brow furrowed. "Why would he do that? He told me to share a cell with Auric and Novak. Nothing else. He hasn't even given me my reformation plan." Not that one could even exist since *I wasn't supposed to be here.*

Her black eyes held mine, her lips pursing as she scrutinized my features one by one. I finally looked at Novak, completely flabbergasted by this female's innate hate for me. "Are you compatible mates?" I pressed.

He locked gazes with me. "No."

"Then why the fuck is she going all territorial on me?" I demanded. Because that was the only explanation I could fathom for her rudeness. Or maybe all Noir were rude. How the hell would I know?

Novak set his fork down and reached for a strand of my hair, bringing it to his nose. I waited for him to say something, to explain, to help me understand this female's clear dislike.

But all he did was sniff, then rub the end across his lips. "Let's go outside, Princess."

My eyebrows shot up. "Are you crazy?" The last time I went out there, it went up in flames. "Absolutely not."

"Actually, it's a good idea. We could all use a little fresh air," Zian said, pushing away from the table. "Especially our sweet bird."

"She does appear to have all her feathers in a twist," Sorin agreed, his lips brushing Raven's cheek.

She glowered at both her mates. "Keep talking and see what happens later."

"I think we all know what will happen later, little dove,"

Sorin replied, pressing his mouth to hers. "Now, let's go play outside, hmm?"

Novak stood and pulled my chair backward with my butt still in the seat. He held out a hand, the decision already made.

When I didn't move to take his palm, he leaned down to whisper, "Trust me."

"No," I immediately said.

His lips curled. "You don't have a choice. Everyone is going to the yard today, including you."

"Seriously, it's starting to creep me out," I heard Raven murmur.

"Me, too," Sorin muttered.

Novak flashed them all a warning look, then refocused on me, his fingers waggling in a taunting invitation.

I could refuse and run back to the room.

Or I could test fate and see what happened.

Option one was the safer of the two, but as I gazed up into Novak's eyes, I realized I craved the second choice.

He'd saved my life once already.

Maybe he'd do it again.

I just hoped it wouldn't be necessary. But something told me we were just getting started.

"All right," I finally agreed. "But if flames shoot up from the ground, I'm blaming you."

He grinned but said nothing else.

I didn't accept his hand, instead choosing to stand on my own, all the while wondering, *How and when did this become my life?*

CHAPTER TWELVE

NOVAK

THE CROWD PARTED FOR US AS WE ENTERED THE YARD, THE other Noir recognizing the royals among them. And I didn't mean Layla. While she was a sight to behold, her title meant nothing here.

These Noir bowed to me—their unequivocal king.

I'd killed enough of them to gain respect where it was due. And I'd only participated in two death duels to date. But all it took to make them kneel was one show in beast mode. My wings weren't typical, and they'd only sharpened over time.

Sorin and Zian had followed a similar path, taking down several Noir while I served time in solitary. Now they were firmly marked as princes of my court. Meanwhile, Layla was just the pretty ornament, but I'd show her how to become a queen unlike any other. If she let me.

And Raven, well, she wasn't my responsibility. Zian and Sorin would handle her titling, whatever it would be.

So long as the other Noir bowed and stayed out of my way, I didn't really care.

Layla kept her chin high beside me, but I sensed her subtle shiver as her attention drifted to the infamous labyrinth. Then she took in the rest of the yard with another shudder, her blue eyes sharp.

I studied her profile, wondering what she sensed out here. When her lips twisted to the side, I took that to mean nothing yet.

Most of the inmates were in their own circles, socializing, exercising, or stretching. I wandered closer to the cliff, my wings catching the breeze.

Oh, I miss the sky, I thought, tipping my head back to bathe in the sun. It was a quick indulgence, one meant to refresh my senses before I put them to better use. But when I lowered my gaze, I found Layla studying me. An adorable shade of red touched her cheeks, providing her with an almost natural blush as she shifted her gaze to survey the yard.

I brazenly touched her wing with mine, making it known that I'd seen that little glimpse of interest in her gaze. *Nice try, Princess.*

She took a bold step to the left but wasn't brave enough to castigate my purposeful action.

Stroking one's wings was a sign of affection meant for mates. Her stepping away was a clear rejection. Yet it only intrigued me more. I always did fancy a good challenge.

"Anything amiss, little dove?" Sorin whispered to Raven.

The dark-haired female gave a slight shake of her head in the negative.

Layla glanced at her, then folded her arms around herself as she took in her surroundings again. Her discomfort was palpable, as was her disappointment when she didn't find Auric.

It seemed highly out of character for him to wander off and leave his charge unattended. Yeah, he was pissed, but he wasn't the type to shirk his responsibilities.

I'd followed him to the breakfast hall earlier, but I hadn't entered, choosing instead to wait for Zian and Sorin. Much to my surprise, Layla had arrived first. I'd nearly intervened when those idiots put their hands on her, but she'd handled it on her own, earning another smidge of respect from me.

A princess with a warrior's heart.

Mmm, a decent pairing indeed.

I just needed to crack that haughty exterior first. Her comments about mating below her station had amused me immensely.

She saw me as beneath her station?

How cute.

I couldn't wait to make her bow and beg.

At least her commentary had told me why she and Auric weren't yet an item—she didn't find the Nora Warrior worthy of her. Perhaps her brush-off was what drove that stick so far up his ass.

However, I suspected it went deeper than that.

He was a man of duty and honor, and surely, fucking the royal heir didn't fit into his skewed view of life.

Now where are you? I wondered, glancing around with Layla. There weren't a lot of places for him to wander off to. I'd seen him briefly in the cafeteria, watching as Layla had taken a seat at my table. Rather than march over and demand she leave, he'd held my gaze and told me without words to watch her.

It was a test of some kind, one that had surprised me. A century ago, there wouldn't have been a question regarding my helping him with such an assignment. But then I'd Fallen, killing any and all trust between us.

Or perhaps not.

Because he'd left me in charge of her care with a subtle nod before ducking out of the cafeteria.

Layla hadn't seen him, likely because he knew how to blend in with his scenery better than most Nora. He hadn't wanted her to notice him, allowing him a chance to observe. But now I wondered where he'd flown off to. I'd expected him to continue monitoring this little test. However, I didn't sense him nearby at all.

I clicked my tongue, causing Layla to frown at me.

Ignoring her, I waited.

And a few seconds later, I smiled when Clyde's familiar claws tugged at my jeans as the tiny rodent climbed up my leg.

Layla jumped back, her sapphire gaze round as Raven said, "Mousey Mouse!"

I rolled my eyes. His name was not *Mousey Mouse*. This was just his exterior to help him blend into the prison. Beneath all that fur lurked a predator who would eat her alive if he didn't find her adoration so cute.

His beady black eyes met mine as he perched on my shoulder.

I don't suppose you've seen that arrogant Nora Warrior flying about somewhere? I asked him.

I'd met my little shifter ally while in solitary. He'd called himself a Blaze—some sort of fiery, dragon-like being from another sector of Nightmare Penitentiary.

Apparently, the tiny demon could read my mind—a trait that would have earned his death under normal circumstances. However, he'd used his telepathic ability to warn me that my enchanted window-like wall was actually cursed and would slay me if I tried to fly through it.

We'd become fast friends after that. I'd even sent him to check up on Zian and Sorin a few times, which was how I'd learned about their new pet, Raven.

Had it not been for Clyde, I might have killed her during our first meeting. She'd been bloody and covered in my cousin's scent. I'd thought the worst until I realized she was the female Clyde had told me about.

Clyde whispered in my mind, his darkness communing with mine. Auric was nearby, but in a precarious position.

A new section of the reformatory? I asked, clarifying Clyde's commentary.

He chittered out loud, causing Layla's eyes to go wide.

"I still can't hear him," Raven grumbled. "It's like he's been corrupted by Novak."

Wrong, I thought. *He just temporarily allowed you mental access to help protect Zian and Sorin. Now that I'm here, it's no longer needed.*

Clyde growled in agreement.

Yeah, I know. I owe you. But tell me more about this new section.

He gave me a general map, telling me where Auric had gone. Something about being promised a phone. I nearly rolled my eyes.

He fell for that?

Clyde essentially shrugged.

The Nora Warrior was smarter than that. Perhaps he'd used it as a chance to see more of the prison. *I'm surprised he left Layla alone.*

Clyde glanced at the female in question, chittering again.

She took another step back, amusing me. *I think she's afraid you might bite her.*

Clyde squeaked—his version of a happy agreement. Then he gave me directions on how to locate Auric.

My gut told me that he was walking right into a trap.

Stubborn Nora Warrior.

He clearly hadn't received the message that he was in hell with the rest of us, meaning his rights were officially revoked.

I'd pity the bastard if I weren't so fucking annoyed. Because now I needed to go ensure his safety before he met with whatever fate lurked in wait.

I couldn't torment him if he was dead.

Thanks, Clyde, I said.

He chirped again, his scales momentarily taking over his fur.

Layla gasped at the sight, causing me to smirk. *Show-off.*

I swore the little demon winked before scurrying back down my side to dart across the concrete and sand and into a little hole.

"Nice, uh, pet," Layla said.

I looked her up and down, my lips curling at the gorgeous sight before me. "Yes. I'm rather fond of her as well," I replied, brushing her wing to underline my taunt.

Her lips curled down, my insinuation not yet clear. Or perhaps it was my intimacy that irked her. Regardless, her frown was rather cute.

I leaned in to inhale her sweet scent. "Now be a good *pet* and stay here," I added, driving my point home, before looking at Zian. "Guard her."

I didn't wait for him to reply, nor did I acknowledge Raven's commentary regarding my voice. But I did pause to glance over my shoulder at Layla after she muttered something unflattering at my back.

She didn't like me calling her a pet.

Too bad. She hadn't earned her title of queen yet.

Her hardened stare also told me she didn't appreciate being lured into the yard just to be left with strangers. It seemed she'd already forgotten that I was a stranger as well.

Clyde, I called, clicking my tongue again. *Watch the girl for me.*

I trusted Zian to keep her safe, but I knew he would pick Raven over Layla if forced to choose. However, Clyde would protect her to his last breath if I required it. And he couldn't easily be killed.

His little nose twitched as he peeked out from his hole, confirming he'd heard me and would stand watch.

Thanks.

He responded by giving me an update on Auric's location. It seemed he'd found some sort of recently renovated room with windows.

Great.

I tucked my wings into my back and headed down the stairs into the heart of Noir Reformatory.

The prison resembled a living, breathing entity that constantly shifted and changed. A hallway could lead one direction today and somewhere entirely different tomorrow. Portals appeared without preamble. And no known map existed, likely because it would constantly require changing.

Magic thrived in these walls, and not all of it was related to angelkind. While in solitary, I'd learned about some of the other realms inside the entity known as Nightmare Penitentiary. Noir Reformatory was just one wing.

Using the directions from Clyde, I wandered by our cell to the end of the hall and beyond it to a corridor that hadn't been there this morning.

Fresh paint tickled my nose, the concrete walls recently furnished.

Light shone at the end, indicating the windows Clyde had mentioned. My lips curled down. Those shouldn't exist this far underground, telling me they weren't real. Which I supposed meant they'd be similar to the window in our cell that showcased a false view of the ocean.

All right, I thought, tracking Auric's wintergreen scent. *Let's see what has you so distracted.*

CHAPTER THIRTEEN

AURIC

I DRUMMED MY FINGERS AGAINST THE COUNTER, WAITING FOR the Nora Guard to return. He'd caught me on my way back to the cell earlier, stating he had a package for me from the Reformer.

I'd asked if it was a phone, and he'd shrugged, telling me to follow him and find out.

So I'd followed, and now I stood in this recently renovated reception-like lobby with fake windows and too-white floors.

There'd been some sort of scuffle with a prisoner that had distracted him, leaving me to wonder if he even remembered leading me here. I didn't have a watch to know how long it'd been, but each passing breath left me more uneasy.

Why is this taking so long? I wondered, both at the guard and my current situation. This was supposed to be a quick fix.

Guard.

Reform.

Return.

Leave.

The princess would continue her courting season with

her myriad of suitors, and I would disappear from her life for good. Yet I wasn't even successfully through with phase one—*guard*—because I was standing here waiting for that damn Nora to return. Which left her alone in a prison full of murderous sinners.

She's fine, I reassured myself.

Except I had no real way of knowing that. I'd left her eating with Novak in the cafeteria. Not that she'd seen me. I'd purposefully remained out of view, curious to see what she would do with her tray of unsatisfactory food.

Novak had known I was there. Despite the century lost between us, he still understood my cues. And even while I didn't fully trust him, I knew he wouldn't allow anyone to harm Layla. She was just as compatible with him as she was with me, which created a huge problem between me and Novak but also ensured she had two protectors.

I blew out a breath, counting seconds that turned into minutes.

This was ridiculous.

While I knew Novak wouldn't let anyone else touch or hurt Layla, I didn't trust him not to do something.

He was a sadist. Dark. Menacing. *Violent.*

She'd break beneath him.

And he'd enjoy watching her shatter.

Enough time had passed for them to finish eating, which meant he'd likely taken her elsewhere now. Perhaps even back to the cell, where they would be alone.

Fuck. I palmed the back of my neck and growled under my breath. Whatever the Reformer wanted to give me wasn't worth the risk. I'd already waited for fuck knew how long. It wasn't like those windows were real, and there wasn't a damn clock anywhere in this damn prison.

"Fuck it," I muttered, taking a step toward the door, only

to find Novak leaning against the threshold with an arched brow. "What the fuck are you doing here?" *No, better question.* "Where the hell is Layla?"

"Safe," he replied.

Both my eyebrows flew upward. "Unguarded is not safe, Novak."

"Who says I left her unguarded?" he returned.

I didn't afford him a reply, instead stalking forward with the intent of slamming my fist into his jaw. He had one job. One. Fucking. Job. And he couldn't even do—

A whirring noise sounded behind me, causing me to pause midstep with a frown. *What the hell is that?*

Novak straightened, his amusement disappearing into a mask of stoicism as his focus went to the space over my shoulder. My feathers ruffled in response, and I turned to see a massive black hole forming on the wall.

"What the fuck is that?" I demanded.

"Portal," Novak said, stepping up to my side.

"Portal to what?"

Something roared from the interior before Novak could reply, then a snout appeared that was the size of my head. My eyes widened as the thing snarled and leapt into the room, its head—no, *heads*—hitting the ceiling.

Three sets of jaws snapped at us, the metallic collars around its necks humming with furious energy.

My eyebrows flew upward as a Nora Guard appeared behind it. "Fuck," he muttered, glancing around the room. When his gaze landed on me, his pupils flared. Then he glanced at Novak with a grunt. "Better run, Noir. Beast will think you're a snack."

The "beast" in question roared in agreement, but his beady black eyes seemed to fall on me, not Novak.

And then it lunged.

I jumped backward as an electric current ran through the air, zapping the thing into temporary submission. "Back through the portal," the guard demanded.

But the creature had other ideas.

One of the three heads snapped backward, taking hold of the guard's head and crushing his skull with a single bite.

My lips parted.

Then the three-headed *thing*—which I supposed resembled a hellhound, just much larger, and not nearly as obedient—trained his focus on me.

I jumped backward as one meaty paw swiped forward. Novak darted to the side as well, placing the beast between us.

"Neck!" Novak shouted.

I frowned at him, my dagger falling into my hand.

The portal behind this thing had closed, leaving the two of us alone with the beast and a doorway far too small for it to squeeze through. If we could get to the hall, we could shut the door and lock it inside.

But that required us to get around the damn thing now since it'd blocked our escape path.

Novak had a knife in his hand now, courtesy of the fallen guard, and he went for the throat of one head.

Gold blood splattered all over the ground and Novak's bare torso, causing the beast to roar in fury. However, *I* seemed to be the target of that anger.

Fire billowed out of the creature's mouth, nearly catching my feathers as I ducked and rolled beneath the beast's belly.

Golden gates, I thought, marveling at the insanity of this situation. Where the fuck was this thing even from? It was a creature unlike any I'd ever seen, and I'd fought a lot of mythical creatures over my extended lifetime.

With a shake of my head, I came out on the other side and followed Novak's direction by leaping onto the thing's back and gliding my blade across the throat of a second head.

Shrieks followed, the monster going up in flames all over his body.

My wings reacted to the pending heat, flapping wildly at my back to take me to the ceiling before the fire could touch my skin.

Novak took a similar course, only his burst of wind took him near the windows—which had him bolting forward again and then up.

I frowned at the bizarre action, wondering what had him so fearful of the glass.

The beast rewarded my distraction by striking out one of those angry paws, lined with glowing claws, and catching my thigh in the process.

I cursed, agony licking through my veins at the sharp gash.

It wasn't enough to bring me down, but it burned like hell, causing me to stumble slightly back and into a corner.

The beast's final head growled in impending victory, its massive jaws snapping at me in excitement.

Only, Novak landed on the thing's back, similar to what I'd done before, and effortlessly drew his blade across the thing's throat, showering me in a mist of golden grime.

Ugh, I thought, wiping the shit from my face as the creature fell to the ground with a loud, resilient thud.

Novak stood on its back, twirling the blade, resembling a picture of ease and content despite the gore dripping from his torso.

I kicked the thing's head as I righted myself, only to

flinch as pain shot up my leg. "What the fuck was that?" I managed to ask through gritted teeth.

"Product of Noir Reformatory," Novak drawled.

Both my eyebrows hit my hairline. "*What?*"

He just shrugged in reply.

"Are you telling me this is normal?" I demanded.

Novak merely lifted his shoulder again as if to say, *Yeah.*

"Fuck," I muttered, running my fingers through my tangled hair, grimacing when my hand came back slimy and wet. "This place is a fucking nightmare."

Novak snorted in agreement.

"That thing could have gone after Layla," I said, my heart skipping a beat as my eyes widened. "Oh, fuck. Where's Layla?"

"Safe," he said, repeating his word from earlier.

I jumped forward, ignoring the agony in my leg, and wrapped my hand around his throat. "How the hell do you know she's safe if *you are here*?" I demanded.

"Clyde," he replied, his hand wrapping around my wrist to give it a warning squeeze.

"Who the fuck is Clyde?"

"A Blaze."

I gaped at him. "A *what*?" I'd never heard of a Blaze before.

He didn't repeat himself or elaborate but instead used his free hand to press the tip of his blade to my throat. It was a gesture that said, *Release me*, so I tightened my grasp.

"I left you with her to guard her, Novak. And you couldn't even do that right."

His icy eyes narrowed. "You walked right into a trap. I helped. You're welcome."

"Trap?" I repeated, temporarily taken aback.

He used my distraction to twist my wrist away from his

neck, then leapt backward to land deftly on his feet. His eyes told me the comment wasn't worth repeating. Instead, he bent down to throw me one of the collars and arched a brow.

I examined the flimsy thing, frowning. "No wonder this didn't work." The voltage on the thing wouldn't even take down a Nora, let alone a menace from hell.

Novak released a sound of agreement, then walked over to the slain guard. Likely to take another weapon off...

My eyes narrowed. "What in the gods...?" The Nora Guard's wings were molting, something that sometimes happened in death. Only, the feathers were decaying in a manner unlike any I'd ever seen, and I'd witnessed my fair share of angel deaths.

Novak poked at one of the feathers, frowning as it dissolved into ash. He glanced up at me with an arched brow.

I just shook my head because I had no explanation. The plumes were all shifting to a shade of black, then dissolving into dust.

Novak stroked another, then brought his fingers up to examine the sand-like remains. Then, with a shrug, he stood and headed toward the door.

"Where the hell are you going?" I demanded, trying to follow him. But my damn leg wouldn't let me move nearly as fast.

Fucking canine-like beast, I hissed to myself.

"Novak," I called, flinching as my knee nearly gave out on me. The claws had dug in deeper than I'd realized. I'd survive and heal, just slowly.

He paused with his foot over the threshold and glanced back to watch me hobble toward him. A muscle ticked in his jaw, indecision warring in his eyes.

Then he pocketed his blade—or I assumed it was now his, since the guard no longer had a use for it. It was something I should reprimand him for, but he'd used it to save my life. And I was seriously starting to doubt the legitimacy of the other Nora here. Especially considering that the one behind me was still disintegrating into a pile of black soot.

Novak returned to my side to wrap his arm around my lower back. "Where's Layla?" I asked again, needing more than a "Safe" from him.

Fortunately, he offered me his version of peace. "Yard."

I nodded.

Then I let him drag me down the corridor, around the corner, past our cell, and to the stairs that led upward toward the yard.

A shower could wait. I needed to ensure she was all right first. Because while Novak might be helping me now, I didn't trust his word on her safety. Not when the two males best suited to protect her had just spent the last however many minutes fighting a golden beast.

What if there were more?

What if one was let loose in the yard?

Or had that thing been meant for me alone?

Novak seemed to think this was a trap set for me. I considered the play of events, how the guard had found me and isolated me, leaving me in that room to wait. Then the portal appeared. However, the guard had seemed surprised by his location. And he'd died for his inability to properly control that beast.

But those collars were cheap as fuck.

"The thing didn't come through until you showed up," I pointed out. "Maybe you're the target."

Novak glanced at me with a look that said, *Do you honestly believe that?*

"You have to admit the timing was interesting," I muttered.

He rolled his eyes and kept moving.

"Why did you come find me?" I asked after several more steps.

He seemed to consider not replying, then he paused to look at me. "Because I can't torment you if you're dead."

I narrowed my gaze. "You can't torment me while I'm alive, either."

He reached down to dig his thumb into my gash, his nostrils flaring with electric power. I gripped him by the throat in response, ignoring the agony rippling up my side, and slammed him against the stairwell.

His pupils dilated.

My lips curled into a snarl. "Try again."

He dug his nail in farther, accepting my dare.

I tightened my grasp. "I could end you."

Amusement taunted the edges of his lips, his eyes daring me to proceed. He lived for the challenge and the violence and our innate need for savagery. I could feel him hardening beneath his slacks, his arousal permeating the air with that damn leathery scent.

He wanted to fight.

To fuck.

To destroy.

And that harsh part of his nature called to mine, taunting my warrior half into coming out to play.

I roughly shoved him away, denying him the opportunity, and headed up into the sunlight to check on my charge. My duty. My sole purpose for being in this hellhole.

Each step made me hate her more.

She was the reason I'd found myself in this nightmare.

Those damn black wings.

Repent. Reform. Resurrect.

Three principles I intended to drill into her skull just as soon as I checked up on her and took a damn shower.

Novak's dark chuckle followed me upward, his presence a shadow of my past that only angered me more.

Fuck. This.

CHAPTER FOURTEEN

LAYLA

MY GUARDIANS ARE ASSHOLES.

They'd left me in the yard, alone, with total strangers. Although, I supposed Novak was a stranger, too. But I felt safer with him than others.

Because I'm losing my mind in this place, I thought, shivering, as his scent lingered around me. It was like he'd created a cloak of protection before he'd left me standing here by the cliffs.

Raven had joined me, our eyes surveying the labyrinth below. Her mates were nearby, functioning as proverbial bodyguards. Not that I trusted them to protect me. They'd choose her over me without much consideration.

So I'd just have to rely on myself. Good thing I had some training in the art of self-preservation. Royals were viewed as dainty beings who were meant to be coddled and cherished, but my father had ensured I knew how to defend myself.

I was the sole heir to his throne.

My survival was imperative.

Of course, he'd never expected me to *Fall*. So I wasn't entirely prepared for a prison full of hungry Noir. But I'd figure this out. There was no other choice.

I will fix my wings, I vowed. *Just as soon as I figure out what I did to earn my black feathers.*

"That one's about to get the wire," Raven announced, surprising me from the tense silence as she jerked out a finger.

My gaze went to the indicated direction within the labyrinth. A strange silvery line trembled in the distance, reminding me of a spider's web.

One of the inmates sprang through the labyrinth, definitely moving too fast to avoid the oncoming trap.

Slice.

I winced, but I forced my eyes to remain open, to observe each misstep. I wanted to be ready in case I found myself in that lethal maze.

"My father wouldn't approve of this," I whispered as the Noir's remains were carelessly swept into the ocean. "Fallen are meant to reform." I tilted my head, hearing the naïveté in my own words. "I guess some might be past reformation, but death shouldn't be a spectacle. Not like this."

Raven stiffened, her ebony wings vibrating like I'd said something wrong. "And you? Are you past reformation, *Princess*?"

I squeezed my fingers before me, unsure of how to reply. "I suppose that would require me to know how I Fell," I said softly.

Her eyebrows lifted. "You don't know how you Fell?"

I shook my head. "My wings just started to turn black one day. I thought it was a prank by one of my unruly cousins, or a trick of the light. Apparently, it wasn't." I swallowed and again focused on the labyrinth, but I felt Raven's eyes on me. "It's okay if you don't believe me," I added. "No one else does."

She didn't reply, her lips falling into a flat line.

After several minutes of silence, she whispered, "I know what it's like not to be believed."

I glanced at her. "You do?"

She nodded.

More silence.

"How am I supposed to reform if I don't know my crime?" I asked her, not expecting her to answer at all. "My father sent me here because he trusts my uncle to help me. But I don't see how that labyrinth is helpful at all."

"I don't think it's meant to be helpful," she said.

"What do you think it's meant for?" I asked, studying her profile as she observed the maze once more.

"A training tool," she muttered.

"A training tool for what?"

"Survival." A cryptic reply, one that she uttered with a wince before glancing at her mates. They were standing close enough to hear us but didn't interrupt or speak.

"The Reformer is meant to help Noir regain their wings," I said slowly, considering her words. "But so far, all I've witnessed is intense violence... and survival. I don't understand the purpose."

"Maybe you should consider that the Reformer isn't who you think he is," she replied, her dark eyes glittering with knowledge. While her aura suggested she was younger than me, her midnight irises radiated with experience that far outlived mine.

"How old are you?" I wondered out loud, trying to discern her features and the strange sort of familiarity of her bone structure. She almost appeared regal with that sharp chin and condescending brow.

"Eighteen."

I frowned. "When did you Fall?" It seemed wrong for a female of such youth to be here. Granted, I was only three years her elder and I'd apparently Fallen, too. Unless she also didn't deserve her wings? Was that what she meant when she said she understood what it was like not to be believed?

"At birth," she replied just as a commotion started across the yard.

My lips parted, dismayed by her comment, but she was already turning toward the gasps and snickers. I rotated with her, only to have Zian and Sorin step in front of us, blocking our view.

Frowning, I struggled on my tiptoes to see around the wall of black wings. Then I caught a glimpse of white feathers flecked with gold, and Auric's trademark scowl.

My eyebrows lifted as he approached, the two Noir in front of me stepping out of his way with matching smirks of amusement.

"Lose a fight with a star?" Zian drawled.

"Fuck you," Auric snapped.

"Beast," Novak said, appearing behind Auric in a similar fashion, his torso painted in golden gore.

"A night creature?" Sorin asked, glancing between him and Novak.

What's a night creature? I wondered, but my lips were sealed shut from the murderous rage radiating off of Auric. He glared at me, his violent stare making me shrink back to the edge of the cliff with nowhere to go.

"Good. You're still alive." Satisfied, he nodded. "Try to stay that way for a little while longer. I need a fucking shower." He shifted on his heel, heading back toward the prison with a subtle limp.

I frowned at the sight of his blood, taking a step after him. "You're hurt."

He ignored me and kept walking, but Novak stepped

into my path before I could follow. His irises sparkled with warning. I blinked at him, then checked his torso and legs for injury. He appeared fine. He also appeared to have acquired a blade, the hilt of which stuck out of his pocket.

I swallowed at the dark energy rolling off him and the way it clenched his muscles beneath the sunlight. He stared me down for a minute longer, then took a step back before glancing at Zian.

The two shared a silent exchange of words that left the latter nodding as Novak turned to follow Auric.

My eyebrows lifted. "Seriously?" I started after him, only to have Zian now blocking my way. I narrowed my gaze. "Move."

"I don't recommend joining them, Princess," he said with a cruel grin. He glanced at the golden footprints as the inmates murmured with curiosity. "They need a few minutes to calm down."

I frowned at him. "Why did they bother coming up here if they didn't intend to stay?"

"To check on you," he drawled.

I rolled my eyes. "I'm fine."

"And to stay that way, I'd remain right here," he suggested.

Sorin chuckled at the comment, causing me to glance at him. "Why?" I demanded.

"It's safer," Zian said.

My jaw clenched in irritation. I was really starting to dislike everyone making decisions on my behalf, telling me what was safe and what wasn't, leading me to yards just to leave me alone with strangers, telling me where to stand, how to move, and where to go.

I had a mind of my own.

Something I proved by deliberately stepping around Zian. "I'm going back to my cell."

He caught my arm. "I seriously suggest you reconsider."

"And I seriously suggest you remove your hand from my arm before I remove it for you," I snapped, tired of being manhandled.

He considered me for a moment, then lifted his hands. "All right. Then enjoy your educational tutorial, Princess."

"My what?" I asked, confused by his odd commentary.

But he was already turning to face a smirking Sorin. Even Raven was grinning.

I narrowed my gaze, then started toward the prison entrance, done being the subject of their amusement.

My life, my rules, I decided, stomping toward the building. No more playing by the standards of others. I was a future queen, and it was about time the others learned how to bow. Including Auric.

CHAPTER FIFTEEN

AURIC

THIS PLACE IS SO FUCKING WRONG, I THOUGHT, SLAMMING MY fist against the concrete wall of the shower.

After checking on Layla in the yard, I'd marched straight back to our cell for a much-needed shower. She seemed fine, standing at the cliff with that raven-haired female. I still didn't know what the fuck any of this had to do with *reform*, and I was seriously starting to doubt that I would ever know.

Because this hellhole? Yeah, it wasn't a reformatory at all. It was a fucking nightmare.

My entire body shook with rage. This whole situation had been building out of control, and now it was clear that not only was I not going to get to talk to the king, but somehow I'd found myself as an inmate with white wings.

I needed to figure this out, which meant I first had to calm the fuck down.

A shower would help.

So would some sleep.

Or a bit of rough sex.

I growled at the thought and let my head fall against the wall while the rivulets of cool water ran down my shoulders and back. *Fuck.*

I inhaled sharply through my mouth and squeezed my eyes shut. None of this made any damn sense!

I wanted to maim, kill, and fuck, in that order.

An instinct that only intensified as Novak's scent touched my nose.

Leather and smoke.

Even after a century apart, he still smelled good. Not like a mangy mutt, but like a man of worth.

Yet the black wings at his back told the truth about his nature. Just like Layla's ebony feathers.

However, after experiencing over a week of "reformation," I could see why he hadn't earned back his white feathers. It was impossible in this environment of death and blood.

"Is what happened yesterday normal?" I asked, rotating my head along the wall to glance sideways at him. He stood, leaning against the concrete siding, waiting for his turn with the shower.

Considering we shared a cell now, I supposed he had nowhere else to go to bathe. But I definitely needed the water first. Especially with my wounded leg. Not that he seemed to be complaining.

His gaze narrowed, his lips unmoving.

I arched a brow. "Is that your way of accusing me of something?"

Novak had never been the talkative type before, but now it seemed he never spoke unless he absolutely needed to. Instead, he let his facial expressions speak for him, and right now, they were telling me that I'd guessed correctly.

"What is it you think I've done?" I demanded, pushing off the wall to let the water run down my torso.

He watched the droplets weave along my abs and to my groin, my cock hard and ready to battle. I was a Nora

Warrior. He understood what that meant—we thrived on violence and sex, typically in that order. Well, I'd indulged in my fair share of violence this week. But no sex.

So yeah, I was as hard as a fucking rock. And if he kept staring at me like that, I'd make him do something about it.

He unfastened his pants and kicked off his shoes, accepting the challenge in my gaze.

Or, perhaps, taunting me.

Whatever.

"I don't know what you think I've done," I continued. "But this place is fucked up. Are the other prisons like this, too?"

He smirked and drew down his zipper.

"That's not an answer," I muttered, grabbing the soap to begin lathering myself up as he stripped. I refused to look. It would bring back too many memories and take this conversation to a very violent level.

He'd betrayed my command.

He'd Fallen.

He'd *left* me.

I hated him, and he hated me. Yet we were trapped in this tiny cage, inside a reformatory where death lingered around every corner, just waiting for me to slip up. Or that was how it felt, anyway.

Fucking three-headed demon dog. "What the fuck even was that thing?" I'd asked him before, and he hadn't really answered other than to call it a *product of Noir Reformatory*. I didn't expect him to elaborate now; my question had been more rhetorical than practical.

However, he was right about one thing—it'd been a trap. The more I thought about it, the more I agreed with him.

Coincidences didn't exist in a place like this, and there'd

been too many for me to believe they'd all been circumstantial.

And even if by some miraculous fate it was all an error, that *thing* still existed in this prison. A prison housing the future Nora Queen.

Un-fucking-acceptable.

This place was a damn death trap that seemed hell-bent on killing me.

Because I was here to protect Layla? Or for another reason entirely?

It wasn't as though the Noir liked me much. I was the lead Nora Warrior. Several of the men here had once reported to me, or to one of my lieutenants.

I had enemies.

But Layla... *Fuck.* Layla didn't belong here, just like she'd claimed. Yet her wings said otherwise, which further infuriated me.

Water stung the gash on my leg, making me grind my teeth as I rotated to let it run down my side and leg. The distraction helped, somewhat, and I concentrated on the burn.

Until a soft wing touched mine. While the cell admittedly didn't have much space, Novak never brushed his feathers against anyone or anything he hadn't deliberately intended to.

Intimacy underlined that stroke, causing my eyes to snap up to Novak's gaze. If he wanted to fight, he would have allowed his feathers to shift into razors. That he kept the tips soft meant he had something else in mind.

He stood naked beside me, his hand hovering by the showerhead.

I wasn't sure if he wanted the water for himself or for

another purpose, but I nodded because I didn't trust myself to speak.

Seeing him like this brought back far too many memories. Ones that I wished I could erase.

Sculpted. Lethal.

Everything that sang to my warrior tastes.

His pale blue eyes glimmered, fully aware of where my mind had gone, as he slowly went to his knees in front of me. My cock pulsed at the submissive pose, then I groaned as he pressed the water directly over the gash on my thigh.

I fisted his hair on impulse, my body strung tight from the agony rippling up my spine. He didn't fight me or utter a sound, just took the soap from my hand and used it against my leg while holding the showerhead with his opposite palm.

"I don't need you to do that," I said through my teeth, both pissed at him for taking control in such a way and also turned the fuck on by his current position.

He knew exactly what he was doing to me, too.

Asshole.

But I couldn't release him, even though I tried.

The temptation to guide his mouth to my shaft had my stomach clenching with raw need. I knew how he'd take me, rough and furious. He'd probably fucking bite me, too. Which would only make me come that much harder.

He was a sadist.

Always had been.

And I got off on the pain and the challenge he provided.

I focused on his black wings, reminding myself of his Fall from grace, the wrongness of this lust, and the danger of our situation.

Except the events of the last week and a half—or however long it'd been—ran through my mind, and a spike

123

of something else caused my heart to stutter. *Pity*. Because if this was the life he'd led for the last century, no wonder he'd turned even darker than before.

A place like this would taint even Layla.

It could probably convince me to Fall, too.

We can't stay here, I realized, swallowing. *It's not safe*.

Novak's touch shifted to my hip, the soap caressing my skin as he finished washing the wound with the water. Then he gazed up at me with a familiarity that made my balls ache.

One word.

That was all he needed.

And I'd sink into the welcome sanctuary of his mouth.

So wrong. So fucking wrong. But my dick pulsed for him anyway, my body strung tight with frustration, pain, and anger. *So. Much. Anger*.

My head fell back against the wall, my grasp tightening in his hair.

I needed to pull myself together. Tell him to fuck off. Ignore the urge to *fuck*.

This is all Layla's fault, I thought, miserable. Her scent. Those damn cherries. Even now, I could smell her. Ripe perfection. Sweet. A taunt to my senses that had my groin aching for her cunt.

I closed my eyes. *I'm stronger than this*.

Except Novak wasn't Layla. He knew how to push all my buttons. He knew my body from decades of experience. And a hundred years had made him bolder, wiser, hardening him to this harsh reality.

I should have known better than to leave him unattended on his knees.

And a part of me probably did.

Which was why I didn't yank him away as his mouth

touched my shaft. Why I didn't tell him to stop as he grazed the tip with his teeth. Why I didn't go for my knife when he closed his mouth around my head.

Instead, I growled his name as memories flooded my mind, all of them involving his playing, his touch, his mouth, his everything.

We'd shared so many females.

And when we couldn't find one to put between us, we fucked each other.

Something he reminded me of now with each stroke of his tongue against the underside of my cock.

I cursed, needing to stop this, to yank him away from me, to not give in to the beautiful temptation of his lethal energy.

But I was as weak for him as I'd always been.

Which made me hate him so much more. And Layla, too. She was the reason I'd found myself in this situation. Her damn black wings.

This fucking place.

"Stop," I said, not meaning it.

Novak took me deeper in response, his eyes glittering up at me like diamonds.

He knew I couldn't resist him on his knees. He never knelt for anyone. And even now, he wasn't truly kneeling for me. He controlled every moment, had me wrapped up in his web of darkness, sucking the soul from my heart and drowning me in the pain of my need.

"I hate you," I breathed, my head falling back again. "I fucking hate you."

He drew his teeth along my shaft in response, threatening me with his brutality and strength. That only made me dig my nails into his scalp, forcing him to take me into his throat.

He swallowed.

I cursed.

Then he pressed the showerhead against my wound, forcing me to *feel*. The sharp spike of pain went straight to my dick, throbbing in time with my heart, my pulse singing the song of wrongness.

Lust.

Desire.

Fall.

But him sucking me off wasn't enough to paint my wings black. And even if it were, I wasn't sure I could find the strength to care in that moment.

I needed his brand of pleasure. His penchant for savagery. His shadowy energy. He'd always been that way, even before his Fall. I'd always been drawn to this animalistic part of him. The danger. The strength. The *challenge*.

Becoming a Noir had hardened him, not changed him.

Which would have confused me in any other moment, but his hollowing cheeks distracted my thoughts, forcing me to focus on his wicked fucking mouth.

"Damn you," I growled, furious that he'd sucked me into this position. Yet even angrier at myself for allowing it.

I'd been an easy target, all pent-up rage and lacking an outlet for it.

Then he'd more or less offered his mouth, and now I couldn't stop pumping in and out of his silky throat.

I pictured Layla, her slick pussy permeating the air with that delectable scent.

Then I envisioned her between us, all animalistic sex and brutality. Fuck, she'd shatter between us. Her delicate sensibilities would be destroyed. We'd ruin her forever.

But this place would, too, if we continued to stay here.

Novak applied water to my wound again, aware that it hurt and knowing it would force me over the edge as he swallowed my head once more.

"Fine, you want it?" I said, thrusting harshly into his throat. "Take it."

He growled in response, his teeth tightening in warning. But I no longer gave a damn. I unleashed all my anger into my hips and finished what he'd started, fucking him with an abandon that would break a weaker man.

He dropped the soap to fist his own cock, pumping in time with my movements. Still in control. Still owning me. Still forcing me into that oblivion.

Hatred spewed from my lips, which only seemed to urge him onward, driving us both into a frenzy of violent yearning.

I wanted to strangle him. To take my blade and drive it between his ribs. Then flip him over and fuck his ass while he screamed.

It was fucked up and so damn *hot*.

I detailed it for him, knowing he'd approve. He confirmed it by using the water on my gash one last time, providing just the right amount of agony to shoot me into oblivion. I tightened my hold on his hair, forcing him to swallow every fucking drop.

He wanted this.

I gave it.

And I didn't stop until I was certain he'd taken it all, his icy gaze glistening with restraint and underlined in lazy triumph.

He'd come with me.

His leathery scent was a heady texture in the air, one that mingled far too well with cherry blossoms.

My knees shook, my body finally coming to rest.

I released him with a shove against the shoulder, disgusted and frustrated and way too sated to do a damn thing about it. He chuckled, still kneeling, his pride tangible.

However, it wasn't his reaction that latched onto my attention and held me captive, but the faint gasp from the doorway.

And the overpowering scent of cherry blossoms.

Layla.

Her wide eyes went from me to Novak and back, her pink cheeks and parted lips telling me she'd seen more than me shoving him away.

She'd seen us come.

Together.

Fuck.

CHAPTER SIXTEEN

LAYLA

HOLY. SHIT.

None of my erotic imaginings could have prepared me for the sight of Novak on his knees with Auric releasing all of his violence down his throat. He hadn't seen me in the doorway, but Novak had.

And he'd held my gaze with each swallow. Each pump of his hand. Each spurt of pleasure.

I shivered.

He still watched me now, his startling eyes radiating satisfaction and amusement. He'd held me captive with those icy irises, forcing me to watch every sensual reaction of his climax.

Auric finally found me in the doorway, his expression shifting from violent pleasure to just plain violence as he released a curse under his breath.

Novak merely grinned, then drew the back of his thumb along his bottom lip before effortlessly rising to his feet. He started to shower as Auric grabbed our cell's only towel.

My throat went dry as Novak began lathering the soap along his torso, his irises seeming to freeze me in place.

I couldn't stop staring.

I *needed* to stop staring.

But, golden gates, that'd been unlike anything I'd ever experienced. It had my thighs clenching with inexplicable need, something I knew Novak could smell because he made a show of inhaling deeply.

Auric cursed again, stepping in front of me. "Turn. Around."

Two words.

Snapped under his breath.

And underlined in a fury that made my blood run cold.

I swallowed, my eyes dropping to the water droplets on his chest. I'd marched up here with the intention of delivering a piece of my mind, but now I couldn't remember a single word of my intended lecture.

"*Layla*." He uttered my name with such intensity that my limbs locked into place, refusing his command. Not to be purposely disobedient. I just couldn't move. He'd paralyzed me with his ire, just as Novak had frozen me with his gaze.

These two males were going to be the death of me.

With a growl, Auric grabbed me by the neck to drag me the rest of the way into the room, then slammed the door closed behind me.

Trapped, I thought. *Oh gods, I'm trapped.*

The heady cologne of smoky evergreen and sex swirled around me like chains, locking me in place even more.

Imprisoned by lust. Driven to madness by their scents. Fallen for reasons I didn't understand.

"Layla," Auric said, his hand still on the back of my neck but his grip less severe than before. His voice had also dropped an octave. "Look at me."

I am, I thought, my eyes practically glued to his chest and the seductive drops of water sliding down his sculpted form.

His thumb brushed my pulse, the gesture almost

gentle. "Lay," he whispered, using a nickname from my youth, one I hadn't heard him utter in years. "Breathe, sweetheart."

The endearment made me shiver, but his words caused me to frown. *Breathe?*

His forehead met mine, causing a funny feeling to flutter in my chest. One that burned a little. Actually, no. It burned a lot. Like a hell of a lot. To the point where my limbs began to shake, my frigid form thawing beneath an inferno of agony.

"Inhale," he said, his opposite arm circling my waist, hugging me to him while his lips hovered far too close to mine. I could feel his breath on my lips, his presence intoxicating and perfect.

My skin prickled as my stomach dipped in anticipation.

But still I burned.

Everything started to sway.

His irises swirled with dark dots.

"Come on, Lay." His soft words tickled my lips and stroked my heart.

Lay, I thought, delirious. *He just called me Lay again.*

"Auric," I mouthed, my voice not working.

I have no air, I realized, my chest tight and my lungs screaming in agony. I blinked in confusion, then gasped and nearly fell over from the overwhelming scents hitting my senses.

His arm flexed along my lower back, holding me to him. "Good girl," he breathed. "Again."

I didn't really understand what he meant or why he'd felt the need to praise me, but my insides quivered as a result. Auric rarely ever delivered words of encouragement or pride. So I knew he meant it whenever he bestowed a compliment upon me.

I took another breath, the inferno inside me flickering to a simmer, my limbs seeming to function once more.

"Good," he said, his thumb brushing my pulse. He didn't release me, his lips still a scant inch from mine.

It would be so easy to angle my head and taste him. *So close*, I thought, sighing against him. *So, so close.*

He held me like that for several minutes, his wintergreen essence surrounding me in a protective cape that was all Auric.

Yet I sensed the leather fringes, Novak's fragrance acting as an exterior line that coated me in a similar cloak of guardianship.

My nose twitched, the hairs along my arms dancing on end.

Something was happening here.

It made my heart hammer inside my chest, turning my thoughts to ash.

Auric's grip tightened, his fingers sliding into my hair as he closed his eyes and exhaled. "Sorry, Lay," he said, surprising me. "You were never supposed to see that."

It took me a moment to realize what he meant.

Novak and Auric.

I shivered again, my thighs clenching, causing him to growl. "Don't," he warned. "Don't do that."

"She can't help it," Novak replied, shutting off the water and yanking the towel from Auric's hips.

My eyes widened as I realized what that meant.

Naked Auric.

Holding me.

His manhood... is... oh, my, gods... there... right there...

Auric didn't release me. Instead, he kept his forehead against mine and reminded me to breathe. "I need you to relax, Lay," he said in a far too gentle tone. "I need you to turn it off."

I started to shake, unsure of what he meant.

He's touching me, I thought, sensing his hardness against my lower belly. My *bare* lower belly. "Au-Auric," I managed to say, my throat resembling sandpaper.

He hushed me, being uncharacteristically gentle as he steered me toward a bed. My eyebrows lifted, my heart thudding wildly in my chest, but rather than push me onto the mattress, he released me to grab his pants and yank them over his still-damp thighs.

Novak merely smiled in amusement while he used the towel to dry himself.

I tried to shake myself out of this daze but found myself unable to focus on anything other than their mingling scents.

Auric cupped my cheek to force my gaze to his blown pupils. "Go up in your bunk. Don't come back down, no matter what you hear."

I gaped at him. "What?"

"Do it now," he said, his tone a touch stronger than before.

When I didn't immediately obey, he pushed me toward the ladder. Not roughly, but sternly.

Rather than watch me comply, he turned to face Novak.

The two of them squared off.

Then Auric slammed his fist into Novak's jaw.

I scurried up the ladder to get out of their way just as the two began to spar.

Oh gods...

Light and dark danced through the room, their wings a tangle of feathers that seemed to bleed into the other. My legs clamped closed, my body on fire all over again at the sight below.

How the hell could I reform under these circumstances when all I wanted to do was jump down and engage in the ultimate sin?

I bit my lip.

My mother had once warned me to avoid temptations, stating it could lead to potential heartbreak. Because, unlike most Nora, I wasn't afforded the option of a choice.

Oh, I had my courting season—which I should be attending now rather than suffering in a cell with two virile males—but everyone knew my father would be the one to ultimately choose my mate. And try as I might, I couldn't deviate from the path set out before me.

According to him, I provided an unerring moral compass for my subjects. I also represented the foundation for the future of the monarchy in all things, especially when it came to my intended mate.

Even so, relations below my station weren't exactly a Fall-worthy offense—that I knew of, anyway—but they were certainly frowned upon.

And these two males were compatible. Which meant that if I slept with them, a mate bond would very likely fall into place.

Disobeying the Nora decree?

That might warrant a Fall from grace.

My future mate had to be of Nora Royal ranking, from one of the approved dukedoms. Not a warrior, or worse, a Noir.

I dug my palms into my eyes and forced myself not to watch any longer.

Lusting would only lead to sinning.

And sinning would lead to Falling.

I needed to reform, not worsen my status.

One of the men snarled as the other grunted, followed by my bed frame shaking as they brawled on the mattress below.

I pulled my pillow over my head.

Don't look. Don't listen. Don't move. I chanted those three statements over and over until finally the room began to quiet.

But the scents remained.

An intoxicating blend of leather, smoke, and wintergreen.

I didn't know who'd won. All I knew was that I was on the verge of losing everything. I curled into a ball. Closed my eyes. And tried to dream of another life.

Only to fall headfirst into a fantasy world where status meant nothing.

A world where I could play with whomever I wanted, however I wanted.

And I drowned in an exotic mixture of ice and dark blue waves.

CHAPTER SEVENTEEN

LAYLA

ENDLESS DAYS AND NIGHTS OF LIVING IN A CELL WITH TWO virile male angels.

Filled with sensual torment.

Novak boldly showering in the nude.

Auric working out in the corner.

A door that refused to open.

A window that never displayed anything besides a warm sun over rolling waves.

No concept of time, other than to know more than twenty-four hours had passed. Perhaps much longer than that. Every time the guards stopped by with food, Auric demanded to know why the doors were still locked.

"For your safety," they kept saying.

The guards claimed that some beasts were running rampant through the reformatory, thanks to a faulty portal, so we'd all been locked down as a result.

"Bullshit," Auric had muttered, summarizing the situation nicely.

I sighed, staring up at the ceiling as the two males started to spar. *Again.*

They kept doing this, falling into some pattern only they seemed to understand. Their history became more and more apparent with each skilled jab and kick and punch. It allowed them an avenue for release of some kind, but not like the one I'd observed the other day, or whenever that'd been.

I swallowed as their scents mingled around me, suffocating me in their alluring cologne. The pillow between my thighs did little to relieve the ache brewing there—an ache that grew worse every day. And their continued bouts of wrestling did not help the matter.

Auric growled at Novak.

Novak snarled back.

And the two crashed into the corner by the shower, their masculinity and violence adding a seductive quality to the air that only made me burn hotter.

They both had knives, but they weren't using them. Only fists.

My nose twitched as an iron-like smell joined their intoxicating mix.

Blood.

I rolled onto my side to study them and arched my eyebrows at the teeth marks on Auric's shoulder.

That was probably why he'd practically thrown Novak into the shower. Now he had the other man pinned against the concrete, his forearm across his throat and his other hand at Novak's hip.

Growls emanated from their chests.

Then Novak reached over and turned on the water.

Auric hissed and took a step back, his jeans soaking through from the showerhead.

Novak merely smirked and yanked his own pants down before sending them off to the side with a wet thunk.

My eyes rounded as he fisted his cock beneath the spray,

his movements measured and slow rather than fast and cruel.

He gave himself a few pumps, then went for the soap.

Auric ripped off his own pants and joined him, the two males breathing heavily and squaring off beneath the single showerhead.

I whimpered at the sight, causing Auric's eyes to flash up to me. "Don't. Watch."

Novak chuckled.

I squeezed the pillow tighter, my heart hammering in my chest.

Then a click at the door sounded, causing Auric to stalk over with a demand of "What day is it?"

The guard at the door replied by shoving a tray of food at Auric's bare abdomen.

"I want to talk to Sayir," Auric added.

"Sure," the guard drawled. "I'll let him know."

Then he locked us in.

Again.

Novak walked over and casually took an apple from the plate and carried it back to the shower.

Still naked.

Both of them.

And hard, too.

It was all some sort of nightmarish fantasy come to life. My ultimate sin in a cage.

Novak washed his dark hair, the strands tickling the bottom of his ears. Then he opened his eyes to give me a smoldering look that screamed invitation as he took another bite of his fruit.

I shivered, only to be distracted by Auric holding up a sandwich for me. He hadn't bothered with his pants, likely because he intended to shower next. The gash on his leg—

something I'd noticed during one of their bouts in the shower—probably needed cleaning again.

I didn't know how he'd earned the wound, but suspected it had something to do with the golden goop they'd been covered in the other day.

The thing that concerned me was that his wound hadn't fully healed yet. He was a Nora Warrior and built to sustain and recover quickly from damage. But that mark on his thigh hadn't disappeared yet. Fortunately, he seemed to be moving all right. And he certainly held his own with Novak just fine.

More than fine, I thought.

"Stop watching," Auric said in a low voice. "It only worsens your scent."

"*Improves*," Novak corrected him in his deep, sultry tone.

"Don't start," Auric snapped.

Novak bit off another chunk of his apple, then tossed the rest of it to Auric—who deftly caught it while balancing the tray with his opposite hand. He made a show of taking a bite before setting it down.

My insides threatened to combust.

So I focused on my sandwich, only lifting my head when a slight chittering sounded through the room.

Auric was in the shower now, and Novak was wringing out his pants, but he dropped them when his little mouse friend jumped onto the fabric.

"Is that a mouse?" Auric asked, picking up his knife.

The little beast on the floor released a threatened breath of pure fire in response, causing Auric to halt midstep.

"What the fuck is that?"

"Clyde," Novak said patiently. "A Blaze." He held out his hand for the thing to climb into his palm, then he stood while focusing on the small creature.

"What's a Blaze?" I asked, my voice soft with disuse.

Novak glanced up at me. "A demon from another realm."

I frowned. "Another realm?"

He didn't reply, his attention returning to the mouse in his palm.

Well, not a mouse. He had scales now, reminding me of a miniature dragon. *What realm is it from?* I wondered, swallowing.

I knew other supernaturals existed in alternate worlds, but I'd never really met any. Noir and Nora kept to themselves, residing in a plane of existence that was somewhat linked to humans—a mortal species that worshipped our kind.

After a few minutes, Novak nodded and set the demon on the floor. It scurried off into a small hole without a backward glance, causing me to frown after it.

Novak pulled on his pants, then picked up Auric's and tossed them to him with a commanding look. "What's going on?" Auric demanded.

"Culling," Novak said, sliding his knife into his pocket as the demon reappeared. It trotted over and dropped a metal object on the floor beside Novak, gave a chirp, and ran off again. He bent to retrieve the slender metallic pick, then eyed the door as screams echoed down the corridor.

I shared a glance with Auric and rolled off my bunk to land on my feet with the help of my wings at my back. He pulled on his pants, his attention on Novak as the dark-winged angel went to the door to fuss with the lock.

"What are you doing?" Auric demanded, zipping up his jeans.

I thought it was pretty obvious *what* Novak was doing, so I opted to ask, "Why are you trying to unlock the door?" I crept forward for a better view as I added, "Are we not safer in here?" Because it didn't sound all that much safer out there.

"No," Novak said as the lock popped. He straightened and grabbed the handle. "We are not safer in here." The door opened and an alarm blared, but Novak didn't react to it. Instead, he grabbed my wrist and yanked me out of the room.

"What the fuck?" Auric demanded as he leapt through the threshold after us.

Novak's death grip on my wrist made it impossible for me to hold my ground, so I ran along with him while tucking my wings into my back. If he wanted to hurt me, he had a much better opportunity to do that in the cell. This was about survival. And despite everything, I trusted Novak when it came to matters of life and death.

"Novak!" Auric snapped. "What the hell is happening?"

I noticed he didn't try to stop us. He could have easily grabbed me and yanked me backward but instead chose to follow us down the corridor. Most of the doors were open with the cells empty inside, making me frown.

We'd been told we couldn't leave for our safety, yet clearly that'd been a lie.

Or they'd emptied this wing for some reason.

No, some of the cells did have inmates inside them.

"Novak?" I asked as the stench of charred meat hit my nostrils. We appeared to be running toward it, not away from it. Each step made it stronger. "What is—"

Novak jerked to a halt as one of the cell doors burst open, releasing flames into the hall. I shrieked, and he yanked me behind him to shield me with a wing as Auric's feathers caressed mine from behind.

"Fuck," Auric muttered.

Novak glanced over my head, his expression saying, *No shit.*

Auric nudged him. "*Run faster.*"

Novak snorted in reply, then yanked me along with him after the worst of the blast relented. Auric ran with us now, his palm a brand against my lower back as we sprinted toward the only known exit.

Novak gave him a single nod as he sprinted toward the stairwell doors.

Which were locked, of course.

I was starting to understand what Novak meant by *culling.* It was like that day outside when the inmates fought for their survival.

"There is no way my father would approve of this," I said in a rush as Novak began picking at the lock. He had it open in less than two seconds, before grabbing my wrist again and taking off up the stairs.

I really need to learn how to do that, I thought, reflecting on his lock-picking skills.

Sunlight flooded onto the platform at the top of the stairs, making my heart soar with anticipation. *Outside. Yes. Fresh air. Please.*

We spilled onto the courtyard, all three of us panting from the escape below. Auric's palm remained against my back as Novak continued to hold my wrist. They urged me forward, away from the prison entrance and toward the cliffs.

The temptation to just take off hit me square in the gut, the need to escape this place stronger than ever before.

"This isn't about reformation," I whispered, looking at Auric and then Novak. "This is about extermination."

Novak shook his head, disagreeing.

"Then what is it about?" I demanded.

"Survival," he replied as flames erupted from the stairwell exit we'd just come out of.

Auric growled, and Novak observed in his deadly silence.

I gaped. "This is madness."

"On that, we agree," Raven said as she approached with her mates.

"Oh my gods, you're alive!" I replied, actually happy to see her. I wasn't sure what cell she lived in or why it elated me so much to realize she was okay, but I felt a little lighter knowing she'd survived that inferno. Probably because she was the only one here I could call a friend. Sort of. Not really.

Gods, I hate this place.

"I don't die easily," Raven responded.

Novak used his grip on my wrist to tug me toward the cliff. Auric must have agreed, because he pressed me forward with his hand on my back, the two of them manhandling me in their own way.

For once, I didn't want to yell at them. Their presence was just too soothing to fight. Instead, I found myself leaning into them as we stopped near the edge, their eyes locked in some sort of understanding.

"Clyde?" Zian guessed as he approached with Sorin and Raven right behind him.

Novak dipped his chin in confirmation.

"Useful pet. He warned Raven, too," Zian said. Then he huffed a humorless laugh. "Right. Because you told him to."

Novak grunted, which I supposed was his version of an affirmative, before drawing his thumb along my pulse and sliding his palm to mine. I should have stepped away or dropped his hand, but the heat of his skin sizzled along my nerve endings, caressing me in a manner I didn't really understand.

"You smell infected," Raven said as she eyed Auric, her nose scrunching.

"And you smell like a wet dog," he returned. "Your point?"

Zian growled. "Watch it."

Auric rolled his eyes. "All Noir smell like wet dogs."

Novak extended his wings to give them a subtle flutter and arched a brow.

Auric's hand tensed against my back.

I cleared my throat, suddenly uncomfortable with the staring match between them. They seemed to be doing this more and more, as though they were taking each other's measure without words.

A muscle ticked in Auric's jaw.

Novak's gaze narrowed. Then he abruptly looked at Raven. "Heal him. Now."

Her eyebrows shot up. "Uh, hard pass. He's an ass, and I don't take orders from you."

"Wait, you can heal?" I asked, impressed. "That's a very unique gift."

"For a Noir? Yeah, I suppose it is," she drawled.

"I meant for anyone," I clarified.

"But especially for a Noir," Auric added, his voice holding a note of interest. "That's considered a divine gift. Interesting that a Fallen would possess it."

Raven rolled her eyes. "Are you questioning my goodness, *Nora*? Oh, but of course you are. White-wing superiority."

Her comment reminded me of what she'd said the other day. "You Fell at birth. How?"

"What?" Auric asked, his eyebrows drawing down.

"That's impossible."

"So is becoming a Noir without sinning, yet Layla's here," Raven returned, lifting a shoulder. "Oh, but I'm guessing you don't believe her, which is why you won't believe me either. Right."

"Prove your purity by healing him," Zian suggested. "I'll enjoy the shock on his face."

"Personally, I'll enjoy watching him accept the help of a Noir," Sorin added, sounding amused. "We're all beneath you, after all. Right?"

Auric's feathers ruffled, his chiseled jaw hardening even more.

I pressed a palm to his chest before he could speak. "How bad is it?" I asked him. I hadn't gotten a good look at his leg but had noticed his injury the other day while he stood naked in the shower. "Is it infected?"

"It's fine," he gritted out through his teeth.

Novak snorted, his wings fluttering again and this time touching mine as he stared Auric down. The Nora Warrior growled. Novak growled right back.

I swallowed, unnerved.

Then Zian said, "Sweet bird, do what my cousin asks. Please."

"Why?" she demanded. "I barely know him. And I don't particularly like the other one, either."

"Something's coming." Zian glanced at the prison while he spoke, the flames still bursting from the doorway. "We need our health."

"We have our health," she retorted. "They're not my or our responsibility."

"Allies, little dove," Sorin interjected. "Besides, he could be the *key* to our survival."

She scowled at that while Auric grunted. "I'm not your

ally."

"Not yet," Zian agreed, locking gazes with his cousin. "But I suspect you will be soon."

Novak dipped his chin just once, signifying his agreement, then squeezed my hand and cocked his head just enough to catch my attention.

I twisted my lips to the side, then looked at Auric again. "Did running hurt?" I asked him. He didn't appear to be limping, but I knew his pain tolerance was rather high given his warrior sensibilities.

His jaw clenched. "No."

Novak just stared at him, making me wonder if he sensed a lie in Auric or something else entirely.

I cleared my throat. "What aren't you telling me?"

Auric's palm left my lower back as he folded his arms. "I don't owe you any explanation."

"You do if you're wounded and incapable of properly protecting me," I returned.

"He's definitely infected," Raven put in. "I can smell it."

"Infected with what?" I asked, giving up on Auric and focusing on the one who seemed to have at least some answers.

But she shook her head. "I don't know."

"Poison," Auric finally said. "Something from the beast."

Novak almost looked proud of him for saying it, which left me wondering if he'd known all along or had merely guessed now.

Raven frowned, lifting her hand to hover near Auric. "May I?" she asked.

"Yes," I said.

Auric glanced at me. "I'm fairly certain that question was for *me*, Princess."

"No. I was asking her," Raven said. "Compatible mates

and all that." She glanced at me. "Trust me. I really don't want him."

I snorted. "Neither do I."

Auric just rolled his eyes. "Lovely. Both of you. Like I'd degrade myself in such a manner."

Novak coughed, and I suspected he was trying to hide a laugh. His feathers brushed mine again, and while I knew I should probably step away from him, I couldn't. He also still held my hand, which he reminded me of by drawing his thumb sensually across my knuckle.

Raven pressed her palm to Auric's chest, making him growl in annoyance. Then his gaze dropped to her wrist as his eyebrows shot upward. "Well, I'll be damned."

"Likely," Novak murmured.

"Fuck off," Auric snapped.

Sorin chuckled. "It's like we've fallen into the past, Z."

"Right?" Zian smirked. "We're just a little more colorful now."

"Shut up," Auric demanded. "Both of you."

"Keep talking to my mates like that, Nora, and I'll stop what I'm doing," Raven threatened. "And trust me, that'll make it hurt a lot more than it previously did."

Auric clenched his teeth, his gaze moving heavenward before falling on the prison. Then his nostrils flared. I followed his focus and understood why. The flames had shifted to an odd blue shade, signifying intense heat.

They were destroying everything inside.

Which left me wondering where they intended for us to sleep.

"Almost done," Raven said, her voice slightly strained as she closed her eyes.

Some of Auric's tension appeared to leave him, but he never once took his attention away from the building. The hairs along his arms had all risen, as though he sensed something we couldn't. Or perhaps it was just the healing energy warming his skin.

"There." Raven dropped her hand and shook it out, then visibly shivered. "I have no idea how you were walking, let alone *running*, with that inside you. A few more days and you would have been dead."

"Impossible," he muttered. "Our kind don't die that easily."

"They do when beasts from other realms infect us," she retorted, shuddering again. "That was some fucked-up magic."

"Did you know he was infected?" I asked Novak.

He lifted a shoulder, neither confirming nor denying it.

"Yes," Auric muttered. "He told me I needed a physician. I ignored him."

"When?" I didn't recall this conversation at all. I would have been on Novak's side for this.

"While you slept," Auric replied softly. Then he took a step toward me, placing his hand at my back again. "Something's coming."

Novak made a sound of agreement, his gaze following Auric's to the building.

"What is it?" Raven asked, stepping into Zian's side as all of us watched and waited.

No one spoke, but the energy around us shifted. I faced the ocean, sensing something in the distance. Auric turned with me, then Novak, their expressions grim as a dark shadow formed over the water.

A squadron, I recognized. At least a dozen angels, all led by my uncle.

He flew over our heads and landed in the center of the

yard. Auric took a step forward, only for Novak to whip around me and push him back with a hand on his chest.

The two of them locked gazes. Novak's expression was almost pleading in nature. Whatever he was trying to convey seemed to register, because Auric nodded, then placed his hand on my back again.

Sayir scanned the inmates in the yard, his dark gaze finding mine, and a spark of fury lit his eyes.

"Who did this?" Sayir demanded, his black-tipped white wings flaring.

He stalked over to a small group of Nora Guards who'd been standing near the side of the yard. I hadn't noticed them before but suspected they'd been there the whole time, not caring at all that the prison had just ignited in flames.

It confused me greatly. Nora were meant to protect. But these guards seemed hell-bent on pain and violence, making me wonder how they'd not Fallen yet.

Something was seriously broken with the entire system if I could Fall with no explanation and Raven could Fall at birth, yet these monstrous guards could remain Nora even while watching prisoners die in unfair battles.

Sayir grabbed one by the wing and slammed him to the ground.

"This is a disgrace." Quiet lethality underlined that statement. "Every misstep sets us back. And it seems that one happens every time I turn around."

Novak and Auric shared another of those glances. This time, I followed their expressions. *Disbelief.*

They didn't trust Sayir.

And frankly, neither did I.

One of the guards stepped forward. "Sir, if I may—"

"You may not," Sayir snapped, fluttering his wings as he

forced his calm demeanor to wash over his features. "I'll perform a proper investigation later. For now, we need to contain the inmates and clean up this mess." He waved a hand. "Knock them out."

"Shit," Zian muttered.

"You'd better not knock me out," Auric said in his most regal tone. He stepped forward. "I am not an inmate."

Sayir glanced at him and waved his hand. "Right, of course. Don't touch the Nora Warrior."

I grabbed his arm, my nails digging into his skin. "Auric."

His focus fell to mine, his blue eyes gleaming with promise. "Trust me, Lay," he whispered, palming my cheek.

Novak brushed his wing over mine, repeating the same vow as I met his calm, pale gaze.

I swallowed, my heart skipping a beat.

Then something hit the air.

A scent that made my nose curl up in disgust.

Auric narrowed his eyes, noting my distress. Then he caught me as my legs gave out, his strong arms holding me aloft as the world began to swim beneath a swirl of black color.

"I've got you," he whispered. "I've got you, Lay."

His evergreen scent kissed my senses.

And everything went dark.

CHAPTER EIGHTEEN

AURIC

I'D NEVER SEEN ANYTHING LIKE IT.

Every Noir in the courtyard wilted to the ground, including the sleeping angel in my arms. I pressed two fingers to Layla's neck just to confirm her steady pulse.

Alive.

Strong.

Sayir barked orders at the guards, completely ignoring me. I gently set Layla on the ground beside Novak. He'd fallen with his arm outstretched to catch the princess.

I couldn't blame him.

She was gorgeous. Especially like this, with her lips slightly parted and her fuchsia strands sprawled over her wings. The black feathers were a stark contrast against her pale skin, a sight I would have considered beautiful if I didn't know their meaning.

She looked so innocent.

But looks could be deceiving.

I drew in a breath, then let it out, and surveyed the courtyard. No other visible threats were around, and I needed to talk to the Reformer while I had the chance. But I would be intelligent about it. Not angry. Not accusatory. Just *observant.*

Because I didn't trust him not to knock me out "by accident." Everything here operated under erroneous circumstances, and I wasn't about to be one of his "unintentional" victims.

However, Layla and Novak had almost perished with me. That differed from the previous events—the ones that seemed to target me more than anyone else.

If Novak hadn't realized we were undergoing another culling, we might have died in that cell together. I'd have to ask him more about the Blaze creature later and how it communicated with him. Obviously, it was via some form of telepathy. But I wanted to know more.

And I wanted to talk about what it all meant. Was someone trying to kill Layla now, too? Or had she been the target all along? Perhaps they'd wanted me out of the way to more easily get to her.

Regardless, one thing was clear—I didn't trust Sayir or his guards.

But that didn't mean I couldn't try to squeeze some information out of them.

Starting with how the fuck he'd put all the Noir to sleep.

Bodies littered the ground, and while they were all breathing, it was still an eerie scene. I picked my way through them to the Reformer, who had his back to me.

"We're not sure what happened," one of the guards began.

The Reformer's wings fluttered, and my stomach heaved as if the world had just tilted, although I had no idea why. "You'll find out," he demanded, his voice lethal. "Or you'll burn with them. Half of my investments have just gone up in smoke."

Investments?

An odd word to use for inmates slated for reformation.

Sayir growled as he continued berating the guard. "One more misstep and I'll rip your wings off." He gripped the guard's wing and yanked hard, taking a few feathers as if to demonstrate. The Nora already had crooked stems, the feathers splaying out in odd directions, so I imagined this was a common reaction from the Reformer.

At least they didn't turn to dust like the other one, I thought, recalling the dead guard from the beast attack.

"Sayir," I said, keeping my voice calm. As the leader of the Royal Guard, I was entitled to information, but the Reformer had already proven not to care about my title or well-being. So I'd try a different approach, one of praise. "I don't know what you just did to the inmates, but it was impressive."

The Reformer turned to regard me with one raised brow. "I merely engaged a spell tied to the Noir inmates."

Interesting phrasing, I thought. *Noir* inmates.

Shouldn't all Noir be inmates? I wanted to ask. But instead, I nodded and allowed him to see my surprise. "I didn't realize you possessed that ability." Some Noir and Nora maintained magical talents, such as the healing spell Raven had performed. "Was knocking them out imperative for the next step?"

He nodded. "Yes. We'll be moving facilities, and I'd prefer to avoid any potential hysteria and unrest that may follow."

"I see. Do you need any assistance?" I offered. "I'm happy to help move the inmates to the transport." *Primarily the ones I want to see untouched,* I added to myself.

He studied me for a long moment. "I didn't authorize what happened here."

"I never said you did," I replied. But it was interesting that he felt the need to say that about this incident, and not any of the others. Everything else was a mistake or an error. Yet his word choice suggested those "errors" had been "authorized," whereas this one was not.

"I will find out what happened," he added.

Damn right you will, I thought. But out loud, all I said was "Good." I didn't follow it up with a demand. I didn't threaten to tell the king. I merely held a blank expression and again asked, "Do you want my assistance?"

"That would be appreciated," he said after a beat. "The transport will be here momentarily. We'll need to secure the prisoners on the plane, then I'll accompany you all to the new prison."

"How far away is it?" I wondered out loud.

He lifted a shoulder. "Space is relative." He turned away to face his guards, more orders dropping from his lips, leaving me to ponder his cryptic statement.

I continued considering his words as the plane arrived. And after every last inmate was loaded into the cargo bay, I still wasn't sure what he'd meant.

Space is relative.

Because of the portals? I wondered. *Or something else entirely?*

I took a seat beside Layla's prone form, her eyelashes spanning her porcelain cheeks as she slept rather peacefully on the floor. Novak lay on her other side, his dark hair swept off his forehead and his expression blank. Not innocent. Not even harsh. Just... stoic. It reminded me of a time when he used to stand among my ranks, never giving anything away with his eyes.

Always loyal.

Always respectful.

Always quiet.

What made you Fall? I wondered at him, not for the first

time. He'd been a remarkable warrior, quick with a blade, and lethal in the most beautiful aspects of the term. Then he'd Fallen, his body forever cloaked in an edge of darkness.

I shook my head and sighed, my head falling back to the metal siding behind me.

This wasn't like the plane I'd arrived on—no rows of seats or passenger areas. Just a lot of open space, suggesting this typically contained large cargo or boxes, not inmates.

But it worked well to lay everyone down. I'd used belts to secure the prisoners to the floor. At least the ones I'd been responsible for carrying. Which had included Layla, Novak, Raven, Zian, and Sorin, in that order.

The Nora Guards saw to all the others, throwing most of the bodies onto the plane bed without care. I'd tried to situate most of them as they retrieved more inmates from the ground, but after seven or eight, I'd given up and focused on those I cared about most.

Mainly Layla.

And, begrudgingly, Novak.

I'd provided some care to Raven as well, feeling it was a bit of a requirement considering she'd healed me. Sorin and Zian received what was left of my concern, which wasn't much. But at least they were safe and buckled.

"Long day?" Sayir asked as he moved toward me on the plane.

I'd sensed his entry, had even observed him from the corner of my eye, but had purposely not outwardly acknowledged him. I'd gone about this all the wrong way, demanding my right to a phone, not so subtly threatening to express my frustrations to the king, and overall disrespecting my "host."

If I wanted to find answers and to make sure Layla and I survived, I needed a completely different tactic.

Not that the disrespect and threats hadn't been deserved —they absolutely had been, and I still felt that way—but Sayir required a different approach. Something more cunning. More *complimentary*.

I needed him to stop trying to kill me. Assuming that was his goal, anyway.

Regardless, the previous method wasn't working. So I'd test this angle and see what happened.

So I sighed again, infusing as much exhaustion into that sound as I could while he sat down across from me. His gaze flicked to Layla before settling on me once more.

He wants to talk, I thought. *Good.*

"I've had better days," I finally said, responding to the question he'd asked upon reaching me.

His shrewd gaze narrowed slightly, indicating his distrust. Likely because of the shift in my approach. The last time we spoke, I'd demanded an audience with Sefid. He probably expected the same now, particularly as Layla had very nearly died in that fire. Which meant he found my calm approach suspicious.

Right.

I considered my words carefully, searching for a way to put him at ease. To make him think I'd changed my tactic for a practical reason.

"I'll admit," I started slowly. "My frustration over this situation might have been misdirected, causing me to react in manners outside my typical behavior."

I couldn't actually apologize but needed to sound contrite. And it wasn't necessarily untrue. I had taken a few frustrations out on Novak. I'd also been quite cruel to Layla.

"I see," he murmured. "I imagine being compatible with a female you have no right to touch can be difficult as well."

Of course he would know that, and the gleam in his dark gaze told me he rather liked my torment.

"Yes," I said. "That plays into my frustration."

Not a lie. Smelling Layla and not being allowed to taste her was a forbidden temptation that often haunted my dreams. Especially now that we were forced into such close quarters with one another.

"I've also been charged with her safety," I added. "Which has proven more difficult than I anticipated." It took serious effort not to show how I felt about that in my tone, but I managed a calm voice.

"Reform is all about survival," he said as he slowly slid down to the floor across from me and stretched his wings out along the metal siding. "Only the strongest will make it through."

I pretended to ponder that. "No point in reforming the weak." Not a statement I fully believed, but I could see in his expression that it was one he wholeheartedly supported.

"Exactly," he agreed.

"How does Layla fit into this?" I asked him, wanting to draw him into a useful conversation. I didn't consider her weak. I knew she was a survivor. But did he consider her strong enough for whatever insanity he had in store for her? Was there even a plan?

"Ah, to understand that, we'll need to discuss how to help her reform," he said as the plane's engines roared to life.

No shit, I wanted to say. Instead, I merely smiled and increased my voice to be heard over the rumbling around us. "I would very much like to hear those plans."

The doors slammed shut, causing Sayir to glance sideways. Two of the Nora Guards stood sentry at the front near the cockpit, their backs to us. But I noted the stiffness in their shoulders. The Reformer had given them all a proper set dressing-down outside, stating that none of them were safe from his wrath. Once he determined who was at fault, they would pay.

I was beginning to think he truly hadn't meant for this to happen. He kept muttering about his investment being a waste of effort. I'd pretended not to hear him while I'd helped load the plane. But I'd added that to my pondering list with his commentary about space being relative.

I glanced out the window over his head, then retrained my focus on him. "Well?" I prompted.

He smiled. "Do you understand how a Nora Falls?" he asked.

"They sin," I replied drolly.

"Do they?" he countered. "Define *sin* for me."

I stared at him. "An immoral act," I stated flatly, not keen on this waste of time. All Nora knew what caused the Fall— a truly heinous act that blackened the spirit.

"Do you think your Layla is capable of an immoral act?" he asked.

"She's not *my* Layla," I corrected him. But as to his question, I wasn't sure how to answer.

Did I think she was capable of the Fall? No, I really didn't.

However, her wings were solid black.

I'm innocent, Auric, she'd said on several occasions. *I don't deserve to be here.*

My jaw clenched as I recalled her tone, that broken quality a plea to my senses that I fought to ignore. But some part of me whispered, *What if she's telling the truth?*

"Perhaps she's not yet yours," he murmured, causing me to frown as the plane lifted into the air with the use of the thrusters below.

It was too loud for speaking at a comfortable volume, forcing me to wait for him to continue. Or, more accurately, to wait for a further denial. Because Layla would *never* be mine. Compatible we might be, but we were not of the same caliber. She was a royal. She would marry within the dukedom, as was her due.

Assuming we figured out how to fix her Fall from grace.

I glanced down at her, my fingers brushing through her silky strands. *So beautiful. So innocent.* Did I believe she could engage in an immoral act? Honestly, no, I could not. But the evidence lay at her back.

My throat worked to swallow, my heart skipping a beat in my chest as the plane began to level around us, the clouds kissing the windows outside.

We were moving at incredible speeds, the turbulence enough to make my stomach twist with unease.

All these angels were immobile and unaware.

If something happened now, they would all perish.

Except Layla, I thought, drawing my thumb along her cheek. *I won't let anything happen to you.*

"Perhaps she's not yet yours," Sayir started again now that the engines had calmed to more of a stable rumble rather than a deafening roar. "But that doesn't tell me if you believe she's capable of an immoral act. What would you say if I'd asked you that a month ago?"

"About her committing a sin?" I asked, ensuring I followed his question.

"Yes."

"I would have laughed," I answered honestly.

"Yet you're so easily convinced that she's Fallen as the result of some wicked deed now," he mused. "Does that not seem strange to you?"

"Everything about this situation is *strange* to me," I

retorted, my patience thinning. "She claims she's innocent. Her wings say otherwise. And besides, it's been some years since I've truly known her." Who knew what depravity she'd indulged in during my absence?

But where? I asked myself. *Where did she find that depravity? She was surrounded by chaperones and golden gates.*

"Perhaps immoral acts are not how one Falls," he suggested after a beat of silence.

I narrowed my eyes. "What are you trying to imply?"

"What do you think I'm trying to imply?" he countered.

Always riddles with this cryptic asshole. I nearly growled but instead said, "I thought you wanted to discuss the plans for her reform."

"Yes, to do that, one must understand how she Fell."

"And do you know how she Fell?" I asked, genuinely curious.

"Of course," he replied. "I imagine I would need to in order to reform her, yes?"

My jaw ticked. "Are you going to tell me more?"

"Not until you understand what causes one to Fall."

"I'm over a hundred years old, Sayir. Nora Fall by sinning. There's nothing else to it."

He arched a brow. "So it's a sin to disobey a direct order?" He looked at Novak and then at Zian and Sorin. "That's how they Fell, yes? By defying your order?"

"They did much more than that."

"Did they?" he pressed. "Explain."

"They were under orders to kill a known assailant. They chose to allow that person to live and, by doing so, helped the culprit commit additional crimes against the Nora. It's a sin to go against the orders of a commanding officer because it implies one is against all of Nora kind."

"Ah, and there you have it," he said, smiling. "The true cause of the Fall."

I frowned. "A sin." Just like I'd said.

"No."

He didn't elaborate. Just declined my comment, causing me to puzzle over what I'd just said.

"To go against all of Nora kind," I repeated slowly.

His lips curled. "And now you're learning."

"That's just one of many sins."

"Is it? Or is it the ultimate sin?" He flashed me an indulgent smile. "Isn't it interesting how killing a Noir isn't a sin, yet countering a direct order is?"

"Some Noir are irredeemable."

"Yet, I could have sworn that causing the death of another was an immoral act," he replied. "Surely the gods frown upon us snuffing out the lives of others."

"Says the man responsible for several dozens of lives in this prison system, and that's only this week," I countered.

Something in his gaze darkened. "I've already said today's episode wasn't authorized."

"What about the culling in the yard before?" I retorted. "Or the beast I ran into while waiting for one of your guards?"

"Unfortunate situations, I assure you," he replied smoothly.

"Were they authorized?"

"I think we're losing focus, Auric. This is about Layla, yes?" He stretched out his long legs to cross them at the ankles. "She needs to consider any and all acts, including thoughts, that might have led to her Fall. Such as, I don't know, being against a certain edict from her father. Sefid is, after all, the one who creates our laws. I think a reflection of her opinions may shed light on how she can repent."

I stared at him. "Are you saying she Fell because she disagreed with King Sefid on something?" Because that was insane.

"I'm saying he makes up the rules, and an attempt to break those rules could lead to a Fall." He smiled then. "Figure out the cause, repent, and be reborn as Nora. Isn't that a beautiful story?"

"What *rule* could she have broken?" I demanded.

"Ah, now you sound like you don't believe she's Fallen. How fascinating."

"Stop fucking with me and speak plainly, Sayir. How did she Fall, and how do we fix it?"

He sighed loudly. "And here I thought we were finally having a productive conversation."

"It would be more productive without your penchant for riddles."

"Are they riddles or *plain* words that you are failing to understand?" he countered, a hint of annoyance in his tone. "I can't tell you how to fix this with steps, Auric. Although, I daresay I did provide several suggestions already. Perhaps you need to consider if she should be reformed. Maybe being a Noir was her destiny all along."

My eyebrows flew upward. "Are you suggesting that the heir to your brother's throne should be a Noir?"

"I would never suggest that," he replied, his lips curling. "But there are other suggestions to consider."

"Which are?"

"Are you always this obtuse?" Sayir wondered aloud, arching a brow.

I opened my mouth to ask him if he was always this fucking cryptic, when movement along the wall caught my eye. *Clyde.* The little mouse demon thing—*Blaze*—crawled over the window, its beady eyes catching and holding mine for a brief moment.

Sayir glanced upward, following my distracted stare, only for the little demon to blend right in with the wall. My lips parted at the display of power. He'd either gone invisible or taken on a masterful chameleonlike ability.

When Sayir lowered his gaze, the Blaze appeared again and made a show of tapping on the glass. Or rather, gesturing to it. He didn't make a sound.

"I'm not obtuse," I said slowly, trying to engage in the conversation while also attempting to follow whatever Clyde wanted me to see. "I'm just trying to discern what Layla has done and how to fix her." I clenched my jaw, thinking what I really wanted to ask: *I'd also like to know how all this violence is meant to help Noir reform.*

"True reformation can only happen in the face of death," he said after a beat.

I arched a brow. "Meaning?" I really hoped he wasn't implying that Layla had to nearly die to qualify for his version of reform. Granted, she'd already faced death at least two times in his reformatory, so maybe that was what he meant.

In which case, he was insane.

"Why reform one who isn't worthy?" he countered.

"Are you saying Layla isn't worthy?" I asked, my skin prickling with the words. She was absolutely worthy of so much more, and if he said otherwise, my entire calm façade would burn to ash.

"I'm speaking in general terms—why reform a weak Noir?"

"Is that the point of your cullings?" I wondered out loud. Was that how he justified this madness? That it was a way to weed out the weak whom he didn't find worthy of his brand of reform?

"It's a reasonable training exercise," he replied.

Training exercise? "For what?"

"Reform," he answered simply.

And has it ever worked before? I wanted to demand. In all my years, I couldn't recall ever actually meeting a reformed Nora. Instead, I said nothing because I had no idea how to reply to that. All I knew at this point was that I needed to get Layla as far away from him and his antics as possible.

"I think you're focusing on the wrong aspects of our conversation, Auric," he continued. "And by doing so, you've completely missed the point."

"Have I?" I wondered out loud, glancing at the window again. *What the fuck is that?* I thought, my eyes threatening to widen at the black cloud we were flying into.

"How a Nora Falls," Sayir murmured. "Why Layla Fell. How to fix her. It's like you've not been listening at all."

My stomach protested as the black cloud swallowed us whole, painting the windows in an ebony shade. "What's going on?" I demanded.

Sayir followed my gaze, then shrugged. "Going through a portal, I imagine."

"A portal? *In the sky*?"

"It's the quickest way to travel," he explained.

"Where is this new reformatory?"

"Does it matter?" he countered as the sky reappeared outside the windows. "We already know that the only way out of here is through reform, right?"

Or one of those portals, I thought, trying to better understand the technology. Those didn't really exist in our realm. They were created with another form of magic, one I was very interested in learning more about.

"Of course," I said out loud, keeping my ponderings to myself. Not that I would confide in the Reformer.

But maybe in Novak.

I glanced at him just in time to see Clyde slip into his pocket.

If Sayir saw it, he didn't comment. But then, his eyes weren't on Novak. They were on my hand, watching as my fingers stroked through Layla's hair.

I considered stopping but couldn't. For whatever reason, I needed her to know I was here, offering comfort where I could. So unlike our first flight, where I'd essentially refused to look at her, let alone touch her. But my anger had morphed into something else. Confusion. Annoyance. *Longing.*

Fury still existed as a thin layer on the top, eager to act out. However, beneath it were a myriad of emotions all battling for purchase.

Had Layla truly Fallen because she disagreed with her father on something? I would have to ask her if she recalled anything in particular.

And Novak.

Was I truly the reason he Fell? Because he'd disobeyed my order? I'd spent a century assuming it was the aftermath of that incident that had earned his Fall—not the singular act of defying me, but its consequences. The very notion of it churned my stomach, a sense of wrongness settling on my shoulders.

None of this was right.

Sayir was fucking with me.

No, *distracting* me.

Clyde had wanted me to see the portal, to know we weren't just hopping over to another island but perhaps leaving the realm entirely for a new one.

To where? I wondered, glancing out at the too-blue sky.

I wasn't meant to know.

But that didn't mean I couldn't pay attention.

Not much I could do with the blue sky, but once we landed, I'd take in our surroundings. I'd learn. And maybe I'd use that information... to escape.

Because I didn't believe Sayir for a minute that he had a plan for Layla's reform.

His idea of repenting involved cullings and poisonous monsters.

He might not have ordered this last execution—a notion that carried much doubt—but he'd authorized the others. I was sure of it.

We couldn't stay here.

Not if we wanted to survive.

I made a vow to keep Layla safe. So I would. Even if it meant defying every rule set before me.

Would my wings turn black as a result? Or was that just more of Sayir's inane babble?

I guess we'll find out.

CHAPTER NINETEEN

AURIC

Sᴀʏɪʀ ᴄᴏɴᴛɪɴᴜᴇᴅ ʜɪs ᴄʀʏᴘᴛɪᴄ ᴄᴏᴍᴍᴇɴᴛᴀʀʏ ᴜɴᴛɪʟ ᴡᴇ landed, ending with a relieved "Ah, yes, much, much better."

I glanced out the window to see the rock formation ahead and arched a brow. "A cave network?"

"Much more durable and reliable than the last prison, I assure you." He unbuckled himself and slid effortlessly to his feet. "I actually own this location. Unlike the Nightmare Penitentiary one."

"Nightmare Penitentiary?" I repeated.

"The prison network we just left," he explained. "I thought I'd try outsourcing. As you can see, it didn't work out well. Too many supernaturals in one network, I think." He lifted a shoulder, then walked away before I could ask any clarifying questions. Not that I had one. I was too busy gaping at him.

He'd *outsourced* the location?

No wonder that prison had been in shambles.

It also explained the monsters—and Novak's pet.

Why would King Sefid send his daughter to the most unstable reformatory? There were others in existence. Were they too full? Or had he wanted her to attend the location his brother was currently monitoring?

Because it seemed Sayir had been closely supervising this last prison, perhaps because of all the errors that had occurred.

Maybe he hadn't sanctioned the killings at all, but had been trying to prevent them from getting out of hand.

My mind liked that notion, but my gut told me it was wrong.

Nothing about this situation felt right. And all of Sayir's comments had left me uneasy. Something about the Fall wasn't adding up. Because he was right. I did find it very hard to believe that Layla had done something worthy of her black feathers. The fact that she was insistent upon her innocence only enhanced that instinct.

If she'd truly Fallen, she would feel unrepentant about her act and wouldn't mind admitting it. So why claim innocence when her lies were written into her wings? Because she truly believed in her innocence.

Or she was playing a very dangerous game.

If it turned out to be the latter, then I'd leave her to her fate and quit on the spot. The fact that I could feel that way so resolutely only further confirmed her truth, because I would never proclaim such an ultimatum unless I knew without a doubt that there wasn't a chance of it coming to fruition.

I loved being a Nora Warrior.

No female would ever change that.

Yet, I would throw down my sword if I found out she'd played me for a fool.

"Auric," Sayir called from the exit as his guards opened the doorway. "We're ready to move the prisoners inside."

I nodded and unbuckled myself before standing. Then I bent to gently unfasten Layla's straps.

A Nora Guard appeared beside me. "Boss says to get the girl and lethal one in a cell first."

"I'll take care of the princess," I said, underlining that final word with steel. She wasn't a *girl*. She was a *royal*. A future queen. A female to be revered. Not some ordinary prisoner.

I silently watched as two more guards gathered some inmates at the back, rolling them onto stretchers and not being too careful about it. I winced when one of the inmate's feathers snagged on the contraption, breaking several of the stems. Those would ache when he woke up.

Fortunately, the Nora Guard who retrieved Novak did so with far more care, rolling him onto a stretcher without damaging any plumes.

Rather than place Layla on one of those things, I lifted her into my arms. Her head rolled against my chest, her cheek warm and her brilliant hair shining like the fire we'd escaped earlier.

"Follow me," the guard said, sounding rather agreeable.

Perhaps my little chat with Sayir had put some of these nitwits at ease.

Or maybe I was walking into another trap.

A little nose poked out of Novak's pocket, the whiskers twitching subtly before disappearing inside again.

The guard didn't notice, but it had me studying our surroundings as we stepped off the plane onto a thick pad of grass. There was no sign of the ocean here, just mountains, trees, and thick gray rocks.

My nose twitched as I inhaled, trying to discern our location from the scents around us. But cherry blossoms filled my nostrils instead, causing my abdomen to tighten with want.

She'd gone into her courting season, which only

enhanced her scent. It told the world she wanted a mate, calling all potential matches to her side.

Including me.

And Novak.

A breeze tickled my feathers, the chilly air different from our previous location. Humidity didn't seem to exist here. And I suspected we were at a much higher altitude as well.

Energy hummed a few yards to the left as another portal opened between two metal rods sticking up from the ground. A set of guards stepped through a second later with a steel box in their grip. They carried it over to the wall of rock, set it down, and stomped back to the shimmering area they'd just entered through.

One of them rotated his wrist, causing a screen to appear above his watch. It seemed to be a list of some sort. He scrolled through it, selecting something, and nodded as the magic vibrated through the air.

Or not magic, necessarily. An electric current of *something*. Technology, maybe. But it sparked the portal back to life, allowing the two men to step through it, only for the void to disappear a second later.

"Yo!" the guard yelled from several feet away. "I said to follow!"

Right. I'd stopped walking when the portal had appeared. With a shake of my head, I picked up my pace and rejoined the Nora. "Sorry. I've never seen anything like that."

"The portals?" he asked.

"Yeah," I said. "That's incredibly useful."

"The Reformer built them," he explained as we walked toward a cavern-like entrance in the mountain. It stood over three feet high, the awning composed entirely of granite. "They're useful to go between all the prisons."

"Why didn't we just take one of those here instead of the plane?" I wondered out loud.

"The only portal on the grounds right now is the one you just saw. Easier to jump through the sky connection with the cargo than to carry prisoners through one by one." He stopped at a panel camouflaged into the entryway. I memorized the code he typed in, as well as the series of commands he added next.

Then I stepped back as the rock began to shift, revealing a doorway that led to a surprisingly furnished hallway.

If I hadn't seen the exterior, I would have thought we were entering a proper building. There was fluorescent lighting, polished marble floors, and pristine white walls.

The guard led the way, the wide interior large enough for me to fully expand my wings without touching the ceiling or the sides. Novak's cot rolled effortlessly over the ground as well, not hitting a single bump as the Nora dragged him toward our destination.

We went through another set of gates—with a second code I memorized.

And then we turned into a new corridor lined with steel doors.

Our new accommodations.

The Nora led us all the way to the end, opening the door with a swipe of his card and revealing a room I would expect to stay in at a hotel, not at a prison. I arched a brow. "This is certainly an upgrade."

"This prison is typically used for those on the edge of reform," he said. "Like a class-one prison for those who have committed minor crimes. It was the closest one within hopping range, and also significantly less populated than the others."

I studied this guard. He'd been rather informative, and

almost respectful. "What's your name?" I asked him. I'd not seen him before. Or maybe I had and just hadn't noticed. It wasn't like I'd spent much time studying the guards.

"Jerin," he replied.

"Nice to meet you, Jerin."

"You're only saying that because I actually answered your questions," he replied, taking Novak over to the sole bed in the room. While it certainly was large enough for the three of us, I wasn't thrilled by the prospect of what it insinuated.

I'd just sleep on the floor.

And Novak would, too.

"Or maybe because you've realized your new digs has a private bathroom," he added with a grin.

"Both are adequate reasons to be pleased by your acquaintance," I said, lowering Layla onto the mattress as far away from Novak as possible. The only reason I let him remain there was because I assumed he wouldn't be waking up anytime soon. Sayir likely wanted to unload everyone into their respective rooms first.

Later, I'd sleep by the door, and he'd take the spot by the window. It wasn't barred, but I suspected it wouldn't be easy to break either. It might even be enchanted like the ones at the old prison. Regardless, I didn't trust that entryway. So he'd guard it, like I'd guard the door.

"Need any help with the other inmates?" I asked, wanting an opportunity to learn more about our surroundings.

"Sure," he replied, the stretcher already at the door.

I followed him back out, noting his codes along the way and surveying every inch of the interior with each trip in and out.

I also noted where Raven, Sorin, and Zian went—into

the cell two doors down from ours, their room similar but not quite as large.

Once we were finished, Sayir met us in the hallway. "I'll release them from their sleep in an hour or so, then a meal will be delivered. We'll have to determine a new schedule as well."

"If you need any assistance, let me know," I offered, wanting to take advantage of any chance he would provide me with to understand more about this prison. For example, if it was going to suddenly breathe fire, I'd like to know how to escape and where to go.

"I'll keep that in mind," he murmured. "For now, just keep an eye on Layla. And consider asking her to discuss Nora rules in depth. Search for whatever she might disagree on. Perhaps it'll help facilitate the reform, or shed light on an opportunity."

It seemed like he was offering me a plan without specific tasks, or perhaps hinting at a solution without providing the explicit ingredients. Rather than demand he elaborate, I merely nodded.

"I'll be locking down the doors in five minutes," he added. "I suggest you be inside her room when I do."

I dipped my chin in acknowledgment and headed back to our new quarters.

Layla and Novak hadn't moved. Rather than nudge the latter to the floor, I merely sat on the bed and watched the door.

It closed and locked, just as Sayir said it would.

Then I waited for something to happen. Anything. Maybe another fire, or bullets, or a toxic gas, but all remained quiet.

Except for a little scratching sound that drew my attention to the only table in the room. I crept over and crouched, expecting to find something nefarious. But it was only Clyde digging a hole into the plaster of the wall. He poked his little head out, gave me a look, and went back to work.

"I'm going to assume you're planning to take a look around and report back," I said, standing again.

He squeaked in reply.

I accepted that as an affirmative and glanced around the cell, searching for anything else out of the ordinary.

No cameras.

No listening devices.

Proper lighting, with switches to turn things on and off.

An actual workout area—near the window—with a pull-up bar, weights, and a bench for chest presses.

The toilet functioned normally. The shower had hot water and was big enough for two angels with their wings spread. There was even soap by the faucet.

Like a hotel.

Even the linen was soft.

I sat down again beside Layla, my fingers immediately drawing through her silky hair. She would be thrilled by the shower when she woke up. Not to mention the privacy of the door.

My lips actually curled. I couldn't wait to see her reaction.

Then I frowned as I recalled that she didn't deserve to be pleased. She'd Fallen.

Or had she? I wondered, sighing.

I ran my fingers over her silky wings, unable to comprehend how something so perfect could be wrong.

It isn't wrong, some part of me whispered. *She's every bit right.*

Yet I'd been cruel.

A complete ass.

I'd ignored her when she tried to talk to me. I'd shut her out. I'd blamed her for my desire. I'd hated her for this situation.

Well, perhaps it was time I attempted to do something else. Something new. Something like... listening to her.

CHAPTER TWENTY

NOVAK

CHERRY BLOSSOMS.

I inhaled deeply, allowing the refreshing scent to consume me. Fuck, I wanted a taste. She was so close, her feathers nearly brushing mine.

My dick hardened in anticipation, my skin tightening with the need for release. I groaned, rolling onto my side.

"Don't," a deep voice said. "Or I'll shove you onto the floor."

My brow furrowed as I tried to escape the fog of a deep sleep.

Another deep breath nearly drowned me in Layla's natural perfume. Then Auric's evergreen cologne hit me square in the gut.

My hands curled into fists as molten need seared my insides. *Fuck.* I nearly growled in frustration, but a rumble from Auric had me forcing my eyes open. He sat up against the wall, his long legs stretched out and crossed at the ankles.

Between us was Layla.

On a bed.

A very large, comfortable, soft mattress.

Built for three, maybe four, angels.

I blinked at her, noting the intimate weave of our feathers, then watched as Auric ran his fingers through her fuchsia strands. It was a rhythmic caress, one underlined in possession.

Mine, each stroke said.

I allowed my wing to stretch, locking my feathers more intimately with hers. Auric narrowed his gaze at the movement, and I dared him with a look to tell me to stop. The tic in his jaw told me he wanted to, that if I so much as touched her with my hands, he would break every bone in my body.

I welcomed the violence. *Craved* it. And I almost reached out to lay my palm on her exposed midriff just to prove it.

However, his sigh held me back. It wasn't a sound of frustration but of resignation.

I rolled fully onto my side and tucked my arm under my head, allowing him to maintain the superior position on the bed. Not that I felt inferior. I just didn't want to pull my wing away from Layla, which I would have to do if I chose to sit up and rival his relaxed stance against the wall.

"You remember that time in Cromwell," he started slowly, his focus on his fingers as he combed through Layla's hair. "When that game turned out to be so much more than we realized?"

I grunted. Yeah, I remembered that. We'd played with a Valkyrie, only to have her try to kill us afterward. It'd been some sort of experiment on her part to test her strength. She had not appreciated the results. Or I assumed she hadn't, since she'd lost her life in the process.

"Do you recall what we found afterward?" he asked.

I glanced around, wondering if he meant what I thought he might. *Recording devices*. The bitch had recorded every second, including our romantic encounter. We never did

177

find out where that livestream had gone, which meant a video existed somewhere of the two of us playing with and eventually killing that Valkyrie.

Our new room didn't appear to have any obvious recording devices in it, but there were certainly some admirable upgrades. I arched a brow as I returned my focus to him.

"I didn't find any either," he said. "But I wanted your opinion."

Well, that was interesting. He could have just asked.

With a shake of my head, I told him I didn't see anything. Of course, I hadn't examined the room all that closely, but there wasn't anything lurking in the obvious spots. And considering the bed covered nearly half of the room, I'd expect it to be within view of my vantage point.

"I was just thinking of that incident because of something Sayir said to me on the plane," he added. "That ritual was a test of power, right? To prove self-worth. There's nothing Valkyries hate more than a weak link."

My eyes narrowed, uncertain of what point he was trying to make.

"Sayir said only the strongest deserve reform, that it requires facing death and surviving." He looked at me then. "But I'm going to guess you've survived quite a few of these incidents over the years, yet you're nowhere near reformed."

I stroked my black wings for emphasis, daring him to issue an insult. I'd given up on reform decades ago. A new life existed for me among the Noir, one as a feared being no one wanted to tempt into a fight.

Better than trying to earn back my white wings.

What would be the point now anyway? There was no longer a place for me in the Nora world. They'd given up on me. So I survived. I fought. I killed. I ruled.

"He told me you Fell because you disobeyed my command," Auric continued, seemingly oblivious to the lethal warmth growing inside me. The need to *hurt*. "I've always thought you Fell because of what happened after you made your decision. That rogue Noir went on to kill several Nora only hours after you refused my order. And it was your job to prevent that very situation. As a result, you paid for his sin."

I stared at him, his version of events causing my heart to race. "No." That wasn't what happened at all. "He was innocent."

"He went on to kill seven Nora. *And* he was a Noir. How the hell could you think he was innocent?"

"They took his mate." I knew this because I'd witnessed the aftermath. "And my wings turned black *before* he killed them."

Which was how I knew that breaking my oath was the cause of my Fall.

Warriors were duty-bound to protect the Nora and to obey commands no matter what. But I'd spoken to my target that day, had learned his intentions, and hadn't been able to kill him.

My instincts rarely guided me in the wrong direction, and they had been screaming at me, telling me the situation was all wrong.

It turned out I'd been right.

And I'd Fallen because of it.

No, *we* had Fallen. Because Sorin and Zian had chosen to follow me instead of carrying out the assassination. I hadn't even needed to tell them what I knew. They chose brotherhood over warriorship. And they'd paid the ultimate price as a result.

We'd spent the last century blaming Auric, wondering

how he could issue such a compelling demand that he knew I would never follow through with.

Death and I were old friends. But I did not kill innocents. He knew that. Yet he'd sent me after a rogue Noir with no propensity for violence, just a need to save his mate.

It'd been the first time I had ever questioned how a Noir truly Fell, because I knew to my very soul that the man I'd been sent to kill did not deserve such a fate.

There were too many inconsistencies, the first of which being that my target lacked a name. All Noir were well known and documented because they were incarcerated. But this one wasn't in the reform system at all, his identity completely his own.

It had intrigued me enough to want to learn more about him, particularly his name and how he Fell. Most of our assignments were to capture, not to kill. So whatever this man had done must have been horrible indeed to deserve such a sentence.

Yet as I'd watched him, preparing for the assassination, I couldn't detect a single sinful trait about him.

Which was why I inevitably trapped him for an interrogation and demanded to know how he'd Fallen. He'd responded that not all Noir were born as Nora. And for whatever reason, I'd believed him.

Then I'd helped him locate his mate in a nearby village. *A female Noir*, I'd marveled. And not just that, but one also free from the prison system. No identity or case regarding her Fall. A mesmerizing situation that should not have been possible. It only further solidified my cause not to act on the order. Because nothing about it felt right.

Sorin and Zian knew my side of the story now, only because I'd felt it was their due, considering the sacrifice we all made as a result of my choice. I suspected they hadn't believed it all until they met Raven. Maybe not even then. But I knew they believed it now—not all Noir Fell.

And looking at Auric in this moment, I decided he needed to understand and believe that truth as well.

So I told him what happened that day, how I'd met my mark and learned more about his heritage and plight. And I told him what happened after, how my wings turned black. I'd flown back to the Noir, shocked by my deformed plumes.

But he'd already started his journey to the village.

And when I saw what waited for him there, the broken rogue female Noir with her tangled, fiery hair and damaged black feathers, I knew I'd done the right thing by allowing him to live.

Those Nora deserved their fate.

"I've always wondered how they maintained their white wings after raping the poor female near to death, yet I Fell for allowing her savior to live." I looked at Auric, noting the shock in his gaze. "Does that seem right to you?"

He said nothing for a long moment, his throat working visibly over each swallow. I dropped my gaze to Layla, noting her uneven breathing. Her eyes were still closed, her body otherwise still, but I knew she was awake and listening.

Rather than draw attention to it, I met Auric's gaze again, daring him with my eyes to say something.

"They should have Fallen," he whispered.

No shit, I thought.

"Noir or not, no one deserves that treatment," he added. "But all this time, you thought you Fell because I issued an edict to kill him. No, I mean"—he held up his hand to stop me from correcting him—"you assume I knew about what had happened and that I'd demanded the kill to stop him from seeking his mate. And, as a

LEXI C. FOSS & JENNIFER THORN

result, my command resulted in your Fall. Like I set you up."

"Did you?"

He scoffed. "You know me better than that."

"Do I?" I countered.

"Fuck, Novak. I would never do that."

"And I would never Fall," I tossed back at him. Then I added insult to injury by returning his statement. "*You* knew me better than that."

Layla's fingers curled just slightly, her discomfort at being trapped between two pissed-off men showing in the subtle movements of her body. This time Auric noticed, his brow coming down.

But rather than call her out on her pretending to sleep, he looked at me once more. "I had no idea, Novak. The command came from King Sefid. I gave you that mission because I trusted you to handle it."

I studied him, noting the sincerity in his expression and hearing the veracity in his tone. He wasn't lying.

Which meant I'd held the wrong person to blame for over a century.

If King Sefid delivered that edict, then it was because *he* knew what had happened to that rogue Noir and his mate. Why would he allow such a fate?

"We never found him," Auric added softly. "The rogue Noir, I mean. We never found him."

"Good." Otherwise, my Fall would have been in vain. I'd have to let Sorin and Zian know as well. Thinking of them reminded me of Raven and her ties to Sayir. What else had the Reformer told Auric? I voiced the question, wondering if he would tell me.

He responded with a summary of their conversation and

also mentioned the portals we'd flown through and the doorway outside.

"Your pet came, too," he added, pointing to a table. "He's burrowing over there."

Clyde telegraphed a quick negative in my head, disliking the term *pet*. I smirked. Then I cocked my head to the side. "Did Sayir mention Layla being his key?" I asked Auric.

"Key?" he repeated.

Yeah, I didn't think so. It seemed we were sharing stories tonight, so I added another to the pile. "He told Raven that Layla is the key to his plans."

"What plans?"

"Some sort of revolution," I drawled. "Or that's what we think is happening. He's creating an army. The cullings are a way to remove the weak and retain the strong. He's been experimenting for decades, perhaps longer."

He sat up straighter, no longer lounging against the wall. "And you're just now telling me this?"

I merely smiled. "Would you have believed me?" I wasn't entirely sure he did now, something his silence seemed to indicate.

Layla had stopped breathing between us. Yet her eyes remained closed.

"Why did Sayir tell Raven this?" Auric eventually asked, his tone holding a note of disbelief.

So I looked him dead in the eye, wanting him to see the truth of what I was about to say. "Because she's his daughter."

CHAPTER TWENTY-ONE

LAYLA

"*WHAT*?" AURIC SNAPPED, CAUSING MY EYES TO FLY OPEN.

I'd been pretending to sleep so I could listen to their conversation, but now I was just as startled as Auric.

Raven was Sayir's daughter?

That made her my cousin.

My. Cousin.

Holy wings! My eyes were wide open now, something Novak seemed to find amusing. His feathers tickled mine, the intimacy of their strokes rivaling Auric's fingers in my hair.

Well, he'd stopped combing my strands a few minutes ago, his touch now resembling more of a brand than a sensual brush.

"How are you feeling?" Novak asked me, ignoring Auric's reaction.

"She's my cousin," I whispered.

"Yes," he confirmed.

"How?"

He lifted a shoulder. "Her story to tell."

"She said she Fell at birth," I breathed. "That's why she believed me when I said I hadn't done anything worthy of a Fall."

"I still think that's impossible," Auric muttered.

Novak made a noise, then rolled off the bed to explore the room. Or I assumed that was what he'd chosen to do, because he started moving the few items of furniture around, then disappeared through a door.

My eyebrows lifted. "Is that a bathroom?"

"With a full shower and heated water," Auric confirmed. "Yeah."

Novak wandered back out with two glasses in his hands. He held one out for me and the other for Auric.

"Thank you," I said, suddenly very thirsty. I finished almost half the contents before he returned with his own glass.

He settled beside me again, this time with his back against the wall like Auric, leaving me somewhat lying between them. I'd gone up onto my elbows to drink. Now I wanted to sit up as well, only their spanned wings left little room for me to rival their positions. So I chose a spot in the center with my feathers pointing at the foot of the bed.

A comfortable silence fell as we all sipped our water, which was actually cool and refreshing, reminding me of a glacier.

"How did he knock us out?" I asked, referring to whatever Sayir did to us in the courtyard.

"He said it was a spell," Auric replied. "But I've never seen an enchantment knock out so many angels at once before."

Novak studied him for a moment, then brought his cup to his lips once more, drinking instead of talking. It'd been rather interesting hearing him speak earlier. His deep voice had been almost soothing, even when his words were anything but.

"He said it was necessary to move all the inmates to the

new prison. Did you hear me telling Novak about the plane?"

"Yes," I admitted. "I heard everything."

Novak's lips twitched while Auric narrowed his gaze. "Eavesdropping isn't a very attractive trait, Layla."

"Neither is belittling a royal, Auric," I returned.

He considered that and nodded. "You're right."

I blinked. "I am?"

He leaned forward, then drew his fingers through my hair once more, this time all the way to where it ended along my upper arm. I shivered as he grazed my skin, his touch electrifying. It was such an intimate stroke, one meant for friends or lovers. And it lulled me into a state of comfort, almost eliciting a sigh of contentment.

"Do you know why you Fell?" he asked softly.

And there went my contentment. I narrowed my gaze. "I didn't do anything wrong." Not that he would ever believe me. I wasn't even sure why I tried anymore.

He wasn't fazed by my comment. "I didn't ask if you did anything wrong," he murmured, his words still impossibly gentle. "I asked if you know why you Fell."

I frowned. That had been on my mind every single moment of every single day since I'd been cast out of my home. "No," I said, resolute in my innocence. "I have no idea why."

Auric twirled a fuchsia curl around his finger, catching Novak's interest, but the Nora didn't even seem to be aware he was touching me. "If you were listening to our conversation, then you heard how Novak truly Fell. It wasn't by breaking some sort of moral, but breaking a command."

Yes, I'd heard that part. It had confused me because it didn't seem right. Why would he Fall as a result of not following through with an edict? Particularly one that seemed to be encouraging harm where it might not be due.

"What was the last thing you did before your wings turned black?" Auric asked, his gaze intense.

I bit my lip, overwhelmed by Auric's question. Not because I didn't know how to answer, but because he'd actually questioned my Fall. And not in a condescending or belittling manner, either.

"It wasn't overnight," I began. "The tips turned first."

Like the Reformer's, I thought. Although, his feathers hadn't progressed like mine into full black. If rumor was to be believed, his wings had always been that way.

"I thought it was some sort of prank or a trick of the light," I continued, realizing how naïve I'd been. "Then one day they just changed completely. I didn't even realize it until you saw me and..." I trailed off as my heart twisted.

I'd been so excited to see him at my doorstep.

Then everything had gone to hell. And his eyes... Oh, Nora, his eyes had radiated such hatred and disgust that I'd felt my chest crack beneath the pressure of his glare.

Only, he wasn't looking at me like that now.

No, he was watching me with interest and listening to me for what felt like the first time.

What had changed? Why did he suddenly care again?

"So it was gradual," Auric said, glancing at Novak. "But your feathers turned black all at once."

Novak nodded, confirming his statement.

"Hmm," Auric hummed, his hand dropping to the bed as he captured my gaze once more. "What were you doing before the tips changed?"

"Preparing for my courtship season." I hadn't enjoyed it. None of the Nora from the dukedom smelled right to me, yet I had no choice but to let them court me. Yet all the while, I knew it would be my father who would choose for me. I'd tried to maintain a positive outlook, to do as he requested, but it hadn't been easy. Not when I knew what a potential mate should smell like.

Because of Auric.

And now Novak.

"Did you fuck any of the suitors?" Novak asked, his blunt question making me blush and Auric growl.

"Of course not," I managed to reply before quickly finishing my drink. Auric held out his hand for my glass, then set it on the table beside the bed. He'd placed his there as well. "I didn't touch any of them," I added, just in case they wanted to explore other avenues of questioning. "Not even a kiss."

"So that's obviously not it." Auric sounded so certain and superior that I couldn't help rolling my eyes.

"It's not like sex is a sin," I muttered. "If it were, I would have Fallen a long time ago."

Auric froze. "*What* did you just say?"

Novak chuckled. "Sweet, but not innocent."

"Stay the fuck out of this," Auric hissed.

Novak merely smirked.

The two of them locked gazes, their aggression enhancing their scents and filling my nostrils with an intoxicating mix of leather and evergreen and *man*.

I swallowed. Maybe sharing this bed was a bad idea. But I couldn't seem to force myself to inch backward to the floor. Instead, I was trapped between them, feeling the heat of their bodies as they engaged in some sort of primitive conversation.

Goading Auric had been a bad idea. But he couldn't possibly think I'd remained untouched all these years, right? I was twenty-one. I had needs, too. Just like him.

Which I was so not going to think about right now, or I'd start envisioning that shower scene from the other day.

Clearing my throat, I attempted to return to the conversation at hand. "I did make a point to avoid some of them. It ruffled some feathers, but surely that's not enough to Fall."

The two males slowly refocused on me. Then Novak said, "Unless you violated a direct order."

Auric frowned.

I almost said that didn't make sense, except it did in a strange way.

Technically, the Nora laws—which my father created hundreds of years ago—demanded that I mate within my station.

That decree also mandated a courtship of entertaining appropriate suitors. And while I'd initially participated—until I was taken to Noir Reformatory—I hadn't given all of my heart to the activities.

My mother had warned me in the beginning that it was best not to question the courting rules, and just obey them.

I hadn't fully understood. We were royals. Why didn't I have more of a say in my future? When I'd asked my mother that, she'd merely replied, "Trust your father, sweetheart. He knows what's best for us all." Then she'd patted me on the head and left, but not before I'd witnessed the tears in her eyes.

"Food," Novak said suddenly, causing me to frown.

Half a second later, the door opened, revealing a guard with two trays. Auric went to him. "Thanks, Jerin."

"Yep," the Nora replied, handing Auric the trays. "Sayir's ensured quality food. It's his way of apologizing for all the shit that happened. I suppose he's also hoping well-cooked meals will keep the inmates happy while we renovate."

"Renovate?" Auric repeated.

I glanced at Novak, but his focus was entirely on their exchange, his gaze calculating.

"Yeah, you saw the exterior, right? We can't risk the inmates roaming around until this place is better secured. So you're going to be in for at least a few days, maybe a week."

Auric sighed. "Great."

"Sorry," Jerin said, then stepped back through the door. "I'll bring more in the morning." He locked us all in once more.

At least this door was solid with no windows.

Auric returned to the bed with the trays, bringing the aromas of cooked meat and vegetables with him.

My mouth watered in response, my stomach clenching with the desire to devour everything on those plates.

"How did you know the food was here?" Auric asked, arching a brow at Novak.

Novak gestured to where his pet, Clyde, was busy climbing up the legs of the table. The mouse-like creature sat down with an expectant look. I understood why a moment later when Novak tossed him a small morsel of meat.

The mouse's mouth opened into a wide, dragon-like jaw littered with teeth and caught the chunk in the air. Then he crunched down on the savory bit and swallowed half a second later.

I gaped at it.

And gasped as Novak repeated the gesture, this time with a potato.

That little demon thing had some seriously sharp incisors.

Novak brought a fork to my lips, offering me a piece of

meat next. My stomach growled in expectation, forcing me to accept his generosity. And then I groaned as the tender steak touched my tongue.

Ohhhh...

Novak grinned, while Auric growled. "Careful," the Nora said.

It took me a moment to understand.

Then I caught Novak's dilated pupils as he offered me another bite.

Right. No moaning when trapped with two compatible mates, I thought as I allowed his fork to enter my mouth. *Dear heavens, that's so, so good.*

I nearly moaned again, but I managed to keep it in.

Auric handed me a fork with a pointed look. I accepted it and prepared my own mouthful this time while Novak started feeding himself. He tossed a few more bites to Clyde, then stopped when the little mouse lay on its back with a satisfied snore.

Novak grinned at the sight, then winked at me before taking another bite of his steak.

We continued in silence, then Auric glanced at the bathroom and back at me. "I assume you want a proper shower. I saw hair products in there earlier, too."

"And warm water?" I asked him, recalling what he'd said earlier. "Have we been transported to heaven?"

I meant it as a joke.

He didn't smile.

Instead, his gaze went to my wings, his lips twisting to the side. "Unfortunately, no. But we're going to figure this out, Lay." He looked at me, his expression earnest. "We're going to find out how you Fell, and we're going to fix it."

My heart skipped a beat in my chest.

He believes me, I realized.

I wasn't sure if I wanted to smile or cry. Maybe both.

So rather than say anything, or allow him to witness my reaction, I just nodded and gingerly moved off the bed. He would assume that all I cared about right now was a hot shower and would think nothing more of my reaction.

It was a much safer thought for us both. One that protected me and my heart. And prevented him from ruining what was otherwise a very moving moment.

Auric finally believed me.

For the first time since he arrived at my room, I felt a spark of hope. Not just for my predicament, but for my heart as well.

Maybe there was a chance for us after all.

Assuming we surpassed whatever trials my uncle had in store for us next.

You want to test my will to survive, dear uncle of mine? I thought, glancing up at the bathroom ceiling. *Well, I'll be ready for you when you do.*

Because now I knew how the game was played.

Kill or be killed.

Do or die.

I choose to fly.

CHAPTER TWENTY-TWO

LAYLA

MASCULINE TONES STIRRED ME TO AWARENESS.

Warm. Sexy. Deep.

I nearly moaned, my stomach clenching with a need so fierce that I considered slipping my hand between my thighs to alleviate the ache mounting inside me.

But that would only make it worse.

And *they* would know.

Sharing a bed with two virile, compatible mates was its own kind of hell. It didn't matter that they slept on top of the sheet—while I slept beneath it—or that the mattress was large enough for us to sprawl out without really touching.

Because every night I dreamt of them.

Vividly.

In the nude.

And each time, I purred.

A mating call. For both men.

Oh gods...

I knew what it meant. My mother had told me about how females reacted around their chosen mates. They *purred.*

I'd never in my life made that sound out loud. But I'd definitely made it in my dreams. Which had rendered Auric and Novak defenseless. And that had led to sex.

So. Much. Sex.

None of it was real. But still very, *very* vivid.

Pull yourself together, Lay, I demanded. *It's just a fantasy. It means nothing.*

Lies.

But I chose to believe them anyway. Because there was no alternative.

Biting back a groan, I forced my eyes open. Novak and Auric had already left the bed, but their scents lingered, intensifying my need. The lethal mix of evergreen, leather, and smoke curled around me, bathing me in a sinful promise I could never accept.

These males are going to be the death of me, I decided, sitting up. Sayir had probably trapped us in here for a reason, perhaps to test my resolve and readiness for reformation.

If my Fall had anything to do with rejecting my suitors— which the timing of my black feathers seemed to indicate— then this could all be some twisted form of punishment. Maybe he hoped Auric would Fall in the process, too.

Or maybe not.

Perhaps it was all in my head.

But it did make me wonder about Sayir's ultimate goal. Truth be told, I knew very little about him. His relationship with my father had always been a distant one, something that had never concerned me before. Yet very much did now.

I should ask Auric about it, I thought as I glanced at him and Novak. They were standing by the window, their tones low and quiet, likely in an attempt not to wake me. I hadn't been sleeping well, mostly because of the fantasy-filled dreams leaving me restless.

Auric's gaze flashed to mine, his lips curling into a smile I hadn't seen since my younger days. Warm. Affectionate. Soft.

"Good afternoon, Princess," he murmured.

I crawled off the giant bed. "Hi," I said rather weakly. It was hard to infuse a lot of confidence when faced with the two gorgeous displays of masculinity before me. Rather than meet their gazes, I fussed with my blouse and joined them at the window to glance outside at the midday sun.

"We're trying to figure out what realm we're in," Auric said, informing me of their conversation. I'd overheard a few words but hadn't realized that was the goal.

"Wherever we are, it's beautiful," I said, noting the mountains and green fir trees. They likely smelled similar to Auric.

"Yes," he agreed, then turned to Novak. "It's not a new territory." That must have been what they were debating when I'd approached. "Expansion hasn't been Sefid's focus lately. He's become more focused on protection. There've been some rogue Noir incidents, and the Fall rate has increased."

"Rogue Noir?" I repeated.

"Noir not currently under reform," Auric clarified.

I stared at him. "There are rogue Noir?"

"Several, yes. As I said, the rate has increased."

Why hasn't my father mentioned this to me? I wondered.

Novak looked at him. "By how much?"

"By ten percent," Auric murmured.

"Really?" I asked, my eyebrows lifting. That was quite substantial. "I haven't heard anything about that."

"Because it's outside of the dukedom," Auric explained.

"There's been more disrespect among the servant classes than usual. Your father has been focused on mitigating that problem, which has taken away resources from potential expansion."

"I'm surprised he didn't tell me." He'd been training me to take over the kingdom one day. Why wouldn't he mention the increasing number of Nora Falling?

"He likely wanted you to focus entirely on your courting season," Auric replied, his lips thinning.

I cleared my throat, not wanting to revisit that conversation again. We'd already established that my Fall had something to do with the courting. It was the only active activity in my life when my feathers started to turn. But for the life of me, I couldn't figure out what I'd done wrong.

Auric wanted to dissect my choices.

I preferred discussing the blue sky outside—a trait that gave me pause. "Isn't the sky blue in the human realm?"

I'd never been allowed to visit the world filled with mortals, but I knew of it. They apparently worshipped our kind, thinking we were some sort of gods. My father once told me it was the result of a few angels playing on Earth where they didn't belong, and the rumors and myths had grown from there.

Auric gave me a look that said I wasn't off the hook for my subject change, but then he glanced outside and frowned. "It's possible. But the technology doesn't marry up with the theory. It's far too advanced to be human-made."

"Have you spent much time with humans?" I wondered out loud.

"No. But I'm familiar with their advancements." He looked at Novak. "They've figured out satellite technology."

The Noir's eyebrows rose, his surprise evident.

"They even have telecommunication and electronic waves now," Auric added.

Novak appeared impressed.

"Of course, they're still primitive when compared to the ways of the dukedom, but humans lack our resources." Auric pressed his left hand against the wall and leaned in toward the glass for a better view of the landscape below. "I suppose we could be in the human realm. Maybe the portals are here to bring in the technology needed to properly safeguard the prison?"

He gestured to the guards carrying coils of wire and strange equipment into the entry side of the mountain, as if to punctuate his point.

We observed in silence for a long moment before Auric added, "The only aspect holding me back is the air quality. It's almost too clean to be the human realm."

I frowned. "Are they usually dirty?"

"Not necessarily, but their cities are notorious for their pollution," he replied.

"Oh." My nose scrunched as I considered that. The dukedom valued a clean environment. But we also had advanced technology to help consume waste and redirect natural resources in productive ways.

"I've never met a human," I said, studying the landscape once more. Auric wouldn't be surprised by my comment. He knew I wasn't allowed to leave the safety of the dukedom. At least before I Fell, anyway.

"You're not missing much," he replied. "They're irritating as hell."

"But also interesting," Novak countered.

Auric grunted.

Novak smirked.

"Meeting them is against the rules," I said, twisting my

lips to the side. "At least according to my father." He had a whole list of improper activities for me. Visiting the human realm was near the top.

Novak's wing brushed mine, his alluring gaze holding a wicked note to it as he smiled at me. *You can break the rules with me anytime,* he seemed to be saying.

I should have moved my wing away from his in response. But I didn't.

Because, apparently, I enjoyed tempting fate.

"What other rules did he give you?" Auric asked, his gaze still outside. Either he didn't notice Novak's advances or he was too consumed by the problem to care.

"Just the standard ones," I replied.

"Did he give you any rules about your courting?" Ocean-blue irises locked on mine as one white eyebrow arched.

Right. He wasn't going to drop this. And in truth, he probably shouldn't. But that didn't mean I enjoyed this conversation.

"Escape is a hollow victory if you remain a Noir, Lay," he added as if to provide me with a reason to walk down this discussion path again. "Because your father won't let you anywhere near the palace with those wings. So help us figure out how you Fell. That's the only way to fix this. And we both know it has something to do with your courting. Nothing else makes sense."

He was right, of course. About everything. And I sort of hated him for that.

I stretched my wings as far out of my view as possible, hating the ebony plumes, and tucked them into my back.

Novak's feathers followed, interlocked with mine.

His icy gaze watched me, intense and unnerving. I couldn't tell what he thought of my hopes to reform. Did he want to reform as well? Or had he given up the route of redemption?

He rarely spoke, so it was hard to know. But I suspected it was the latter, that he'd chosen to embrace his dark path instead of venturing back into the light.

Auric turned, noting Novak's wings tangled with mine. Rather than comment, he focused on me. "What rules did he give you about courtship?"

"Just to treat all my suitors with respect and allow them to test our suit," I replied. His nostrils flared at my words, making me realize I'd phrased that badly. "Not... *test*, like sex. But test in terms of, uh, scent. And like dinner. And normal things." I cleared my throat. "He just wanted to make sure I took each suitor seriously."

"And what happened after that?"

"I went into my courtship period," I replied.

"Layla," he said, pushing away from the window to stand right before me. "We are never going to figure this out if you keep holding back."

"I'm not holding back."

"You *are* holding back. Did one of the suitors try to hurt you?"

"What? No. Of course not." That would imply I had let them close enough to touch me, which I hadn't. At all. "They just weren't right."

"Well, did you treat them respectfully?" Auric pressed.

"Of course I did." Initially, I'd actually been excited and nervous for my courtship season. The promise of finally meeting a worthy mate had interested me. Although, it'd mostly intrigued me because I'd hoped it would help me stop dreaming of Auric—something that had happened pretty much all my life.

I'd been looking forward to a new possibility, one that would overshadow my desire for Auric.

Which had clearly not worked at all.

Except for maybe Novak now, but he was an entirely different problem.

"You're not telling me something," Auric said, his tone insistent.

I scowled at him. *There are a lot of things I'm not telling you,* I thought bitterly. But none of those things were relevant. Well, except for maybe... "The suitors became more, um, aggressive as time went on. Or maybe *competitive* is the right word? There were just so many of them." My chaperone had a list longer than my arm. The whole thing had felt entirely overwhelming. And yet not one of them had suited.

Not. A. Single. One.

"Aggressive, how?" Auric pressed, a dangerous tone to his voice.

I'd just told him none of them had hurt me. And it was the truth. They'd just become overwhelming at times.

"They were insistent," I said, trying for a better term. "Like they would insist upon additional meetings even after I stated my disinterest."

Auric frowned.

Novak listened.

"And then?" Auric asked, irritation an electric wire between us.

He wasn't going to stop this nonsense until I gave him specific details.

Fine, then I'd tell him everything, and he'd realize this was all a giant waste of our time.

"And then I told my mother that I had no interest in

meeting with suitors whom I'd already denied," I said, allowing him to hear my own version of irritation.

His expression told me to continue.

"She declined my request, of course. So, in protest, I tore up the schedule my chaperone made for me." Had that been the night my wings started to turn? I couldn't remember. I'd been in such a state that I might not have noticed.

"I'm guessing she didn't appreciate that," Auric offered.

"No. She did not." My lips pinched. "But I was justified. I'd already said I wasn't interested."

"Perhaps, but that doesn't sound all that respectful."

"Then you'll really hate what I did next," I replied.

That arrogant white brow inched upward again. "Which was?"

"My chaperone and mother arranged for a dinner with a handful of suitors wishing to try again. All of them were ones I'd denied before. So I slipped out of the window and hid until they left."

Retelling the story now, I realized how bratty I sounded. But it'd been entirely unfair to me to have to play pretend for a bunch of males I had no interest in pursuing. It also wasn't fair for them either. Why bother courting someone who wasn't interested?

"You hid," Auric repeated, sounding unimpressed.

I shrugged. "Sometimes it's nice to be alone. Besides, it didn't make any sense to see them again knowing we had no future."

Auric studied me. "You're still hiding something."

My jaw clenched. "I'm not sure what you want me to say, Auric."

"I want you to tell me why you hid. Perhaps you spent those hours with your secret lovers since your suitors weren't cutting it for you? You did, after all, state you're not innocent?"

I gasped. "Seriously? You're going to throw that at me now?"

"You're the one who mentioned it."

"After you tried to say I may have Fallen for not being virtuous." A ridiculous notion. Angels were sexual beings. I didn't have to be a virgin on my wedding night. "If that were true, my wings would have turned black years ago."

"Perhaps it was fucking non-suitors during your courtship period that did it," he offered.

My eyes widened. "You're unbelievable, Auric. You know me better than that."

"If that were true, you'd still be a virgin." He folded his arms. "Did you fuck non-suitors during your courtship period?"

If I clenched my jaw any harder, I'd bleed. "No," I spat out. "Not that it's any of your business."

"It is if that's how you Fell," he replied.

I was going to kill him. I was going to take that dagger from his hilt and drive it through his cold heart.

"I'm not sixteen anymore," I told him. "And I was permitted to have relationships. All of them were approved by my father, and I was very single when the suitors started to arrive."

My father had made sure of my single status. Just as he'd encouraged me to date. Because, apparently, the majority of my suitors didn't want a virgin. So it'd never been about me or my wants and needs so much as ensuring I met the satisfaction of my suitors.

"My father arranged my first boyfriend," I added, unable to hold back my bitter note. "He sanctioned *everything*."

A fact I'd learned after that night.

The man whom I'd given my virginity to had been a skilled asset of the court. A male many of the females in the dukedom preferred in their beds.

Learning that had destroyed my entire experience.

But Anthony had felt the need to tell me, to confess he'd been assigned to my sexual training.

Which was when I'd learned the truth about my incoming suitors. They wanted an experienced mate.

I'd understood at the time and had taken it all in stride. But looking back upon it now, I felt a measure of anger toward my father. He'd spent so many years teaching me how to lead, or so I'd thought. Yet he hadn't mentioned the troubles with the rogue Noir. He never discussed expansion. He didn't even talk about how to run the council.

It was always about my courtship.

Leading with a smile.

And choosing the right mate.

"But none of them felt right," I mumbled out loud, more to myself than to Auric.

"What does that even mean?" he demanded. "Their temperaments weren't right? They didn't fuck you right? They didn't kiss you right? What wasn't 'right' about them?"

My wings flared. "I told you—"

But he wasn't done.

"I'm going to break this down for you. We now believe a Fall can be caused by disobeying an edict or an order. And your father demanded you treat your suitors respectfully. But instead, you expressed disinterest, denying second meetings, avoiding dinners, and hiding with gods know who. That doesn't sound all that respectful, *Princess*."

I bristled at his summary. "How was it considered respectful of them to pressure me for a second meeting after I expressed disinterest?"

"How was it respectful to them for refusing their suit without getting to know them properly?" he countered.

"But there wasn't a point," I argued. "It was a waste of our time. We didn't suit."

"Based on what?" he pressed. "An initial meeting?"

"That's all I needed to know they weren't a match."

"Let me guess—because they didn't measure up to a former lover?" He huffed out a humorless laugh. "Your father probably hired your consorts, Layla. None of those dukedom prats could ever measure up."

"It wasn't that," I promised. I knew better than to compare them to my previous boyfriends, if they could even be called that. Because Auric was right. They were consorts.

How did he guess that? Or had he known my fate when he left?

I frowned, not liking that thought at all.

"Then what was it?" He was in my face now, demanding a response. "What could possibly cause you to disrespect your suitors in that manner?"

"I didn't disrespect them."

"You did. And I suspect it's why you Fell. You disrespected them by running off with someone unauthorized—"

"I hid alone," I snapped.

"Of course you did."

"I did!"

He snorted. "All because they didn't suit."

My hands curled into fists. "Yes," I said, even though he hadn't voiced it as a question but more of a derisive comment.

"That's not a good reason to disrespect them."

"They were disrespecting me by demanding another audience when I already rejected them," I countered, wanting to slap some sense into him. Why was this my fault? Why did I have to be the perfect one? The obedient little princess? Why didn't I have a right to choose? They were not suitable. I owed them nothing as a result.

"That's not the point, Layla. They were within their rights to ask you to try again."

"And I was within my rights to say no," I tossed back at him.

"You really weren't. As King Sefid's daughter, you owed it to them to try again."

"But it wouldn't have changed anything," I argued.

"You couldn't possibly know that," he said, his tone underlined in derision.

"But I did."

"How?" he asked, sounding so condescending that my feathers ruffled at my back. "How could you possibly know that, Layla?"

Ugh, this man! My palm itched to meet his face, so all I could do was growl.

"You know what I think?" he said silkily. "I think you were scared that you'd made a mistake and didn't want to admit to it."

Seriously? Did he not know me at all?

"So you hid instead, stating you weren't interested in any of them. When, in reality, you might have sent away your true mate."

"I didn't," I forced out. "I know I didn't."

"And how do you know that? Is it because none of them could make you purr?" he taunted, his tone cruel and cold and so very, very wrong.

This wasn't my Auric.

This wasn't the man I once thought I loved.

This was a monster, a tormenter, a crude beast of a Nora

sent here to elicit all my truths and force me to drown in the despair of my choices.

"Come on, Layla," he continued. "Tell me how you knew."

My palms were going to bleed if I didn't loosen my hands, but I couldn't stop digging my nails into my skin.

Auric stood so close now that we shared the same breath. Heat poured off him in waves, his anger nearly suffocating. "Tell me how you were so certain they weren't meant for you."

I glared at him.

He smiled. "I didn't think you could."

"You know nothing," I seethed.

"Then tell me, Layla. Tell me how you knew, and I'll drop it."

I said nothing, my tongue bleeding from biting it so hard.

Then his lips curled into a patronizing grin as he shook his head in clear disappointment. "You knew better than to behave like that, Layla. They all deserved a chance."

"I gave them one."

"But only one."

"That was all I needed," I spoke through my teeth.

"And yet, you can't tell me *why*." He tsked. "How dis—"

"I knew," I snapped, so riled up I could barely think straight. "I knew they weren't meant to be mine. I knew we didn't need a second meeting. Because none of them smelled like you!" I shouted, the truth spilling from my lips as his evergreen scent washed over me, dousing me in its perfection.

My heart stopped with the admission.

Auric froze.

And Novak whistled, his feathers unlinking with mine.

"I guess she really did know," he murmured, his deep voice a caress to my senses that I didn't want to acknowledge.

So I did the only thing I could do.

I fled.

To the bathroom.

CHAPTER TWENTY-THREE

AURIC

I FROWNED AT THE BATHROOM DOOR. LAYLA HAD ESCAPED into there shortly after admitting the real reason she'd avoided her suitors.

Me.

My scent.

Our history.

Her revelation had floored me into silence, which had then resulted in her fleeing the room to the only private space she could find.

And I couldn't blame her.

I'd been a complete ass, allowing my jealousy to drive my reactions in a conversation that should have been handled with much more care.

But the notion of Layla with another man...

Fuck. I clenched my fists, violence riding my spirit.

I knew her father would have hired her a consort or a paramour, someone to ease her into womanhood. It'd been part of the reason I'd left. I didn't trust myself not to kill that man.

Or *men.*

Gods, she'd probably been with several.

Her father would have wanted her prepared for

matrimony, and given the proclivities of the dukedom, she would have been expected to know how to perform.

Such an archaic approach, but one the Nora thrived upon. Women were rare. They were cherished. But they were also set upon pedestals and expected to perform.

I swallowed and looked at the door again. At some point, she had to come back out, and I still had no idea what to say to her.

In a world where females were outnumbered ten to one, it was extremely common for the females to find several potential mates. I'd expected someone within the dukedom to be suitable for her.

To learn that none of them had been compatible was shocking. And yet, I hadn't felt shocked by her admission. I'd been pleased.

No, beyond pleased. I'd been elated. Because it meant she hadn't found anyone else. Which was precisely the wrong reaction to such a reveal.

Females were expected to mate by their twenty-fifth year. It was just how society worked. It also coincided with the procreation requirements—most females were fertile in their midtwenties. Not all conceived, as it was a difficult process to birth an angel, but chances increased when pairings occurred early in the female's twenties.

With how rare females were in our world, it wasn't uncommon for courting seasons to be notoriously advertised. Nora from all over would venture to the female's location to express interest and see if they suited one another. All it took was a few inhales, and the angels knew whether or not they had a future.

Layla's courting season was famous among the Nora. All the available males in the dukedom would have flocked to her in droves, hoping to be a match for the future queen.

That she hadn't found a single worthy candidate... I smiled. It was wrong, but I couldn't help it.

And one look at Novak told me he knew exactly what had inspired my reaction. Because he felt the same way.

I wasn't sure if I wanted to slam my fist into his jaw or just accept fate. We'd always shared similar tastes in women. It was why we'd often played together in the bedroom. So it came as no real surprise that he was also compatible with Layla.

"We can't do anything about it," I told him. "She has to marry a royal."

He merely arched a brow in response, his expression essentially saying, *You think I intend to play by society's rules?*

"I mean it, Novak. We can't have her."

"Who are you trying to convince?" he countered. "Me or you?"

With that taunting comment, he stalked over to the exercise corner to continue his workout—something he'd started when Layla ran into the bathroom. I'd joined him for a bit, but now I couldn't stop glancing at the door, waiting for her to return.

My feathers ruffled at my back, impatience trickling through my veins and leaving me restless. I wanted her to come out here and face me. However, I had no idea what I would say when she did, which left me preferring she continue to hide.

It was a conundrum that made me feel unbalanced.

I knew what I should say, that she just hadn't found the right mate yet. Except I didn't trust my mouth to form those words.

Leaving her all those years ago had been one of the hardest decisions of my life. And Sefid had rewarded me for it by making me her guard.

Oh, I knew why he did it. As a potential mate, I'd be even more aggressive and protective as usual. And as a loyal Nora Warrior, he trusted me not to act on my impulses.

But every moment in this cage with her ate at my sense of integrity. I wanted her. I'd always wanted her. I just couldn't have her—a fact I easily accepted when I didn't have to see her. Then I'd used her black plumes as a reason to fight my instinct to claim her. However, now that I believed in her innocence, I was right back to wanting her again.

I ran a hand over my face and blew out a breath.

This was a nightmare and a dream come true all wrapped up in a convoluted mindfuck of an experience.

I must have muttered that out loud, because Novak grunted in agreement. Or perhaps he'd read the annoyance in my features.

Even after a century apart, the man still seemed to know me. And if I were being honest, I felt as though I still knew him as well. He'd inherited a few new dark edges, his lethal side enhanced and sharpened by his time spent in the reformatory, but his innate sense of honor still lurked beneath the surface. It was that knowledge that had convinced me of Layla's truth.

Novak wouldn't lie about how he Fell. He gained nothing by doing so. And the fact that I could still see that honesty in him told me he hadn't truly Fallen—not in the way I'd thought, anyway.

I'd seen that massacre shortly after that rogue Noir killed all those Nora.

Novak had been waiting for me there, his expression inscrutable. Sorin and Zian had stood beside him as well, the three of them too honorable to flee.

And rather than ask them to explain, I'd sent them to be

reformed. Their wings told me all I needed to know, and part of me had always wondered whether or not they'd participated in the slaughter. I'd thought perhaps they'd been corrupted by the rogue Noir, seduced into the dark side, but now I knew the truth.

Novak had stood there that day because he'd wanted to see my reaction, to determine if I'd known this would happen. My sending him away without a word or a comment to the contrary had solidified what he thought he knew, giving us both cause to hate the other.

"I should have talked to you," I muttered, more to myself than to Novak. "I should have asked you what happened that day."

His icy irises flared as he looked at me, then he turned to do another round of pull-ups. I translated that to mean he agreed. I almost pointed out that he could have tried to tell me the truth, but we both knew I wouldn't have listened. His wings were black. I didn't need the details; that was for the Reformer to deal with, not me as his commander.

"I never would have sent you on that mission had I known what would have happened," I added, giving him my version of an apology. There wasn't anything I could do to take it back or fix it, but I could choose to believe him now. I could choose to help him, too.

While this upgraded cell certainly met my original expectations, it was still a prison. And I didn't trust the men in charge. Even Jerin, who continued to bring our meals daily, was hiding something. I felt certain of it.

Nothing about this place or this situation was what it seemed.

"Next time Jerin stops by, I'm going to ask if they need help," I said, glancing out the window to take in the mountains beyond. "It'll help me review their security and see what else I can learn on the outside."

Novak didn't reply but dropped to his feet after another round of pull-ups. His expression remained inscrutable, which was typical for him. But I sensed his distrust. While he'd provided me with the information he knew from Raven, he didn't want to believe I intended to help anyone.

Actions always spoke louder than words.

If I wanted his faith in me, I'd have to earn it.

I felt the same about him. But so far, he'd done a reasonable job proving I could trust him. Despite his obvious attraction to Layla, he hadn't acted upon it. He'd even given her space. But I knew he'd jump on her the moment she asked him to. I also wouldn't put it past him to seduce her.

A week ago, that would have infuriated me.

Today, all I could do was sigh.

Another piece of my integrity lost.

Layla chose that moment to open the door, almost as though she heard my armor crumbling into dust. Her fuchsia hair was piled high on her head in a messy, wet bun, the strands curling at the ends. She had on her same outfit, which I suspected she'd just spent the last few hours cleaning and drying because some of the threads looked a little darker than the others, suggesting they were still damp.

But she appeared refreshed and beautiful.

No. Not beautiful. *Stunning.*

Her blue eyes glistened beneath the lights, her creamy complexion a stark contrast to her dark wings. She looked alive. Powerful. Regal.

I wanted to grab hold of that mess of curls and drag her

to the bed, strip each of those freshly washed scraps of clothing off of her, and lose myself in her cherry scent.

Her shoes were by the wall, leaving her calves and dainty feet exposed. She almost appeared fragile as a result, but her athleticism showed in each step as she moved toward the bed without a word.

She was curved in all the right places, toned from years of physical activity, and perfect in every way imaginable.

I knew all of that already, but somehow, everything about her felt new. Almost as if I was seeing her beneath a new light.

Perhaps I was. Now that I'd accepted her innocence, her black plumes no longer detracted from her beauty; they added to it. And I found myself lost in her presence, unable to utter a word.

Because I still didn't know what to say.

"Because none of them smelled like you."

Her words had been a punch to my gut and a sensual stroke to my heart. She refused to meet my eyes now, instead sliding into the middle of the bed, beneath the sheets.

My original intention of Novak and me both sleeping on the floor had never come to fruition. Instead, we'd engaged in an unspoken agreement where we shared the bed with Layla and let her go beneath the sheets while the two of us only used the blanket on top.

It had created a few awkward moments of tangled feathers, but none of us had remarked on it, choosing to ignore the tension and distract ourselves with breakfast or words instead.

Now she looked so small in the center of the massive mattress, her legs tucking into her chest as she curled herself into a ball.

Judging by the sun, it was only late afternoon. Our

dinner would arrive soon. I met Novak's gaze, catching a glimmer of concern in his features before he put on his usual stoic façade.

We had one of those silent conversations where I spoke through my eyes and he somehow understood me.

I need a minute alone with her, I was saying. I still had no idea what I would tell her, but I couldn't just ignore our situation. She'd revealed something important to me, and I owed it to her to do the same.

He studied me for a moment, then gave me a nod before disappearing into the bathroom. The water turned on a second later, suggesting he'd decided on a post-workout shower. Or perhaps he intended to do something else in there.

I wouldn't blame him.

I'd done the same before bed last night.

Layla didn't react to Novak's departure, her thick eyelashes fanning her cheeks as her eyes remained closed.

I sat on my side of the bed, which put me behind her since she'd chosen to face the opposite way. Whether that was meant as a statement or not, I wasn't sure. She typically slept in a ball like this, so it could have just been her preference at the time of lying down.

Regardless, I needed to stop analyzing and start speaking.

Except I had no idea where to begin.

I cleared my throat, uneasy with this strange concept of nervousness. Women never made me feel this way. No one did. Only Layla. Always Layla. She unnerved me in a way unlike any other and left me feeling like a fledgling.

I commanded warriors daily, had escalated to the top of my ranks, only to be brought to my knees by this alluring female.

My lips curled and I shook my head. "I have no idea what to say, Lay," I admitted. "I've been pacing out here trying to find the right words, and nothing sounds right."

She said nothing, but I caught the tension in her shoulders. She expected the worst, perhaps for me to ridicule her for her revelation.

I would never do that.

But I hadn't exactly given her cause to believe I wouldn't. I'd been a right ass from the beginning of all of this, chastising her for Falling, telling her she deserved this fate, taking out all my frustrations and aggression on her like she was some sort of soldier worthy of my wrath.

It wasn't fair. I'd been wrong. And I needed her to know that now.

"Do you know why I left all those years ago?" I asked her, my fingers trailing the edge of her wing in a tender stroke. It was an intimate caress, one meant for mates. I shouldn't have done it, but I was a slave to my instincts, a warrior losing the battle within my very soul.

She remained quiet, but I knew she was listening to me, waiting for me to continue.

"I sensed our suitability," I murmured. "You had a nightmare one night and ran into my room, begging to be held. And your scent hit me right in the gut. It wasn't a gradual sensation, but a shock to my system."

I recalled the night with clarity, my blood heating as a fresh surge of her scent taunted my nostrils.

She'd been so alluring.

So beautiful.

So fragile and small.

Only sixteen years old, a female growing into her prime.

"There'd been no choice," I continued. "I had to leave."

I drew my finger along her wing once more, causing

goose bumps to pebble down her arm. She otherwise didn't react, her response one of silence.

"It was no longer considered proper for me to be your primary guard," I added softly. "But it wasn't easy, Layla. Actually, it was one of the hardest decisions of my life. You're the first and only female I've ever met who is a suitable match. But as a Nora Warrior, I'm not permitted to take a mate. Especially not one of your class and standing."

That didn't stop me from touching her now.

That didn't stop me from lusting after her either.

And it didn't stop me from tracing her spine—a gesture that was considered the most sacred touch between mates.

"You smell like cherries," I murmured. "Sweet and perfect and mouthwatering. I've wanted to taste you for so many years, Lay, but I know it's wrong. Forbidden, really. And I used the excuse of your Fall as a way to distract myself."

I rolled closer to her, my hand going to her hip as I curled myself around her and touched her ear with my lips.

"I'm trying to safeguard your honor," I admitted, the scent of her hair tickling my nostrils and forcing me to take a deep inhale of that alluring, tantalizing scent. "Your father charged me with your protection. He put me here knowing we're compatible, because it would make me that much more possessive. And he's trusting me not to act on my urges."

Which I was clearly not doing now as I pulled her closer, my arm circling her bare stomach as I held her in a way I was never meant to hold her.

"I'm sorry, Lay," I said softly, uncertain of exactly what I was apologizing for. My treatment, surely. And maybe a bit for our situation and the fact that I wanted her more than I wanted to breathe yet couldn't have her.

"I thought you hated me," she whispered, her words barely audible despite the silent room.

"I could never hate you." My lips skimmed her pulse as I hugged her to me from behind. "I hated myself for not being stronger, for not remaining by your side to prevent your Fall. I hate that others have touched you—even though I fully acknowledge it was your right to choose them. But that doesn't mean I like it. And I've wrongly taken my frustrations out on you."

She shivered and tried to rotate in my arms to face me, but I held her still.

"Don't," I said, not trusting myself to look her in the eye. Not here. Not on the bed. Not while holding her so intimately.

She stopped moving, but her heartbeat escalated beneath my mouth. Because my lips were still on her neck, tasting her in the barest of kisses. Tempting fate. Taunting my resolve. Torturing my soul.

"I'm sorry, Lay," I repeated. "So damn sorry."

I needed to release her, to slip off the bed and put myself in a corner as far away from her as possible.

But my body remained locked around her, my arm a heavy weight I couldn't move. And my mouth refused to lift away from her skin. Instead, I traced the column of her throat, my kiss a vow of protection and a promise of a future we would never know.

I couldn't stop. I couldn't think. I couldn't do anything other than exist.

Nora Warriors weren't meant to take mates. We were married to the hierarchy, beings sworn to safeguard the dukedom at all costs. That left no room for romantic connections or wavering loyalties.

But this female *was* the dukedom. The future queen.

Was mating her a true deviation of my oath? Or did it just solidify my purpose that much more?

"Auric," she breathed, arching back into me.

I hummed her name against her neck.

Fuck, she smelled so damn good. So perfect. So *mine*.

My muscles tightened with yearning, my stomach clenching with the need to *take*.

I'm stronger than this, I told myself. *I can't have her. There are rules.*

Rules I hated.

Rules I longed to destroy and to defy.

But I was a Nora Warrior. A commander. The one charged with her safety. I had to be stronger than this. I had to be better. I had to release her.

Only, her arm had fallen over mine, her palm resting on my hand. Her nails dug into my skin, not to hurt but to force me to remain.

She trembled against me, her hips pressing back into my groin in unspoken invitation.

"We can't," I whispered.

"I know," she replied, her voice husky and sultry and oh-so inviting. "Just hold me."

"I am."

"Don't let me go."

"I won't," I promised, the words a murmur against her sensitive skin. I allowed my tongue a taste, her sweet flavor a jolt to my senses.

My pants tightened.

My lower abdomen ached.

My whole body felt as though it were cocooned in flames.

"I've always wanted you," I told her. "Always."

She quivered again. "I've always wanted you, too. No one could compare to you, Auric. It's why I rejected them all."

I buried my face in her neck, claiming her in my own way, pledging to never take it further than this moment, and allowing us both to revel in this sensual peace.

For today.

For right now.

Nothing more.

Nothing less.

Just this and all the unspoken words between us. The knowledge that we could never have more. The understanding of our shared torment. The solace of each other's touch.

I would forever want her.

But I would never be good enough.

A fate I accepted long ago.

A fate I despised now.

A fate I might one day choose to ignore. But not today.

Novak returned in just a towel, his damp hair falling into his eyes as he rounded the bed to look down at us.

He said nothing and everything with a glance. *Some rules are worth breaking,* he was saying with his eyes.

As are some oaths, I returned with my own eyes.

Indeed, he seemed to say as he settled into the bed on the other side of her, his wing spreading to touch us both. *Indeed.*

CHAPTER TWENTY-FOUR

NOVAK

BEAUTIFUL, I THOUGHT, WATCHING AURIC AND LAYLA SLEEP.

He had his arm around her again, similar to how I'd found him earlier after my shower. Only this time, he'd curled himself around Layla while she slept. Almost as if his body had decided it was safe to touch her now without his mind's permission.

She snuggled back into him as well, her face void of the lines that typically troubled her at night. I'd often wondered what nightmares plagued her. Or if it was just the stress of our situation. But now, she seemed rather relaxed. A testament to our evening.

We'd eaten another fulfilling meal. Then we'd discussed a few ideas for escape, mostly involving the portals—which was Auric's idea more than mine.

I'd sent Clyde to inform Zian via Raven. For whatever reason, the Blaze wouldn't talk to my cousin. So he spoke to his mate instead. Something about powers and respect. I hadn't asked him to elaborate because I didn't really care.

However, as Clyde hadn't returned yet, I imagined he was still trying to find a way to tunnel into their room. The rock here was much thicker than at Nightmare Penitentiary. He probably wouldn't return until the morning.

Which gave me plenty of time to continue worshipping the sight before me.

Such strength and beauty. So regal, too.

I reached out to cup her face, my thumb drawing a dangerous path along her lower lip. She sighed in response, her mouth parting in an unspoken invitation.

I wouldn't accept it.

Not now.

But I had every intention of tasting her very soon.

I slowly withdrew my touch, then smiled when her fingers slid into my feathers. She often did this while she slept, her palm seeking the comfort of something soft. Auric always shifted away when she touched him.

I never did.

Nor would I now.

I also had complete control over my plumes—a necessary learning from my childhood—and wouldn't allow any of them to shift to metal beneath her delicate hand. Instead, they remained comforting and plush, allowing her to hold on as tight and for as long as she desired.

It seemed rather perfect to have her between us like this, with his body protecting her back and mine guarding her front. I only wished I could shift a little closer, perhaps slip my thigh between hers.

Now it was my turn to sigh. Because I couldn't do what I wanted. Not yet. I needed her to ask for it first. I might favor cruelty and live for blood, but I would never force a woman.

Seduce, yes.

Demand, no.

And this seductive dance with Layla required a little more time. Some trust, too. It also included Auric, which was a very different sort of complication. Sharing had never been our problem. But until Auric decided to claim her, we would be at a standstill.

I admired his ethics, just as I respected his loyalty. I wouldn't push him. Not too hard, anyway.

I studied his chiseled jaw and nearly reached out to brush his long white strands from his cheek. But I didn't want to wake him. He, too, appeared peaceful. Such an interesting look for him. He rarely ever exuded calmness, his penchant for control resolute.

I like this look on you, I thought, admiring him. *It reminds me of another time. Another day. Another fate.*

Scrutinizing him now, recalling everything he'd said, I knew he wasn't lying. He'd never set us up to fail. Sefid had. The king. I still wasn't sure why. What had he been hoping to gain by that rogue Noir's death? Why allow the Nora to torment that female? What value did they hold for him?

I'd never really analyzed that event for more than what it was—just a male trying to save his mate. But knowing now that the order for the assassination had come from King Sefid himself had me reviewing every detail all over again.

I'd missed something important.

Something pertinent to my Fall, and those of Zian and Sorin.

It would come to me soon—my mind had a natural way of picking apart strategies and finding the heart of the issue. It was how I'd ascertained Sayir's plans to build an army. He hadn't precisely said that to Raven, but I knew it to be true nonetheless.

The question became: How did he plan to use that army? And why was Layla the key to it all?

I took in her beautiful face, my lips curling at her still-parted lips. How I longed to lean forward and slip my tongue inside to taste hers.

And later, I'd guide her down my body to another part of me that yearned for the cavern of her mouth or the cradle between her thighs.

Her body seemed to vibrate in approval, almost as though she could sense my thoughts. Maybe she even dreamt of them.

I smiled at the prospect, then froze as a subtle rumble came from her chest. Not a growl or a snarl. Not even a snore. But a *purr*.

There and gone in a second, leaving me to wonder if I'd imagined it.

Then a subtle flare of feathers drew my focus back to Auric, where he stared at me with his shrewd gaze.

Had the purr woken him? Or had he been the source of the sound?

I was already aroused, leaving me unable to discern if Layla had released a mating call or if it had been something else entirely.

Auric looked down to where her fingers clutched my wings, then slowly returned his gaze to mine.

I challenged him with a cocked brow.

He merely tightened his hold around her waist.

She moaned a little, her body reacting to the warring energy shrouding her petite form. But no purr. Not even a subtle rumble.

Maybe I'd imagined it. Purring mates were a fantasy few males ever experienced.

Raven purred for Sorin and Zian.

I always tried to disappear when that happened.

But Layla... if she issued a purr, I would absolutely stay. Ignoring a female in need resulted in pain unlike any other. Or that was what I'd been told, anyway.

I studied her, waiting for her to call me with that delectable sound. But all she did was sigh.

Auric growled, low and ominous, capturing my attention.

A challenge scented the air, his wings ruffling a bit at his back. Then he leaned down to press a kiss to her pulse.

My abdomen clenched in response. I wanted to do that, to kiss her pulse, lick her neck, nibble her jaw, claim her mouth. And I wanted him to watch me as I did it.

Just as I wanted to watch him take her.

Afterward, we'd both claim her irrevocably. One at the front, one at the back, pumping into her, giving her everything we had to offer and ensuring she took us all to oblivion.

It wouldn't be kind.

It wouldn't be gentle.

It would animalistic. Savage. *Intense.*

She would shatter, and we'd put her back together again. Auric would hold her through her climax, then force me to lick her clean.

I'd draw out another orgasm just to hear my name from her sweet lips. Then I'd kiss her until she passed out in our arms.

A brutal mating. Perfect. Rapturous. *Ours.*

Auric growled again, the sound low and intoxicating. He knew what I wanted. He knew what I was thinking. He knew what I intended to have happen between us.

He could fight it all he wanted. He could fight me. He could fight Layla. He could demand us all to behave and kneel.

But in the end, he would capitulate.

He would bow.

He would beg.

And our future queen would own us both.

I let him see that knowledge in my eyes, and then I underlined our fate with a slight tilt of my lips. *I vow this will happen*, I was telling him. *Just let me know when you're ready.*

His glare told me to fuck off.

My smirk told him no.

And so we battled with our eyes, an entire war raging between us while our angel slept peacefully between us, none the wiser of her eventual fall. I didn't mean the negative kind that painted her wings black—she'd already experienced that. I meant the fall where she submitted to us both and allowed destiny to guide her.

Ours, I said to Auric now. *She will always be ours.*

Mine, his eyes said as he kissed her neck once more.

Ours, I corrected with a mere smile. *You'll see.*

Then I allowed myself to sleep.

And dreamt of bright blue eyes framed by fuchsia strands.

Only it wasn't Layla, but a different Noir.

The female I'd helped to save long, long ago.

On the night I let her mate live...

CHAPTER TWENTY-FIVE

RAVEN

Sorin clutched a chipped piece of tile, using it to scrape another line across the wall.

Seven nights.

I sprawled on the largest bed I'd ever had in my life as I lazed with Zian. "When do you think they'll let us out?" I asked. It wasn't the first time we'd been relocated or locked in our cells for an extended length of time, but I didn't like the tension in the air.

Something was coming.

Something big.

I just couldn't figure out what.

Fortunately, my mates and I found a pleasant way to pass the time. But all of us were itching for some time outside. Some fresh air. Some sunshine.

"No idea," Zian murmured, his palm sliding down my bare abdomen to cup my mound. "Perhaps we should just see how many times we can make you come before the doors eventually open again."

I squirmed, my body still not fully recovered from our last session in the sheets. Which had ended maybe ten minutes ago?

"Zian," I said, giggling as I tried to outmaneuver him.

But he expertly held me to him, his finger sliding through my slick folds to collect my arousal.

He brought his hand to my lips, his mouth at my ear. "Suck."

I did as he asked, moaning as I tasted myself and Sorin's cum in my mouth.

"Mmm, now there's a sound I do adore," Zian said softly.

"Bet I can make it louder," Sorin said as he knelt between my thighs.

"Oh!" I tried to move out from between them, but Zian's arm circled my waist, holding me back against him while Sorin dipped his head to take my clit between his teeth. "*Gods.*"

"Your praise is very much appreciated," Zian whispered. "Feel free to bow and worship us daily."

I wanted to say something witty back, but I couldn't. His hands cupped my breasts as Sorin slid two fingers inside me, forcing my overworked body into a mounting state of rapturous chaos.

These two males always undid me.

Their hands and mouths were everywhere at once.

Because *I* was the one they worshipped.

My head fell back against Zian's shoulder as he held me back against him, keeping me in place as Sorin devoured me below.

Then Zian tipped my chin up and back so his mouth could claim mine.

It only took mere seconds to force me over the edge once more, my orgasm one I swore rattled the prison walls around us.

Or, at the very least, our bed.

Because I was shaking with intensity, my body begging

me to take a break. To rest. To do something other than fuck.

Zian shifted me on the bed, laying me down as he slid over me, his lips a caress against mine, a promise of more.

But he didn't try to enter me. Instead, he held me through the pleasure-induced agony while Sorin stretched out on my other side.

They knew I couldn't go again, that I needed a break, and they were giving it to me. For now. I kissed Zian and then Sorin, our tongues lazy as we gently played with each other.

Sorin drew his fingers through my hair while Zian traced my curves with his palms, petting me, stroking me, lulling me into a peaceful quiet.

Until a scratching sound made my ears twitch.

My brow furrowed, my instincts firing to life. *Another culling? A night terror? Something else?* I sat up abruptly to look around, then noticed the little nose sticking out through a new hole in the floor.

A few crunches later and the mouse squeezed through with a squeak of triumph. Then he ran right up to me with a message. "Novak sent him," I said out loud as he spoke into my mind. I frowned as he continued chattering. "Wait, *what*?"

"What is it?" Zian said, his senses going on high alert.

I held up my hand, needing to hear the rest. Then I scowled at the little creature. "He had no right to do that."

Mousey Mouse—or I supposed he preferred *Clyde*—chirped indulgently in response. I was somewhat pacified by the fact that he agreed with me. At least in terms of Auric. But he fully supported Layla knowing the truth about my parentage.

A stab of betrayal hit me hard in the gut. I wasn't exactly

surprised that Novak had spilled his guts to Layla, but I would have appreciated him allowing me to tell my own story.

Clyde essentially replied that Novak had a good reason.

Then he went into a description of the escape plan the three of them were discussing in the other cell.

That information somewhat calmed me down, mostly because it provided me with insight into their little secret.

Of course, it was a secret Novak had wanted us to know. So I supposed that meant it wasn't really a secret at all.

"I see," I finally said.

Clyde ended his report by saying we should be getting out today, as it seemed the guards had secured the yard enough to allow the prisoners some fresh air.

"It wasn't secure before?"

The Blaze chattered at me, telling me it was not secure at all and, technically, still not all that protected. But the inmates were growing antsy, so Sayir wanted to allow everyone a break outside.

"Interesting," I murmured.

Then I looked at Zian and Sorin, who were both wearing matching expressions of impatience. Because yeah, they couldn't hear Clyde.

So I gave them a consolidated version of the Blaze's report.

"Portals," Sorin repeated. "Interesting theory."

"Sounds like Auric," Zian remarked. "Which concerns me because the whole plan essentially hinges on him finding a way to hack into the portals."

"Better than our plan of just lying here," Sorin pointed out.

"True," Zian agreed.

"I'm also pleased to hear that your cousin actually wants to leave now," Sorin added.

Zian snorted. "You and me both. But it sounds like the princess and Auric are a package deal. So it'll be six of us. That's a rather large number for an escape plan."

"But if anyone can manage it...," Sorin started.

"It's Auric and Novak," Zian finished for him.

They both nodded as Zian ran his fingers up and down my naked thigh.

"So you trust them?" I asked, my wings bristling at my back. What I wouldn't give to be able to extend my wings for a short flight. I missed the air on my feathers and the wind in my face.

Not that I had much experience with it all.

I'd grown up in the system, which limited my time in the sky. But my few experiences were ingrained in my memories, and I couldn't wait to experience them again.

"I trust Novak," Zian said.

"Same," Sorin agreed.

"And if Novak trusts Auric, then it means they've come to some sort of understanding," Zian continued.

Clyde whispered his agreement into my mind, saying the two had discussed Novak's Fall at length. When I said that out loud, Sorin and Zian snapped their attention to the little guy and demanded to know more.

But Clyde just flicked his whiskers at them and darted into his hole.

"I guess that means you'll have to talk to Novak," I said, frowning.

Sorin and Zian shared a look, then scowled at the space Clyde had just occupied.

"At least he told us about the plan." I cleared my throat. "And what Novak has told Layla and Auric."

"Auric must have confided something big for Novak to reveal what he knows," Zian remarked after a long, tense minute.

"Something about our Fall," Sorin muttered.

Zian dipped his chin in agreement. "That's my guess."

"Maybe you can ask him today," I suggested. "Since Clyde says we're finally going outside."

"I hope he's right," Sorin said. "And I hope there isn't a culling."

"Hmm, well, on that note, maybe we should just stay here instead," Zian said, his tone lazy as his fingers dipped between my thighs, making me purr all over again. "I've been rather enjoying our little predicament."

Sorin grabbed his wrist and licked Zian's fingers clean, all the while watching me.

Fuck, my mates knew how to kill me.

"I'll endure this kind of imprisonment any day," I admitted, my body humming to life once more. I loved that they knew how to entice me and how they never seemed to grow tired of playing.

Always indulging.

Always attentive.

Always *mine*.

Sorin's lips met mine, his hands already roaming.

We knew not to waste this temporary luxury by fretting. Just as we knew to enjoy it while it lasted. Death lurked around every corner, and our skills would forever be tested. Because the Reformer wasn't done with us yet.

We wouldn't be safe until we escaped. And even then, we'd be on the run.

And then what? I wondered as Zian's lips skimmed my breast.

Oh, that'll be a question for another day...

CHAPTER TWENTYSIX

AURIC

FREEDOM.

At least for a brief moment.

I inhaled the outside air, allowing it to fill my lungs in an effort to replace the sweet cherry scent. It was futile, of course. Layla's essence swirled all around me, her natural perfume a permanent feature in my life.

She stood several feet away, and still she consumed me.

Novak flashed me a knowing look, his nostrils flaring as he tried to calm his inner desires.

We were entirely lost to the woman. Claimed by her presence. Possessed by her existence.

He and Zian were having some sort of mental conversation, one that only seemed to exist between their gazes. Sorin stood nearby, his arm around Raven. And Layla just tilted her head back, her porcelain features bathed in sunlight.

She smiled in quiet delight.

Novak glanced at her, his own lips curling in approval. As did mine.

"Are you listening to me, cousin?" Zian demanded.

Novak's head rolled as he returned his focus to the dark-haired Noir. They appeared somewhat alike with their sharp bone structure, lean, muscular forms, and black hair, but Novak's eyes resembled ice, while his cousin's irises rivaled the night.

I studied them both for a long moment, eavesdropping as Zian chastised his cousin for detailing a story that wasn't his to provide.

Novak merely looked at him, boredom radiating off his features. He would never apologize. Because Novak didn't do anything without thoroughly considering all angles and consequences beforehand.

Yet another reason I knew he'd opted not to kill that Noir for a good reason. Something I should have considered a century ago but had been too angry at the time to contemplate.

Novak never acted without cause.

Just like he never spoke unless he had something worthwhile to say.

It was part of what I'd always liked about him. Although, he was even quieter now than he'd been during our previous life together. He rarely said anything, using his eyes instead of his voice to convey his messages.

Too soon, our time outside was called to an end, the guards leading us back into our cages after only maybe an hour of sunshine. I wasn't surprised. One glance around the yard confirmed they hadn't fortified the security yet. Had I known how weak the perimeter was, I would have suggested an escape today.

Except I had no idea where we would go or how we would flee.

I needed one of those watches that controlled the portals. And beyond that, I needed some training, too. Hell, we needed a schedule and a layout—something Clyde had provided, except it kept changing with all the construction going on—and a way to ensure all six of us could flee without anyone seeing us.

I'd organized a lot of missions in my time, and none of them held a candle to the complexity of this breakout.

Our primary issue was where to go once we escaped.

We couldn't return to Layla's father, not with her sable plumes. He also wouldn't be thrilled by Novak, Sorin, or Zian. And Raven, well, she would certainly provide an interesting introduction, assuming we could somehow get her past the guards and up to the king's quarters.

I shook my head. No. We needed a much stronger plan, not only for our breakout but also for after our escape.

"Dinner will be delivered soon," Jerin said from the threshold of our room, interrupting my thoughts.

"Thanks," I replied. "And let me know if Sayir agrees to an extra set of hands." I'd offered when we first walked into the yard, after gesturing to all the potential hazards with my eyes. He'd followed my unspoken commentary with a nod of understanding. The place was a ticking time bomb. Once the other inmates figured out the weaknesses, the guards were in for a world of hurt.

It was technically counterintuitive to our escape plans, but I'd prefer no one be able to follow us. Which required a stealthy breakout, something I could more easily facilitate with the appropriate tools.

Like a watch.

"Will do." Jerin shut the door, followed by the click of the dead bolt sliding into place.

Novak stood in the center of the room, while Layla went straight to the bathroom, escaping us both. She'd woken up this morning all flustered and had done much the same— run off under the pretense of needing to wash her hair.

But Novak and I knew what she'd really been doing.

We could smell her arousal, the cherry aroma a flavor on our tongues as she came undone in the privacy of the shower.

I swallowed as that ripening scent met my nose again now, her sweetness a perfume I could easily lose myself in. "Want to spar?" I asked through my teeth.

Novak started stretching in response, his jaw tightening from the knowledge of what Layla was doing in the other room.

If she'd done this before today, I wasn't sure. Maybe something had changed. Or maybe I'd just been oblivious.

Regardless, I felt so much more in tune with her after holding her last night. Like we'd surpassed some sort of invisible barrier that tied us together on a new level. I tried not to overanalyze it. All I knew was it made me much more aware of her than before.

"Her courtship period," Novak said as he straightened up from a leg stretch. "When does it end?"

I blinked at him. "When she finds a mate."

He stared at me expectantly.

I stared back.

"Someone compatible, or someone chosen?" he pressed.

"If it was just the former, then her courtship would have ended before it even started," I replied. "She's known me for years."

"So both," he said as he swung his arm to wake it up. Then he rolled his neck.

"Yeah, both," I agreed, very aware that he was trying to imply something. But if he meant to suggest that Layla had chosen me as a mate, he was very wrong. She knew better than to deem me worthy of her.

He considered me for a moment, then lowered into a fighting stance. "Ready."

I warmed up my arms and legs first, then mimicked his position. "No drawing blood." He still had that knife from the guard incident, and I had my own as well. "Unless it's a punch," I clarified. Because I would happily break his nose if he kept smirking at me like that.

He arched a brow, daring me to make the first move.

I scrutinized our surroundings, deciding my best path forward. We were between the window and the bed, with the workout corner to my left. The small table was behind me. And he just had the wall at his back, as the nightstand was between the mattress and the bathroom door.

All right.

That left him without an escape route—unless he hopped over the bed—and me with a lot more ground to work with.

I didn't want to risk switching positions, as mine was more favorable.

So I stepped forward and ducked to try to swipe his legs out from beneath him. He jumped, using his wings to suspend him a moment longer than necessary, then rolled toward the window while kicking out in the direction of my jaw as I went to stand up.

I leaned back, barely missing his heel—which would have seriously hurt with those thick boots of his—and almost fell on my ass.

He recovered faster, coming at me with his fist, nailing my jaw before I could move out of the way, but I sent my own punch into his midsection, smiling as he let out an "Oomph."

It was a short-lived amusement because my ass hit the floor in the next moment. "Fuck," I muttered, not even sure of how he'd knocked me down that fast.

He remained standing, his expression amused as he

waited for me to find my footing. I used my wings to push myself up off the floor and squared off with him again, my back still to the table and his still to the wall.

But then we started circling, neither of us sure who would strike first.

And then Novak moved, his hand coming for my throat. I went to grab his wrist, except it'd been a fake-out, his knee being the true threat.

It hit my side, no doubt leaving a bruise on my rib cage, and I elbowed him in the face to demonstrate my gratitude.

He grunted.

I growled.

And the violence between us escalated.

Mostly spurred on by Layla's increasing arousal, her scent making it impossible to fucking breathe as she pleasured herself in the shower again.

Novak slammed into me harder. I returned the favor. By the end, I couldn't tell if we were fighting each other to blow off steam or battling over who could charge through that door first to win the prize. Or maybe we were blocking each other from taking something we weren't allowed to touch.

Whatever it was, it ended with us both panting on the floor like we'd just finished fucking each other. Except neither of us was satisfied, and we were both still very hard.

Layla hadn't joined us, likely because she could hear us warring outside the door.

"When I first Fell," Novak started, his words coming out on a sharp exhale. "I spent the first few decades"—he paused to inhale—"trying to reform. I did everything I should. Lived by the Nora code." He stole another deep breath, and his muscles began to relax as he lay sprawled on the floor beside me. "I did everything right. And I never reformed."

I rolled my head toward him. "Then it wasn't right."

He gave me a look. "Or there's no such thing."

My brow furrowed. "Is that how you justify giving up?"

"It's how I justify accepting my fate," he countered, his tone darkening. "Do you know anyone who has successfully reformed?"

I'd wanted to ask Sayir that the other day. Because no, I didn't know anyone who had ever reformed. But I'd always thought it was a personal choice, or perhaps those who had reformed just kept it quiet. However, I was beginning to consider that line of thought to be a bit naïve.

"Zian used to mark those who were close to Falling," Novak continued, suggesting his question had been rhetorical. "Remember?"

"Yes." The Nora had the ability to alter memories—wipe them clean—and was often used to warn those who had done something worthy of a Fall. Like killing without remorse. He'd wipe their minds clean of the event but leave a mark behind to let them know they'd done something very wrong and only had one more warning left. It served as a scare tactic, a way to convince Nora to stay in line.

"Layla was never warned," Novak said. "I was never warned. Why? How do the Nora choose?"

I studied the other man, aware that this was probably the most he'd spoken to me since we'd become reacquainted. "Zian was always given his targets."

"By King Sefid?"

I nodded.

"Like my final assignment," he added, his eyes lifting to the ceiling as he considered that. "What will you do if she can't be reformed?"

His sudden shift in conversation left me blinking at him.

Although, I supposed it wasn't much of a shift since he

seemed to be focused on reform, but his question floored me nonetheless.

"There's no *if* in this situation. She will be reformed."

He said nothing for a moment, then looked at me again. "I did everything right, Auric. Lived by every code. Repented. Begged, even. Thirty-seven years, I tried to reform. And all I earned was heartache and pain. Until I accepted my fate and embraced my wings. So there is definitely an *if*, Auric. A very large *if*."

I swallowed, his tone and words unnerving me. He only spoke when he had something to say. Which meant he'd chosen to tell me these things for a reason.

"You don't think she can be reformed," I realized out loud.

"I don't think she needs to be reformed," he countered. "I think she's perfect as she is. The question is, can you accept her?"

"She's not for me to accept."

"Then you're blind," he replied, sitting up abruptly and drawing his knees upward to wrap his arms around them. "She's chosen, Auric. She's chosen us."

"She hasn't."

He glanced down at me, a smirk taunting his lips. "She has." Two words, uttered with such finality that I wanted to break his jaw just for speaking such blasphemy.

"She's not ours."

"Not officially," he agreed. "What's stopping you? The fact that she's royalty? Well, what happens if she can't be reformed? What does her future look like then?" His dark hair fell into his eyes as he cocked his head to the side. "Or is she to remain on a pedestal forever, trying to reform, just to return her to a world that threw her away without any regard to her royal standing?" He looked off to the side. "Is that what you want, Layla? To remain a princess forever subjected to reform?"

My heart skipped a beat upon realizing that she was standing near the end of the bed, her wide eyes on us.

How much had she heard?

She visibly swallowed, her hand fluttering up to her throat. "I... I..."

"It's a moot point," I interjected. "She's going to reform."

Novak ran his fingers through his thick hair and granted me a rare glimpse into his emotions via the portal of his eyes.

Disbelief.

Anger.

Pity.

All three reactions swirling in his icy irises, allowing me to observe and absorb each one through some hidden connection.

He didn't believe in reform.

Which pissed him off.

And he pitied those who still possessed hope. Angels like me.

"You need to consider what will happen if she can't," he replied, effortlessly lifting himself to his feet. "And we need to decide how that impacts *our* future." He walked up to Layla and boldly cupped her cheek, his thumb drawing over her bottom lip. "Next time, I'm joining you in that shower, little cherry."

She sucked in a breath, her cheeks reddening in response. "Novak..."

"Mmm, yes. You'll sound just like that when you come on my tongue," he whispered, leaning in to press his lips to her cheek.

I shoved off the floor, ready to grab him by the neck, but

he'd already shifted around her, his eyes holding a promise as he glanced back at me before disappearing into the bathroom.

"Not happening," I said, loud enough for him to hear.

"Not your choice," he called back to me, causing my jaw to unhinge.

"She'll never choose you," I muttered, then realized she was still standing there, now with her hand brushing the spot where he'd kissed her. "You can't choose him."

Her nostrils flared. "I can choose whoever I want to choose."

"Not him," I stated, meaning it. "He's not from the dukedom. He's a warrior like me. We're not meant for you, Layla."

"I wasn't meant to Fall either," she returned. "Yet, here we are." She flared her wings for emphasis. "And what if he's right?" She glanced at the door and then back at me. "Thirty-seven years, Auric. That's... that's a very long time. I don't think... I can't..."

She shivered, then wrapped her arms and feathers around herself, her resulting tremble a tremor I felt to my very soul.

"What if he's right?" she repeated. "What if I can't reform? I don't even really know what I did wrong. Let's say it was because I hid from my suitors. How is that a Fall-worthy offense? And further, how do I even begin to reform? Do I send apology notes? Allow those suitors to visit me here? How do I begin to rise from such a clumsy Fall?"

"Layla," I whispered, stepping toward her.

But she shuffled backward in response. "I think Novak's right. I think—"

"He's not. He's not right. There's a way to fix this."

"That's not what I mean," she said. "I think he's right about *you*."

"Me?" I asked, frowning. "What about me?"

"Will you keep me on this pedestal forever? Always waiting for my wings to shift back? Is that the only way I'll be worthy in your eyes?"

"Layla, that's not—"

"I Fell because I rejected some suitors who didn't smell like you," she continued, taking another step away from me. "Or that's the best theory we have, anyway. And if it's true, I'm not sure I want to reform. Because it implies that I have no choice in my future, no true free will. What kind of life is that? Am I meant to serve my position as queen like some pretty ornament?"

My throat worked without sound, my mind too busy dissecting her statement.

Something about it struck me in the gut, my mind whirring through each phrase and trying to discern what had given me pause.

She likely Fell because she rejected some suitors.

Suitors her father had selected for her.

His edict being the reason she was to entertain all the prospects and provide a respectful front.

But as queen, wouldn't those edicts become hers? Wouldn't she be the one in charge of the rules? Which would imply that she could break them at will without risking the Fall because the laws would change with her.

I shook my head, trying to clear the convoluted web forming in my mind.

Except... I was onto something.

How could a future queen Fall if the rules were always hers to command?

Unless our theory on how she Fell was just completely

wrong. However, what else could she have done? This was Layla. Beautiful, innocent, mostly polite Layla. She couldn't touch a hair on another being's head unless they meant to hurt her in kind. And even then, I'd seen her wince during that culling. She hadn't wanted to harm anyone.

I might have spent the last few years away from her, but these last few weeks had told me this female was the same one I'd left behind. My instincts screamed at the wrongness of her feathers.

She shouldn't be here.

Just like she'd said from the very beginning.

She didn't deserve this.

Yet she stood before me wrapped in a cloak of black plumes, her sapphire eyes blazing with power. She wasn't sad or feeling sorry for herself. She was angry. As she should be, because if there was no honest way to reform, then this entire incarceration was a sham.

Did her father know? Or had he sent her here innocently, expecting her to return with white wings?

What had Sayir told him? What exactly had Sefid asked his brother to do?

We had none of these answers, only a myriad of questions. And Novak stating that no matter how hard he tried—of which I had no doubt he spoke the truth—he hadn't been able to earn back the Nora favor.

So he'd embraced the darkness.

Would I accept Layla doing the same? Or would I force her to keep trying? Forever maintaining her higher regard, demanding she return to the Nora way of life.

What sort of future did she have as a Noir?

And further, if she wasn't meant for me, then why did she still smell so good, despite her change in status? Shouldn't she reek like a wet dog, similar to the others?

Same with Novak. Why did he still smell so *right*?

Noir were supposed to be vile, evil angels, all deserving of their punishments.

But for the life of me, I couldn't see how Layla or Novak deserved any of this.

I should despise them, not desire them.

With Novak, it was like nothing had changed, aside from his hardened spirit and darkened wings.

And with Layla, my sweet, charming, stunning Layla... I didn't want her any less than I had years ago. I only wanted her more.

So. Much. More.

"Auric," she whispered, her nostrils flaring. "Say something."

I couldn't.

I didn't trust myself to speak.

"You'll never accept me, will you?" she asked, her voice cracking as she spoke. "Not like this. And not like that, either. As a Nora, I'm superior and untouchable. As a Noir, I'm despicable and unworthy. There's no form I can take that will satisfy you, is there?"

I stared at her, uncertain of how to reply to that. When had this become about my acceptance and desires? Clearly, I wanted her. I'd always wanted her. But I couldn't have her. She was forbidden, even in this form.

"Perhaps that's my biggest sin," she continued, her voice a hush of sound. "Loving you. I shouldn't, I know. But I... I don't know that I'll ever be able to stop. The dukedom... the suitors... they'll never compare. Not after this. Not after knowing you. Not after knowing Novak, either."

She took another step away from me, her back meeting the wall beside the table. She slid down it to sit on the floor, her eyes on her drawn-up knees.

"I don't know how I'm supposed to reform here," she whispered. "I'll never regret rejecting them. They weren't worthy, despite being within my station. But maybe I was never destined for them. What rule says I have to mate within the dukedom? Propriety? My father?"

Her head fell to her knees as she wrapped her arms around her shins.

"I refuse. That's not what I want. *They're* not who I want. And if that's worthy of a Fall, then maybe I was never meant to be queen."

"Layla," I said, her name coming out on a choke of a sound. "You can't mean that."

"Why can't I?" she asked, her sad eyes lifting to mine. "Because it doesn't suit your image of me? The precious little princess incapable of sin?" She gave me a sad smile. "I'm not sure I want to live on a pedestal, Auric. What sort of existence would that be?"

CHAPTER TWENTY-SEVEN

LAYLA

Auric never replied. Not that I really expected him to. I wasn't even sure what I wanted him to say.

Was reform even possible? I didn't know anyone who had succeeded in the process. But I also hadn't known anyone who'd Fallen either.

However, I'd lived my life believing that Noir were vile beings who committed wicked sins and possessed no positive regard for the well-being of others. Upon first glance, that might be true. But for as lethal as Novak could be, he had yet to exude any of the qualities I would have expected of him.

He made his desire for me clear but never pushed it.

He listened when I spoke.

He protected me.

He even helped Auric in his own way.

Thirty-seven years, I marveled. *Thirty-seven years trying to reform.*

Because of a disobeyed order? That seemed a bit overkill. But apparently, I'd Fallen due to disrespecting my suitors. There truly wasn't anything else it could be. It was the first time I'd really disobeyed my father, and even then, it hadn't been much.

I'd hid.

After ripping up my schedule.

But seriously, how was that enough for me to Fall?

I wrapped my wings around myself, still sitting on the floor, watching Auric work out in the corner. He was angry. Or maybe sad. Every few seconds, he glanced at me. But I pretended not to see him.

There really wasn't anything left to say.

Novak was right—we needed to determine a course forward. Even if we escaped, I wouldn't be able to return to my father in this state. So where would we go? Were we just going to hide while I tried to atone for my supposed sins? What kind of life would that be?

And more importantly, what kind of life would I be leading if I did somehow regain my white wings? A life without choice where my father dictated my every move?

I was a future queen. For all my life, I thought that implied I would one day lead. But my father hadn't focused all that much on my leadership, more concerned with my courtship.

It took being here for me to realize that. All I knew was the dukedom. However, the Nora kingdom went far beyond that. The warriors existed to protect us, but they lived outside our walls.

There were servants, too.

And lower classes.

I knew none of them.

I barely even knew myself at this point.

I'd walked into my courtship with hope, expecting to find another suitable match. But none of them were right. What was I supposed to do? Fake a mating? It required a specific scent and bond. All Nora knew that.

Except my mother. She once commented that it didn't

necessarily require compatibility to mate. Well, more specifically, to produce offspring. She just mentioned it could be a little harder to perform.

I'd asked her then if she and my father were true mates. For the life of me, I couldn't remember her actually replying. Instead, she'd shifted the conversation back to my schedule and the specific Nora my father wanted me to meet again.

Warmth touched my arm as Novak slid down the wall beside me, his freshly washed feathers locking with mine as he sat far too close. I looked over at him, startled by his nearness and comforted at the same time.

He said nothing, just watched me with that intense stare of his.

"Next time, I'm joining you in that shower, little cherry," he'd said. His hypnotic eyes seemed to be repeating that statement now, his pupils flaring as he inhaled slowly, absorbing my scent.

My thighs clenched.

He'd known what I'd been doing in the bathroom. Which meant Auric probably did, too.

Because of course. My scent would have practically functioned as a beacon. But could they really blame me for seeking some much-needed relief? Sharing a bed with *two* potential mates was its own kind of torture.

I couldn't have them. Yet I *very* much wanted them. It wasn't just the dreams, but everything about them.

Auric with his blatant authority and commanding presence. He had a soft side, too. One he rarely let anyone see. Usually only me, and not all that often. But that was part of what made it so special. It was how I knew he meant it.

And Novak. He was an enigma. A silent power that

everyone knew was deadly. Yet he'd been so utterly patient and protective, and he showcased an intelligence that I longed to know better.

I didn't love Novak, but I could.

And Auric... I'd given him my heart years ago. Perhaps not on purpose. However, he possessed it nonetheless. Even when he was cruel and angry, he still owned a piece of me. I suspected he always would.

But societal standards made a relationship between us forbidden.

Except, those standards no longer applied. And if Novak was to be believed, they might never apply to me again.

Because my reform was likely an impossibility.

"Did you feel different when you Fell?" I asked Novak, curious to learn more about his transition.

His gaze dropped to my mouth before lifting once more to give me another of those intense stares. "The only reason I noticed my Fall was because my wings had changed color," he murmured. "Everything else felt the same."

"That's how it was with me, too," I said softly. It just seemed appropriate to keep my voice low and quiet, but I knew Auric could hear me just fine. "It's why I thought it had to be a trick of the light. I kept thinking that if I was Falling, I should at least sense something different." But all that happened was the pigmentation of my wings shifting.

"Mine changed all at once." He reached out to stroke my wing, the touch decidedly intimate.

"Mine were just the tips," I admitted. "Maybe two weeks before Auric arrived. I didn't even notice until he, um..." I trailed off, swallowing. I was pretty sure I'd already said this once. And if not, well, Novak could infer what happened after that.

Novak traced one of my feathers while he spoke, his eyes

following the movement. "So soft." He stroked the edge, shifting down toward my shoulders. "Beautiful, too." He leaned forward to inhale, causing Auric to growl from across the room. "And so very sweet." His eyes lifted to mine, ignoring the mounting tension radiating from the workout area. "I think you're perfect just the way you are, Layla."

"That's enough, Novak," Auric snapped. "Leave her alone."

I caught Novak's wrist as he started to pull away, his nearness and energy soothing the ache inside me. "No. Don't." I placed his hand on my wing again, needing his positivity and strength. "Tell me how you tried to reform. What did you mean by the Nora code?"

I'd started listening to their conversation shortly before that moment. Right around the time Novak had asked Auric what he would do if I couldn't be reformed.

"As a warrior," he explained in a low hum of sound, his fingers drawing through my feathers once more, petting and stroking me like one would an intended lover. "Protect the Nora at all costs. Worship the dukedom. Only kill in the name of the Nora way. Remember that the Noir are our enemies. Reform and repent above all else. Pray King Sefid forgives us all."

The last sentence was uttered in a hush, his long lashes splaying over his cheekbones for a moment before lifting to capture my gaze once more.

"Do you think your father forgives your Fall?" he asked. "Or do you think he is testing you by having two unworthy yet compatible mates locked with you in a cell?"

My eyebrows lifted. "A test?"

"To force you to learn from your mistakes of disrespect," he added. "By taunting you with real prospects he believes are below your station." He cocked his head. "What a terrible situation to bestow upon a daughter. Forcing her to face the two mates she should never have, just to return her to a dukedom full of incompatibles."

His eyes slid upward to Auric, who had come to stand over us with his hands fisted angrily at his sides. But his expression held a note of surprise, one likely rivaled by my own.

"Do you think my father would do that?" I asked, not really sure who I was talking to. Maybe to myself. More likely to Auric. "But wouldn't that punish you both as well?"

"At this point, I probably deserve it," Novak replied, his lips curling into a smile that revealed two subtle dimples that disappeared in his next breath. "But I doubt Auric deserves such a fate." He looked up at the warrior once more. "A faithful commander to the royal service for over a century. Handpicked by the king himself to guard his only daughter. I can't imagine why he would wish to torture you in this manner."

"Yet the punishment suits the crime," he replied, his voice gruff with emotion. "Force Layla to survive two viable mates who could never be suitors, just to teach her how to properly respect the rules. A twisted, cruel flirtation with fate."

"Indeed," Novak agreed, his touch slipping from my feathers to brush my breasts as he ventured to my other wing.

I shivered, aware that his stroke had been intentional, because I could see the calculated gleam in his eyes.

Temptation.

Yearning.

Destiny.

"Auric is a loyal warrior. He won't break his vow. But no such rules apply to me," Novak continued. "I'm the trump card in this wicked deck of fate." His breath was on my neck, his lips skimming my pulse. "Do you suppose that means I'm within my rights to seduce the female who is meant to be mine? Because I don't believe in the rules. Not anymore. And propriety died in me a very long time ago."

I trembled, his heat beckoning me to lean closer to him and to angle my neck to grant him better access to my throat.

"Novak," Auric warned.

"It's not your decision to make," Novak mused, his tongue licking a path up to my ear. "Layla has a choice. She's always had a choice. The answer to her reform is in rejecting her desired mates. And even then, who knows if reform will ever even happen? Will she be tormented like this for months? Years? Decades? Perhaps even eternity."

He nipped my earlobe, his breath hot against my skin, causing goose bumps to pebble down my arms. "Novak," I whispered, a plea in my voice. One I didn't fully understand. I wanted him to stop. But I also couldn't bear the notion of him pulling away from me now.

Auric uttered his name again as well, his anger a whiplash to my senses. But it wasn't enough to pull me out of Novak's spell. His leathery scent wrapped around me in a blanket of invitation, his essence calling to mine and pulling my soul to the surface of my body, begging for a date to play.

"An eternity of waiting," he breathed. "What if we waste all that time waiting for a reform that was never destined to exist? We're supposedly in a prison full of those who are on the edge of reform, or that was what Auric mentioned the purpose of this place being. Yet everyone in the yard today was someone from our previous reformatory. Are those special reformers being kept somewhere else? Or do they simply not exist?"

He pulled away to stare up at a smoldering Auric, the two men entering a battle of looks and quiet glares.

"Have you known anyone to reform?" Novak asked him after a beat. "Anyone at all?"

Auric's jaw ticked. Then finally he said, "No."

My breath caught in my throat.

Auric was over a hundred years old—closer to two hundred—and he'd never known anyone to be reformed? Anyone at all?

"Neither have I," Novak replied. "Not a single one."

I swallowed. They were similar in age, and Novak had been surrounded by Noir for... "How long have you been a Noir?" I'd heard how and why he Fell, but didn't know the exact timeline.

"Over a century," he replied. "And I've known hundreds of Noir. None of whom ever came close to reform. Nor were any of them guided toward it. These prison camps are not meant to rehabilitate or prepare an angel for some sort of re-ascension. We're being trained for an entirely different purpose. *War*."

Auric was shaking his head. "It doesn't make any sense."

"I never said it did," Novak returned. "But that doesn't make it any less true."

"So I'll never be reformed," I whispered.

Even if this was all some sort of messed-up punishment meant to make me appreciate my purpose within the dukedom, there was no guarantee of how long it would last or that it would even work.

As Novak said, I could be in this misery for an eternity.

Or I could embrace it.

What kind of queen would I become then?

And what kind of queen was I destined to become otherwise?

Which one do I want to be? I wondered, shivering as Novak released me to slide effortlessly to his feet. "Dinnertime," he said just as someone started to unlock our door.

My stomach twisted.

But it wasn't a hunger for food.

No, I was craving something else entirely.

Leather and evergreen topped with cherries.

A forbidden sort of mix, one that was becoming harder and harder to avoid sampling every day.

CHAPTER TWENTY-EIGHT

NOVAK

I SMOOTHED MY THUMB OVER LAYLA'S FOREHEAD, TRYING TO calm the lines that had formed there while she slept. She relaxed considerably beneath my touch, her lips parting on an alluring sigh.

The poor thing was exhausted from her fourth night of tossing and turning.

We'd been allowed outside for only one hour a day for the last five days in a row. Each time, Auric scanned the perimeter for improvements to security and frowned upon finding none.

I suspected that was the point.

The guards weren't preparing this prison for protection. They were up to something else. Not a culling or another match, but a game of sorts.

Not only had they moved us to these improved accommodations, but they were also feeding us heartily. They provided exercise areas in our rooms to maintain our endurance. And they granted us an hour a day outside to witness just how poorly this reformatory was being guarded.

Something was definitely about to happen.

And I was prepared for whatever they had in store.

Layla might not have chosen me yet, but I accepted her as mine. Auric made a noise, one that told me he strongly disagreed. Or, more likely, did not appreciate the way I was touching Layla while she slept.

I met his gaze over her shoulder and deliberately stroked my thumb across her forehead once more. She released another breath of contentment, causing his lips to curl down into a severe frown.

Just because he hadn't decided to keep her didn't mean I couldn't.

I'd happily share with him.

So long as he treated her well.

He lived under this misconception that she could reform at any minute, but I knew it was never going to happen. She'd Fallen. There was no coming back from that. And I wasn't entirely convinced that Falling implied anything inherently bad about an angel.

After a century in purgatory, I'd learned that there were several decent Noir. But we were bred to hate each other, taught to be competitive, and trained to kill.

Beneath that, though, there were hearts that beat and emotions that reigned.

Layla was proof of that. "Has she changed?" I asked Auric in a low voice, not wanting to disturb the sleeping beauty between us. "Or is she the same woman you knew before?"

He said nothing, but I didn't push for words. His silence confirmed what I already suspected.

No. She hasn't.

Because a Fall didn't alter an angel other than the wings. Which left me wondering if we even knew the real cause. Disloyalty, likely. But something told me it went much deeper than that. Our meager understanding barely skimmed the surface of the truth.

Perhaps Layla was somehow tied to that deeper knowledge.

I drew my thumb to her temple, then down along her jaw to her elfin chin. "She's perfect just the way she is," I whispered, meaning it.

Auric remained silent, but his expression told me he was lost in thought. That'd been his perpetual state these last few days.

Every night, he held Layla, as he was doing now with his arm around her waist. But he couldn't convince himself to do anything more.

Which was truly a shame considering how ready Layla was for us.

Even now her nipples were beaded beautifully beneath that thin, gauzy shirt. And the aroma of her need permeated the air with sweet, succulent promise.

I wanted to nibble a path down her body to the delicious juncture between her thighs. Alas, I required an invitation to taste her. And I couldn't do more than dream until she chose to issue that invitation.

Soon, I thought, closing my eyes. *You'll be mine soon.*

And maybe Auric, too.

If he ever figured out how to dislodge his head from his ass, anyway.

I slid my palm to rest upon Layla's hand over my wing, covering her fingers and holding her to me. Then I let sleep take me once more.

Only, a soft hum stirred me several minutes later.

No, not a hum but a *purr*.

My eyes opened once more, taking in the calm lines of

her face and her soft breaths. Had I imagined it? Like the other night?

I strained my ears, listening, waiting, *yearning*.

Auric cleared his throat, his expression strained.

And she purred again.

My heart skipped a beat at the alluring sound, my body rousing to awareness in response to my mate's call. *Yes,* I thought. *Open those eyes and beg me, sweet cherry.*

But instead, she whined, discomfort spoiling her features as she tucked herself into a tiny ball. "No," she whispered. "No."

I froze. "No?" She was calling us to her and denying us at the same time. Because of propriety? What society demanded of her? Twisted fate? This punishing game? I looked at Auric and saw the same confusion in his eyes.

"Layla?" he whispered, his arm still around her abdomen. "Are you all right, Lay?"

I studied her face, noting the harsh lines of her mouth and her crinkled brow. Another purr burst out of her, this one louder and more insistent. She panted with it, her eyes squeezed shut.

"She's dreaming," I said, pressing the back of my hand to her forehead. "And she's burning up."

Except she started to tremble in the next second, her purr growing more intense. Auric growled in response. "Stop, Layla."

A whimper escaped her mouth as a tear slipped from her eye. I palmed her cheek, wiping away the droplet with my thumb. "Wake up, little cherry," I purred back at her. "Let me see those pretty blue eyes."

Her purr intensified, making Auric groan as his arm tightened around her. "*Fuck,*" he cursed, his head falling to her shoulder. "*Layla.*"

I drew my thumb across her bottom lip. "Time to wake up, sweet one. Before you kill Auric with that alluring call."

He snarled at me, making me smile. But that smile turned into a grimace as she released another sensual rumble, my groin tightening with the desire to claim what was mine.

She moaned, her body beginning to convulse from the pleasure of her dream. If she came undone between us in this state, we would not be able to hold ourselves back from taking her. I could see the restraint being tested in Auric's arm, his muscles bulging as he fought not to act, his teeth so close to biting down on her shoulder.

Tension lined my body as well, driving my actions, beckoning me to play with the female who had so clearly chosen us.

But it wasn't time yet.

She wasn't awake.

And I valued her consent, wanted her to beg, *needed* her to say my name as she came. Not some dream figment, even if it was a version of me. That male could never compare to the real thing. Not when she hadn't yet experienced what I had to offer her.

"Grab her tit," I said. "Pinch her nipple."

Auric glowered at me. "Fuck off."

"It'll wake her up," I replied, my tone urgent as her quakes began to crest into a beautiful state of oblivion. "*Now, Auric.*"

I counted to two, ready to do it myself, but he cupped her plump breast and gave it a squeeze. Then I captured her mouth and drew my teeth along her lower lip.

She came to life between us on a gasp, her purr cutting off as awareness drew her into the present. Then her thighs squeezed together as she released a sound of protest.

"Wh-what are you doing?" she asked, her voice breathy and possessing a husky quality that I would forever fantasize about.

"Waking you up," I said against her mouth, pulling back just enough to see her eyes. "You were purring."

"Purring?" she repeated, mouthing the word.

"Mmm," I hummed, nuzzling her nose. "Good dream, perhaps?"

She shivered, her tongue slipping out to dampen her lips. "I... I... I need to go to the bathroom." She tried to squirm out of Auric's grasp, but his arm was solid around her, his face still buried in her shoulder.

And his palm had not yet left her breast.

My lips threatened to twitch. It seemed the Nora's control was hanging on by a thread, and each shift of her body was only making it worse. "Stop. Moving." The two words came out muffled but strong against her skin, Auric's tone underlined in command.

"Let me go," she said, not listening to the warning in his voice.

"I wouldn't keep wiggling," I warned, brushing my knuckles against her overheated cheekbone. "Just take a few breaths."

She shuddered instead, her pupils overtaking her blue irises. Her plump lips glistened in warm welcome, drawing my focus to them.

Magnificent, I thought, taking in the sight of her mounting arousal. She appeared only seconds away from imploding, just by remaining between us.

Another of those delicious whimpers escaped her, followed by a subtle purr that she desperately tried to swallow. She'd denied her urges, and now they were demanding compensation in full.

"Layla," Auric breathed, tension lining his tone and body.

"I-I can't." She practically vibrated with need, her nostrils flaring as she took in our scents. "P-please."

I couldn't tell if that was a plea for us to grant her space or for something else entirely. Her expression told me she wasn't sure herself.

Auric's lips went to her neck, his expression an intriguing mixture of pain and resolve. Had the warrior finally realized the futility of denying his desire? Even if Layla managed to rise from her Fall, she'd still be ours. And there wasn't anything society or her father could do about it.

His mouth traveled up to her ear, causing her pupils to dilate even more. She uttered his name on a purr, then squeezed her eyes closed as though to hide from her own need.

But it was too late.

I could see the change overcoming Auric, his features tightening with a desire that rivaled her own.

Gone was the obedient Nora Warrior, replaced by a man who scented and knew his mate.

They had a history far deeper than the beginning I'd established with Layla, something I respected between them and endeavored to achieve in time. I lusted for her now but hoped it would grow into something more. A bond. Perhaps even a deep friendship.

Zian and Sorin seemed to share that with Raven after knowing her for barely a few months. Why couldn't I develop a similar relationship with Layla?

I withdrew my touch from her face as Auric shifted, guiding her to her back so he could hover over her. She stared up at him with an apologetic look, one that morphed to surprise as he touched his forehead to hers.

"Layla," he whispered, the name reverent on his tongue. "I'm not strong enough. I'm trying, but my duty is to the crown. To *you*. My Layla."

"What are you saying?" she asked, her voice so incredibly soft.

I went onto my elbow beside them, giving Auric the space he needed with Layla. Of course, he was so lost to her that he barely noticed my presence. His hand cupped her cheek as he lifted his forehead from hers to stare deeply into her eyes.

"Tell me to stop," he said, ignoring her question. "And I will. But tell me to continue, and I'm yours."

Her breath feathered out of her, time standing still as she processed what he was telling her.

I said nothing, observing the exchange, wondering what she would do.

She claimed to require someone from the dukedom, yet none of those suitors fit her true requirements. And while she might eventually meet one of circumstance, she also might not. Which would mean she'd wasted valuable time with her true mates. *Us.*

Layla swallowed, her fingers trailing up Auric's arm to where he cupped her face. "Mine?"

"Always," he vowed. "I shouldn't keep you, Lay. It's wrong. Forbidden. Against so many rules. But my loyalty has always been to you. If you choose me, then I choose you. Always you."

CHAPTER TWENTY-NINE

LAYLA

MY HEART STOPPED.

I was drowning and I couldn't breathe, too consumed by Auric's intense blue eyes to do anything other than stare.

Always you.

Those two words spun through my mind on repeat as I echoed them back at him. I'd always wanted him. Always dreamt of him. Always yearned for him.

I knew it was forbidden.

I knew it was wrong.

I knew I could be falling headfirst into the trap my uncle had set for me.

But nothing could stop me from lifting my mouth to Auric's and kissing him as if my very life depended on it.

If this was all just some wicked punishment to teach me the value of respecting my suitors, then it had failed in its purpose. Because what I found in this room was a dream come true.

Two compatible mates. One of whom I'd craved for more years than I desired to count. And the second was a man I shouldn't accept, a Noir with a lethal edge and a darkness to him that would surely taint my lighter side.

Together, they were the worst kind of forbidden.

A proverbial "fuck you" to the kingdom that had raised me.

A kingdom that had cast me out without a second glance or any words of encouragement.

A kingdom that had embraced my Fall and sent me here to suffer.

What did I owe them if they felt this was a more desirable fate than helping me learn from my Fall? To punish me with two exquisite male specimens, just to see if I was strong enough to reject them.

No.

I chose to *accept* them.

To embrace them.

To *kiss* them.

First Auric, with a searing passion underlined in years of pent-up lust and need. He unleashed it all upon me, his tongue a dominant presence in my mouth, demanding I return his ardor. And I did. Oh, how I did. With a determination and a passion unlike any I'd ever experienced.

This was fate.

This was how I should feel when a male touched me, kissed me, stroked me.

Oh gods. I was falling apart before we'd even started, his palm against my cheek a brand that set my very soul on fire. And his mouth... his mouth should be a sin in itself. Full lips, wicked tongue, a rhythm meant to seduce and to claim.

I groaned against him, arching my hips, seeking more friction, seeking *him*.

A smoky tendril of leathery fragrance tickled my nostrils as though to remind me it wasn't a *him* but a *them*.

I shouldn't, but I wanted them both.

It was immoral. Cause for a Fall. And yet, my wings were

already black, so why not finalize my state? Would it even matter? There were no specific rules that said I couldn't mate below my station, just that finding a suitable match among the dukedom was preferable.

But none of them fit.

Not like Auric and Novak.

I chose my heart. My spirit. My destiny. I chose defiance.

I threaded my fingers through Auric's hair and held him to me as I unleashed all my feelings into our kiss, telling him with my mouth that I accepted him, wanted him, intended to keep him.

His groan vibrated against my chest, and I responded with a purr. *Mine.*

My mates.

My future.

My *choice.*

Fuck your punishment, Sayir, I thought. *Fuck it all.*

I'd done everything right. Followed every rule. Bent over backward to acquiesce and accept my fate. But it was never my destiny to live, just one chosen by another. My father. And with every swipe of my tongue against Auric's, I realized how true that was.

He'd taken away my true match, forcing me to accept another. Then he'd rejoined us as some sort of twisted test. Or perhaps I was overthinking it all, and I'd Fallen for disobedience already.

It no longer mattered.

This was what mattered.

Leather. Evergreen. Smoke. *Mates.*

Auric's hand slid down to cup my breast again, his palm possessive and hot over the thin fabric of my shirt. I longed to feel more, to experience his mouth and teeth and tongue all over me.

And Novak.

Oh, I wanted him, too. Needed to tell him, to show him, to ensure he knew he was just as much a part of this as Auric.

Assuming he chose me, too.

I pulled my mouth away from Auric to stare into those alluring, icy eyes. So much intensity. So much savagery. I shivered beneath his gaze. Then I reached for him and pulled him to me. "Kiss me," I demanded.

"No," he replied, his smile cruel against my mouth. Then he tugged my lip between his teeth and bit down. I cried out in surprise, which made him chuckle darkly in response. "Auric?" He glanced at the other male, his eyes narrowing as they engaged in one of their infamous silent conversations.

Auric's thumb circled my nipple through my shirt, his body hot alongside mine as I stared up at the two men hovering above me.

I swallowed.

Were they going to reject me? Realize the forbidden quality of this relationship and leave me alone to please myself?

My lips curled down at the prospect.

I'd chosen them.

They were compatible.

I wanted them.

They were *mine*.

They couldn't walk away. They couldn't say no. They couldn't decide suddenly to leave me in this agony of want and need. That wasn't how this worked. Or was it? Did they have an equal opportunity to choose?

Yes, of course they did.

They should.

Just as I should.

LEXI C. FOSS & JENNIFER THORN

But they wanted me. I could smell it, taste it in the air, *feel* it against my hips. Their bodies had aligned on either side of me, caging me beneath a wall of hot, *hard* male.

Whatever battle they waged now wasn't in regard to willingness or accepting me as a mate. It was about whether or not they wanted to share. Or maybe, no, maybe it was about *how* they intended to share.

Because they weren't angry so much as calculative. Communicating some sort of unspoken agreement with their eyes, deciding their next move and leaving me to writhe in agony between them.

My dream had been so *hot*. So intense. So overwhelmingly sensual.

And they'd woken me before I could climax, leaving me aching with *need*.

A taunt. A way to ensure our prolonged pleasure. A game of wickedness.

A game I would win.

Because I had something they did not.

I could purr.

And I did. *Loudly*.

Both of them slowly turned their heads toward me, their expressions equal parts feral and intrigued. Novak's lips even twitched at the sides, approval radiating from his gaze.

"Do you need something, little one?" he asked, his voice smooth like velvet. His hand slid beneath the sheet to rest on my lower abdomen, his touch a brand to my bare skin. A molten claim. A promise for so much more. "Tell us what you want, and we'll consider giving it to you."

"Consider?" I repeated breathlessly.

"Mmm," he hummed, leaning down to kiss the edge of my mouth. "You're still purring, Layla. Such a glorious, hypnotic, mesmerizing sound." His lips trailed across my cheek to my ear. "Tell us what you want," he said again. "Tell us how to worship you."

My legs squeezed together, my core burning with a need only they could satisfy. "Kiss me," I said again.

"Where?" he asked, his lips brushing mine. "Here?" he guessed, his palm slipping deeper into the sheets to my shorts and lower to the place aching for a man's touch. "Or maybe here?" He tilted his head, then pressed his mouth to my neck. "Or is this what you desire?" He nipped my thundering pulse as Auric bent over my chest to nibble my nipple through my shirt.

"Oh!" I bowed off the bed.

"I think she wants to be kissed here," the Nora Warrior said, his hot breath weaving with the strands of my top.

I wanted to strip. To free my body. To invite them to touch every inch of me. To claim them. To *explode*.

Novak's fingers skimmed the top of my shorts, his thumb popping open the button before he deftly dragged down the zipper.

I wore nothing beneath.

Which elicited a low growl of approval from him as he ventured inside to stroke my bare skin. "She's soft," he said almost reverently, his fingers slipping lower. "And very wet."

Auric made a sound against my breast, his teeth grazing my stiff tip. "What do you want us to do to you, Layla?"

It warmed a certain part of me to realize they were both willing to please me. *Together*. Like it wasn't even a question that they would share. Because they knew I desired them both. Was it my purr? My eyes? My scent? Whatever the cause, I was grateful, as I didn't think I could choose if forced.

How strange that Novak had become a part of me in such a brief time, his presence one that completed me in an unexpected way. He empowered me, listened to me, and provided me with an uncanny confidence to take what I wanted.

Auric... Auric was my heart. My home. My joy.

Together, they made me feel whole.

I whispered that knowledge out loud, telling them that my soul recognized its match. Our fates were interlocked, and I didn't want to fight it.

Perhaps it was a naïve decision on my part.

Or maybe it was the right one.

Regardless, I accepted it. I owned it. And I told them what I wanted. *Them.* "Everything," I breathed. "I want everything. Everywhere. Every touch. Every kiss. Every sensation. Make me yours. Claim me. *Take* me." My chest reverberated with the call of my soul, demanding their compliance, aching for them to accept me.

Their mate.

Their chosen.

Their female.

Auric released a low sound in his throat, the animalistic quality of it sending a quiver through my body and causing my stomach to clench with need.

"Everything," Novak repeated, his lips caressing my ear, "is a very dangerous proposition, Layla." He skimmed his mouth along my neck to my pulse as his fingers ventured deeper into my shorts to slip through my folds to the very heart of me. "Have you ever been with two men at the same time before?"

I shook my head, my lungs constricting as I reminded myself to breathe. Auric's lips sealed around my nipple through my shirt, his tongue circling my peak as Novak slipped two fingers inside me.

A jolt shocked my spine, my body enslaved by their touch, their mouths, their very presence.

Then Novak slipped out of me, his fingers guiding back toward my other entrance, making me freeze. "What about here, sweet cherry?" he asked. "Have you ever been taken here?"

I shook my head again. "Only..." I swallowed, my mouth suddenly dry. "Only in the front."

"In your pussy," he corrected. "I see." His lips went to mine, hovering, tasting, taunting. "Has a man fucked your mouth?"

This time I nodded, only a little, the movement causing my lips to brush his in a tantalizing tease. I wanted to close the gap between us, to truly kiss him, but he pulled back to smile.

"Good girl," he said, pleased by something I didn't quite understand.

Because I'd sucked a man off before? Or was he pleased with me replying?

His fingers reentering me below left me without an answer and derailed my thoughts entirely, cascading me down a hill of sensation that had me feeling unbalanced. Overwhelmed. Teetering on the edge.

I grabbed his wrist, holding him to me, demanding without words that he never stop touching me there. He responded by kissing my jaw. Then Auric lifted and captured my mouth, his tongue even more insistent than before, branding me with his essence and demanding my compliance.

I submitted with a whimper, losing myself to them and the electricity thriving through my veins.

So close.

So hot.

So intense.

My legs spasmed, my muscles tightening in response to the sensations building within me. I moaned into Auric's mouth as flames trickled over every inch of my being.

More, I thought. *I need more.*

"Shh," Novak hushed, his mouth against my throat.

I must have issued that demand out loud.

I didn't care.

It wasn't enough. But it was too much all at once. I couldn't think, couldn't breathe, couldn't *move* beyond pressing myself into them, begging them with my touch to give me what I desired.

Auric slipped his hand beneath my shirt, his palm against my bare breast. Then he pinched my nipple, sending a ripple of ecstasy through me that met Novak's hand below as he settled it firmly over my mound.

No. *My clit.*

Oh gods...

He applied just enough pressure, just enough strength, to taunt me into dancing over the cliff into the oblivion awaiting me below.

And I fell.

Oh, how I fell.

Down, down, down, floating in a cloud of rapture meant only for the heavens above. And yet it caressed every part of me, drowning me in the sensual bliss of climax and leaving me panting for more.

My kiss with Auric morphed into something violent, my need clawing at him to act, to do more than just touch and caress. I dug my nails into Novak's wrist, then captured a fistful of Auric's silky white-blond hair with my opposite hand, holding them to me, forcing them to feel the quakes of my pleasure as I tempted them into joining me.

They groaned in unison, their feral energy cloaking me in a fiery blanket of passion. Auric squeezed, causing me to arch off the bed, and Novak speared me with a third finger. But it wasn't enough. I needed them. Their claim. Their intimate touch.

I drew my nails up Novak's arm to the back of his neck and released Auric's mouth to seek Novak's kiss. This time he allowed it, his lips firm and knowing against mine. Everything he did was strategic. Every touch. Every nip. Every lick. I lost myself to his tongue, almost too consumed to notice Auric kissing a path down my neck to my breasts.

But his teeth skimmed my nipple as he unknotted my shirt, pulling it away from my neck and back and dropping it somewhere on the bed or the floor.

Novak swallowed my moan, his mouth issuing demands of his own as Auric continued licking a path down my body and taking the sheet with him. I shuddered and trembled as goose bumps fled up my arms, anticipation warming my blood. Then I groaned in disappointment as Novak rolled away from me, only to sigh as he returned beneath the blanket.

Auric shifted as well, the sheet a barrier neither male desired between us.

Warmth and expectation flooded my senses as both men continued driving me into a state of delirium.

Novak's tongue was inside my mouth, his damp fingers tracing my hard nipple and painting my skin with my arousal. The stimulating caress left me shaking and yearning and panting for more.

Auric tugged my shorts down, the fabric whispering along my thighs to leave me naked and open and ready. But both men only wanted to taste.

Their lips and teeth and tongues were everywhere,

starting at my mouth, then my neck, my chest, my abdomen, and then Auric's head disappeared between my thighs for a long, sensuous lick that had me screaming his name.

Novak bit my breast, forcing me to utter his name as well, and I gave up trying to understand reason or reality and just let them devour me.

A sea of euphoria washed over me, intoxicating my being and leaving me a breathless, wanton shell of a woman lost to the desires of her mates.

Oh, but they weren't mine yet.

I needed them inside me.

Their essences mingling with mine in the most intimate of ways.

"Please," I whispered. "Please."

Novak chuckled, his face disappearing between my thighs next as Auric went to his knees beside me, his hand at the buckle of his pants. "Is this what you want, Lay?" he asked, his sapphire orbs intense and aware.

An important question.

A last chance to escape.

Because once he entered me, the deed would be done. He would be mine and I would be his.

Yes, I thought. *Yes.*

I couldn't imagine another fate.

If he accepted me with my black wings, then I accepted him. He considered Noir beneath him, vile creatures with sinful proclivities. Yet he still wanted me. How could I not want him in return? He was noble, a warrior, the epitome of good. I couldn't imagine a more suitable mate, our stations in life be damned.

"Yes," I breathed. "Yes."

Chapter Thirty

Layla

"Yes," I repeated for the third time, my back arching as Novak drew my clit into his mouth.

I looked down, noting the smile in his icy gaze.

He knew that response was for him, too. He wouldn't ask. He wouldn't take, either. He relied fully on the answers my body provided, his intuition uncanny and almost eerie. Yet so very right.

I slid my fingers into his hair, holding him to me as I enjoyed the pleasures of his tongue. *Yes, yes.* I would say it a thousand times. A million if they required it.

But the sound of a zipper told me it wasn't needed.

Auric removed his pants first, leaving him as naked and as vulnerable as me. Yet he didn't appear vulnerable at all, but powerful. Built. Strength personified. I pushed myself to my elbows, wanting to take him all in as he knelt beside me on the bed once more. So proud and beautiful, sculpted in every way, resembling a statue of perfection.

I leaned forward to take him into my mouth, his cock a picture of temptation I couldn't ignore. Balancing on one elbow, I angled to take him deeper while I wrapped my free palm around his base, noting his impressive size and virility.

"Now there's a beautiful sight," Novak said, approval

darkening his tone as he removed his tongue from my slick flesh.

"Trust me," Auric said, weaving his fingers through my hair to hold me to him. "It feels even better than it looks."

"I imagine it does," Novak replied, a zipping and rustling sound following his words. "Just as I imagine you intend to take her first."

"I do," Auric agreed, his voice strained as he fed even more of himself into my mouth, forcing me to take just another inch. I relaxed my throat, accepting him and watching his reaction with intrinsic fascination.

This was Auric coming undone. No more control. No more thinking. No more concerns. Just unadulterated decisions founded in pleasure and forbidden cravings.

I hollowed my cheeks, wanting to feel more of that power piston into my mouth, but he pulled away with a curse, his grip on my hair almost harsh. "No," he said. "Not yet."

I purred in response, the hum meant to be a demand for *more*. I wanted to taste him just as he'd tasted me. I wanted him inside me. To lick up his essence. Devour him like he'd done me. *My turn.*

"Patience, Lay."

I'd show him patience. My hand was still on his shaft, and I gave him a little pump, using the moisture I'd left on his head to smooth the motion down his length and back up again.

He growled.

I snarled.

And he yanked me up to my knees by my hair, forcing my mouth to meet his as he aligned my thighs. It happened so quickly that I was shocked my body knew how to obey, and then I was too distracted by his hardness against my abdomen to care. I wanted that inside me. I wanted him to—

Oh...

Novak's chest met my back, his presence a dark shadow to my senses, surrounding me in his smoky aura.

Both of them were naked now.

Both of them were hot.

Both of them were hard.

Both of them were going to fuck me.

I shivered with the knowledge, my legs going weak. Novak's hands on my hips held me in place while Auric's fingers in my hair angled my head to better receive his brutal kiss. It was almost violent, yet gentle. As though my warriors were trying to be tender, to cherish me and hold their harsher natures at bay.

That wasn't what I wanted.

I wanted them.

Their masculinity. Their ferocity. Their *souls*.

"Take me," I said, then bit down hard on Auric's lip. "*Now*."

Novak chuckled against my neck, then he sank his teeth into my skin, just like I'd done to Auric, only his bite pierced my skin. I flinched, then moaned as his tongue laved the open wound, tasting my blood.

Auric's chest rumbled in displeasure, whether at me or Novak, I couldn't say. But then he leaned down to add his tongue to the wound, his growl turning into a groan. "I want to mark you," he whispered darkly. "I *need* to mark you."

He didn't give me a choice, his lips already moving down to my breast. Novak's palm circled my throat as he pulled me back, forcing me to arch and present myself to Auric.

Then his teeth sank into my breast, drawing a gasp from my throat.

Novak's grasp slid upward to my chin, and he guided my lips back to his, kissing me soundly while Auric traced a seductive path to my nipple.

I grabbed his head, my opposite hand going to Novak's wrist where I'd left indentations from my nails. *A marking*, I realized. I'd marked them both in my own way. I intended to do it again now.

By biting Novak's lip just like I'd done to Auric.

Both men growled.

The energy heated between the three of us, boiling my blood and slickening my thighs. I purred in welcome. No. *Demand*. I ensured they knew I'd chosen them, that I would not allow any other outcome in this situation other than a full claiming.

Novak's arm slid around my waist, holding me upright as his other hand remained on my jaw, his mouth devouring mine. Then Auric moved away, making me whimper at the loss of his warmth. Only for Novak to guide me forward on my knees, straddling Auric's prone form.

Heavenly gates, I thought, my mind short-circuiting beneath the hunger mounting between us.

"He's ready," Novak whispered in my ear as he carefully tilted my face toward Auric. "Wrap your hand around his base and take him inside you."

Electricity zipped up my spine, my body convulsing both from his words and the sight of Auric sprawled out before me. His blue eyes practically glowed in the moonlight streaming in through the window, a beacon daring me to inch forward and accept Novak's demand.

All those muscles flexed as Auric shifted, his cock hard and proud and *mine*.

I stared at him, trying to decide if this was all still a dream or reality.

If I woke up tomorrow and found out this was all just a fantasy, I'd die. Because I couldn't imagine a life without this, without him, without *them*.

I had no idea who I was anymore. No clue how I'd found myself here, in this situation, trapped between two desirable men. But I thanked the fates for granting me their favor.

My palm went to Auric's abdomen, my legs straddling his thighs. Then I inched higher until my heat engulfed his hard length.

I shuddered, the perfection of that intimate kiss enough to almost throw me into another climax. *Almost*. I needed him inside me. To feel him. To ride him. To indulge our baser instincts and to make him mine.

I allowed him to see my intentions in my eyes.

He responded with a dare in his own.

This was my decision. My choice. My desire. He wouldn't force me. Instead, he would watch... and wait... and allow me to make that final move.

I lifted up just enough to reach between us, then I angled him upward and sank down on him without preamble, without drawing it out, and without any hesitation. His chest rumbled in approval as he sat up enough to wrap his palm around the back of my neck and pull me down to him.

His kiss invigorated me, forcing my hips into action as I accepted our mating with an eagerness unlike any I'd ever experienced.

No paramour could teach me this.

It was all instinctual. All natural. All *us*.

I rode him hard. I clawed at his chest. I screamed his name. And then I groaned as Novak fisted my strands and pulled me back to kiss him while I kept pace with Auric inside me. The latter cupped my breasts while the former held my hips, forcing me to take more.

Harder.

Faster.

Harsher.

It was hungry, intense, insanity.

Novak's hand slid to my lower belly, his thumb finding my clit and tipping me over into a cataclysmic orgasm that stole my ability to think and breathe.

Auric cursed, his body tensing beneath me as I forced him to follow me into an extraordinary oblivion. Novak released me, guiding me down to kiss Auric once more, our bond snapping into place and securing us together for eternity.

A beautiful union.

Fate bridging our souls.

Intensely exquisite pleasure.

"Auric," I breathed, my lips a caress against his, memorizing every aspect of the moment, cherishing the gift of his protection and devotion.

He kissed me soundly, returning the feelings with his tongue as he gently thrust in and out of me, prolonging our experience and reveling in our joining. Then his hands went to my hips, pulling me off him and angling me in offering to the male behind me.

He didn't intend—

Oh!

He did.

Oh gods, he *did* intend for Novak to take me like this, on top of Auric, entering me from behind and driving a scream from my throat. So deep and hard and fierce.

Novak was wider than Auric, his girth providing a different sort of sensation, making me feel even fuller, and a little bit pained. But it was exactly what I needed, my body accepting him with several internal clenches, desiring more... more... *more*.

I went to my hands and knees, only for my arms to buckle as Novak pushed me back down. "Kiss him," he demanded, his fingers in my hair guiding my mouth to the male below.

Auric's grip on my hips tightened as he held me for Novak's assault, his tongue doing wicked things to mine that had me panting between them. The experience was so profoundly intimate that I couldn't concentrate on anything other than the sensations.

Hot.

Sweaty.

Passionate.

Fucking.

A world of insanity with me as the star.

My body hummed with need, my core clenching, begging Novak to break me. To take me. To shatter me into a million pieces and glue me back together again.

Tears leaked from my eyes.

Cries escaped my mouth.

And still it wasn't enough.

Auric's mouth grew insistent against mine, his palms brands against my skin, his grip bruising and steady and so very right.

Novak's lips met the back of my neck, his teeth skimming my nape to the top of my spine. He reached around to squeeze my breasts and tease my nipples. Then one hand ventured lower to where our bodies joined. "Is this what you need, Layla?" he asked, taking my clit between his finger and thumb and pinching just enough to make me jolt.

Auric grinned against my mouth. "Are you going to come again?" he asked. "Are you going to scream?"

I whimpered, my body strung tight like a bow, the tension freezing me in place.

I no longer owned myself. They possessed me now. My mind, body, and spirit. I was theirs. A female claimed, my soul linking to theirs in a perpetual bond that only death could break.

And oh, I felt as though a part of me was dying.

Because I *needed* to breathe. Needed to pant. Needed to *explode*.

Auric's lips left mine, his mouth going to the wound Novak had left on my neck and biting down with a fierce growl that vibrated every inch of my being.

Novak twisted my clit at the same time, shooting me into the stars and blinding me entirely.

I shook.

I screamed.

I died.

Only to be brought back to life with a series of vibrations that heated every fiber of my being, paralyzing me in a state of perpetual bliss as Novak found his release inside me.

I trembled, the spasms unending, his fingers ruthless against my over-sensitized nub, drawing out my pleasure and forcing me to experience every last second of agonized bliss.

His name left my mouth on a plea. Or maybe it was a tone of gratitude. Auric's soon followed, my voice hoarse, my body used, my soul exhausted.

The life drained from my limbs, and they secured me between them, holding me and petting me and whispering sweet words of praise.

It all blended together into a dream.

One that took me under, surrounding me in the depths of the ocean, so shadowy and right.

I sighed.

Content.

Claimed.

Cherished.

And sated.

CHAPTER THIRTY-ONE

AURIC

I COMBED MY FINGERS THROUGH LAYLA'S HAIR, CAREFUL NOT to wake her as I gently untangled her strands. Novak watched, his eyes glimmering in the dark of the night. He faced Layla while I held her back to my front—a position we'd slept in several times now.

But tonight, we were naked.

Gloriously, stunningly naked.

I should hate myself for what I'd done, taking the mating bond with someone so superior to my ranking. However, my soul refused to allow me to feel any guilt.

She was mine.

Just as she should be.

Her bond to Novak should have bothered me as well, except it seemed rather appropriate given our history with each other.

He knew exactly what I liked, even a century after our last session with a woman. Perhaps because I hadn't necessarily changed. But it was definitely different with Layla. We'd cared for her in a way we never had for any other female. We held her now, ensuring she recovered from the intensity of our fucking.

And we hadn't even begun to demonstrate our strength or proclivities in the bedroom.

"You were right to ask about her experience," I said, pitching my voice low so as not to disturb her. "Too much too soon would hurt her."

He nodded, his fingers stroking her feathers, fixing those that had bent a little during sex. She hadn't seemed to notice, too lost to the sensations to realize the harshness of Novak's thrusts.

He didn't know how to be gentle.

And honestly, neither did I.

But we'd tried.

"She's bruised," Novak said, his voice gruff and holding a dark quality to it as he removed his hand from her wing to stroke her hip.

"She'll heal," I murmured, kissing her neck and inhaling deeply. "She did well."

"She did," he agreed.

I looked at him, noting the way his hungry eyes roamed over her curves and down to the luscious space between her thighs.

He wanted more.

I did, too.

However, his hunger seemed almost ravenous.

"When was the last time you experienced a woman's touch?" I wondered out loud, taking in the tension in his shoulders and abdomen. He was rock hard again, ready for another round. Not that I could harshly judge his reaction. Because I, too, was ready. As was evidenced by my arousal pressing into Layla's heart-shaped ass.

"Essexton," he said, his gaze capturing mine. "Barmaid."

My eyebrows rose. "Fuck off." I didn't mean that literally;

I was just shocked by the revelation. That had been... *shortly before his Fall.*

He gave me a look that said he'd heard that thought, even though I'd not voiced it out loud.

"Shit," I breathed. "And you've been stuck in this cell with temptation personified for..." Well, I wasn't sure how long. Several weeks? Regardless, that took a hell of a lot of discipline. And tonight, he'd been almost kind with her, always in control, managing the scene like he preferred to. "She's lucky you're a master of restraint."

This served as yet more proof that he was still the Novak I once knew.

The Noir we were taught to loathe wouldn't have given Layla space to consider an alternative. He would have taken her, forced her to her knees, and bonded her without any regard to her personal choice.

While I knew Novak had had every intention of claiming her, he'd never forced her. He'd given her time to think everything through. And had strategically moved her into the position he desired.

Through truth.

By listening.

And by telling—his statements always ones of purpose and value.

I shook my head, bemused and also not. This was Novak. And there was a reason I'd always enjoyed partnering with him.

Now it seemed we were mated for life.

"For what it's worth, I'm glad it's you," I admitted.

"Even though I'm a Noir?" he countered, a hint of sarcasm in his tone.

"Maybe because you are one," I replied, kissing Layla's neck again before settling my head on the pillow behind her. She had both her wings curled around her, as she seemed to like to do when she slept. I preferred to sprawl mine out along my back, same with Novak.

She released a sigh but otherwise didn't wake. Not that I expected her to. We had a glass of water waiting for whenever she did, aware that she would need to rehydrate. We'd also cleaned up the mess between her thighs.

Fortunately, she wouldn't be able to breed yet. That wouldn't happen for another four years or so.

A fact that made me frown as I glanced around our cell.

Would we still be here in four years? Or would we be somewhere else?

"Even if we escape," I said, thinking out loud, "I don't know where we would go."

Novak considered me for a moment, his fingers stroking Layla's wings again. "She can never go back. Not like this."

"I know," I agreed.

"And I don't believe she can change," he added, reaching out to stroke the edge of my wings by my shoulders.

I glanced backward, half expecting to find black feathers. But they were still white. Pristine and regal. A confirmation that claiming Layla hadn't been worthy of a Fall. But had her taking me as a mate ensured she forever remained a Noir?

I returned my gaze to Novak as he withdrew his touch, his palm going to Layla's cheek as he leaned forward to kiss her forehead. "I accept her this way." He gave me a challenging look. "Do you?"

"Yes." I wouldn't have mated her if I couldn't accept her potential fate as a permanent Noir.

"Good," he replied, a hint of possessive energy rolling off him.

No, not possessive. *Protective*. He didn't like the idea that

I might not accept her. And he had every reason to consider that a possibility. As did she.

"We need to start talking about how to survive as Noir," I said. "There are rogues. We should find them."

He looked at my wings again and cocked a brow, telling me without words that it wouldn't be easy to do that with a Nora Warrior in tow.

"I imagine that will be part of our discussion and plans," I added flatly. "Besides, if rule breaking is enough to Fall, then I should be turning into a Noir any day, right?"

He lifted a shoulder, neither agreeing nor disagreeing.

"You don't think I'll Fall?"

He met my gaze again, his expression calculating and serious. "I'm not sure," he said slowly. "I think there's a lot more to this game than any of us realize. And it's not something we're going to figure out tonight."

"But it is something we'll figure out together," I countered.

He said nothing for a long moment, his shrewd stare assessing. Then he ever so slowly dipped his chin in agreement.

"I mean it, Novak. We're mated now."

His lips curled as he gazed at Layla, his expression almost indulgent. "Yes. Yes, we are." He kissed her forehead again, then nuzzled her nose in a strangely endearing manner.

Novak never displayed feelings. He was a badass with a lethal shadow hanging over his every move. But when he looked at Layla, it was as if he were seeing the sun for the first time.

It wasn't love.

But it wasn't lust either.

It was something else entirely.

And it stirred a fuzzy feeling in my chest, one that almost made me smile. However, I pushed it away in the next moment and cleared my throat instead. "We should sleep." It was late, and who knew what tomorrow would bring?

Novak didn't reply, just continued to study Layla.

I left him to his admiration.

Good night, Lay, I thought to her, my arm firmly around her waist. *Sweet dreams.*

Two words I never should have allowed to grace my mind.

Because this prison didn't promote dreams. It delivered nightmares. And our new one was just beginning.

CHAPTER THIRTY-TWO

LAYLA

LANGUID.

Warm.

Bliss.

I never wanted to move. Didn't want to wake. Desired nothing more than to laze in the arms of my mates for the rest of my existence.

Unfortunately, the sun had other ideas. I could feel it bathing my feathers through the window, beckoning me to rise.

Not that I had anything to do today.

Except... maybe... my mates.

My lips curled. Now there was a good reason to rise.

I'm mated, I thought, almost giddy with the reminder. I probably should have feared the consequences of my decision. But I couldn't. It felt too right. They were mine.

Two dangerous, predatory angels with penchants for violence.

Mine.

I opened my eyes to find Novak watching me, his expression intent. No smile. No frown. Just... Novak.

Studying.

Thinking.

Scrutinizing his next move.

I wasn't naïve. I knew he'd navigated us all into this position. He knew just what to say and when to say it. It intrigued me. Floored me, even. And I was curious to see what he had in store for us next.

Auric stirred behind me, his body coming alive against mine. I resisted the urge to press back against his growing arousal, to tempt him into playing. I wanted him to initiate it, to ensure he held no regrets about our mating.

But a kiss to my neck told me he was content.

And a nibble to my ear suggested he wouldn't mind another round.

Novak's eyes danced with knowledge, his fingers reaching for me. Only, he suddenly pulled back to sit up straight, his posture rigid.

"What is it?" Auric demanded, following suit.

Then a low rumble shook the foundation of our room. I frowned, my brow coming down.

And in the next moment, Novak wrapped around me like a lethal shadow, covering me with his wings as a loud *boom* rocked the prison. The shock wave that followed had me jolting beneath him, my head slamming into his collarbone.

Ow!

Auric jumped off the bed in the next second. I screamed his name, but Novak shushed me.

"The hinges snapped," Auric said, his words muffled from Novak covering me.

"Can you open it?" Novak asked.

"Yeah," Auric replied, a creaking sound following. "Another culling?"

"Clyde?" Novak prompted, rolling off me just enough to look at the floor near the foot of the bed.

That must have been the cause of him sitting up a few moments ago. Or perhaps he'd heard something I hadn't.

The little Blaze crawled forward from beneath the table, squeaking.

Whatever the creature said seemed to relax Novak. He unfurled his wings, leaving me exposed as he gathered my pitiful blouse and shorts. "There's been a breach," he informed us, handing me the articles of clothing, seemingly unharmed from me slamming into him.

"Not surprising," Auric muttered. "This place is more like a hotel than a prison."

Novak grunted in agreement, his gaze sweeping over me as I slipped off the bed and dressed. "Can you walk?"

"I think so," I mumbled, rubbing my forehead and wincing when I found a tender bump.

"We'll have to run, not just walk," Auric said, blocking the doorway. His clothes rested behind him, but he didn't dare turn around. Every muscle tensed along his perfect body, ready to spring into action and defend. Bloodcurdling screams filtered into the room just seconds later, cascading goose bumps down my arms.

"Are you sure we can't just stay in here?" I asked as I wrapped my arms around myself. Running *toward* death and destruction just didn't sound like the best plan.

Auric took a daring step toward the exit, only to be sent stumbling back as a guard rushed into the room. "The inmates are attacking!" the Nora shrieked, his eyes wide with terror.

I nearly scoffed. *And we should care why?*

"Auric," he said, urgency in his tone. "There's something you have to know. The Reform—"

His words died as a blade exploded from his chest. It retracted a moment later, sending blood spurting all over

292

Auric as the guard fell into a heap on the floor. Gurgles sounded from his mouth, followed by a metallic stench that indicated imminent death.

An inmate stood in the doorway behind him, triumph tugging at his lips. The lighting gave the prisoner's eyes an eerie glow. His two orbs were as dark as midnight and speckled with silver stars, accompanied by an almost psychotic expression. He twirled a guard's weapon that now dripped with blood.

From the Nora on the floor.

And likely others.

I recognized him just as he spotted me, and my blood ran cold. A strap ran around the stump of his wrist, evidence of a missing hand.

Horus. The guy who tried to touch me in the yard. The same one who had tried to assault me outside the cafeteria.

He licked a strange splatter of silver mixed with blood from his lips, then grinned. "I thought I smelled ripe pussy," he mused as inmates ran through the hall behind him, their attention elsewhere. His gaze slid to Auric. "And you. Oh, my revenge will be so sweet." He hefted his sword, angling it at Auric's chest. "Maybe I should impale you with this before I put something else in your female here."

Auric's muscles coiled, but something kept him from striking. "What's wrong with your eyes?" he asked, his voice cold and deadly.

So it wasn't a trick of the light. The Noir really did appear mad.

Ignoring him, the Noir stepped inside, his nostrils flaring as his gaze snapped to the Nora on the ground. The guard's pristine white wings were disintegrating into ash.

I frowned at the sight. "What in the name of the—"

But my question was cut off as Horus lunged to the floor.

He clutched his weapon as he mauled the Nora's back, shoving the dust into his mouth like a rabid dog.

Novak raised an eyebrow.

I gagged, the stench of blood mixed something foul, invading our room.

What in the holy gates is going on?

"Something's wrong with him," Auric said, covering his nose as he stepped around the occupied Noir. "He's infected with... something." His gaze slid to me, full of concern. "We need to leave. It's best not to touch him."

I nodded, unable to speak past the lump in my throat.

Auric yanked on his pants and Novak followed suit, then they both pulled on their boots while I laced up my sandals.

"Watch," Novak said, nodding toward the dead Nora.

Auric frowned, then pulled out a blade as he bent to gently remove the item from the dead man's wrist and pocketed the watch. "Good call."

Horus didn't notice, too enthused by his, uh, meal.

Zombified angels, I thought, blinking in dismay. *How...? When...? How...?*

Chaos echoed down the halls, promising that more inmates would be on their way soon.

However, Novak had mentioned a breach. Perhaps they would run toward that? Or they'd all gone insane like Horus. In which case, we needed to use that breach more than anyone else.

Novak grasped my wrist, guiding me around the morbid display on the floor and out into the hall with Auric a step ahead, his white wings gleaming with purity.

Novak released me and pressed against the small of my back, gently propelling me before him as he guarded the rear.

We approached a massive hole through the rubble that

boasted a view of blue skies and evergreen trees. The edges smoldered with metallic debris sparking with magic and energy. Inmates flooded through the opening, escaping outside as the alarms blared.

The last of the inmates ahead of us filtered out into the yard, and another wave echoed from somewhere behind us.

"Hurry," Auric said as he took my hand and helped me step through the gaping hole. I picked my way carefully over the hot stones with my heels. I really envied Auric's and Novak's boots right about now.

A fresh breeze caught my wings as I squinted into the sunlight. The sirens reverberated through the clearing, sending the wildlife fluttering into the air. However, none of the inmates followed suit, including Raven and her mates, who had edged closer to us, their eyes on the others.

Why wasn't anyone trying to escape?

They all seemed to burn with manic rage instead, their bodies painted in blood and gore and *ash. Like the Nora in our room.*

I wanted to ask what it meant, but the macabre scene of the courtyard held me captive. The prisoners were going mad, slaughtering guards in some sort of bloodlust rage.

My nostrils flared as the sour scent of death hit me hard, a harsh contrast to my cocoon of evergreen, leather, and smoke.

"They're not leaving," Auric said, his eyes on the row of inmates forming a wall to block those trying to flee. "They're holding."

"No, they're claiming," Novak corrected, his gaze narrowing at the prisoners taking up ranks throughout the field.

Claiming? I repeated to myself, considering the crowd and tucking closer into Novak's side. "You mean they're taking control of the prison," I realized out loud as I took in the state of dismantling happening throughout the yard.

Dead guards.

Destroyed machine guns.

The strongest prisoners standing their ground, declaring victory over the smaller of inmates. It was a grotesque visual of dominance and war.

All brought on by an explosion.

That doesn't seem right. Something else had happened here. Someone had helped them. But who?

"All white-wings must bleed!" came the battle cry from behind us, followed by a roar of agreement.

Horus exited from the rubble, his pupils completely overtaking his irises.

My gaze slid to Auric, his badge of purity now a beacon that made us all a target.

Raven edged closer, glancing at me before speaking to Novak. "What now?"

"The portal," Novak said.

"If we can get to it," Auric muttered, his wings flaring as the Noir in the yard all seemed to face him, their eyes crazed with murder.

Horus barked orders to the two Noir I'd met outside the cafeteria that one day. Both of them were covered in ash, their dark eyes wild with stars.

As they growled, the stench in the air turned wrong, and other inmates followed suit.

"Slow and steady," Horus said, his lips curling into an evil grin. "Don't want to risk overdosing like that idiot." He gestured to a convulsing Noir on the ground, his lips pulling back into a sneer. "Greedy fool. I warned you not to take too much."

I glanced at Novak, but his calculating gaze was on

Horus and the others. His expression gave nothing away. Nor did it change as Auric backed closer to us.

"Don't let the ash touch you," Auric said, his voice low with deadly calm. "Don't breathe it in. And by all the gods, don't digest it." He glanced at Raven and then at Novak.

Wordless conversation flashed between the males, with Sorin and Zian focused primarily on Novak. The latter nodded as if agreeing with his unspoken decision.

Novak shoved Raven closer to me as he turned, facing the inmates from behind.

The command was clear.

Keep her safe.

I wasn't sure what he'd said to my Noir cousin to win her to my side, much less protect me, but she sniffed the air and crouched. "Stay close," she said, and I obeyed.

For now.

Even if Novak trusted her, I sure as hell didn't.

I saw how all the inmates looked at Auric, and we were terribly outnumbered. We couldn't afford any mistakes.

The hairs along the back of my neck stood on end as the wall of inmates started to move. All eyes were on Auric.

"If you're going to do something, cousin, you'd better do it now," Zian said as Sorin guarded the other side.

Novak grinned. "Is there a limit?"

Zian smiled. "No limit."

"Brilliant," Novak drawled, cracking his neck. "Let's play."

CHAPTER THIRTY-THREE

NOVAK

"Kill the Nora!" the one-handed Noir commanded as if this were his kingdom.

A misconception that needed to be remedied.

Auric just sighed, his blade ready in his hand. I hadn't even seen him sheathe it, but I wasn't surprised he'd grabbed it in the room. He rarely went anywhere without it.

A flood of inmates ran toward him, and I yawned. This wouldn't last long. Auric knew how to dole out death and proceeded to show me how his skills had improved over the years.

He had always been a force to be reckoned with. But now? Yeah, he practically flew as he cut each offender down before they could so much as touch him. And yet, his feet never actually left the ground.

I nodded. *Not bad.*

Then another swarm of inmates joined the fray, their rage palpable and underlined with a savagery that called to my inner beast.

That's my cue, I thought, grinning as I flared my wings and launched myself into the wall of bodies.

Let.

I twisted the neck of a Noir.

The.

I grabbed a knife from his belt.

Games.

And rammed it through the heart of another Noir.

Begin.

I reveled in the sensation of death, blurring through bodies as I used the edges of my wings to slice off their heads, my feathers sharpened into a razor's edge when I entered this state. Even with their strange ash enhancements, they didn't stand a chance against me.

This was my power—the reason others knew to bow before me.

Because I didn't need a weapon. I *was* a weapon.

I resembled the God of Death and War. If such a being existed. I didn't allow this side of myself to show often, but clearly, someone needed a reminder on why the Noir considered me a king.

Blood sprayed through the air, coating me with red as I glanced back to check on Layla. The female was growing on me, and we were nowhere near done. If ever, really. As I intended to keep her. And if anyone harmed her, I'd wear their entrails as a necklace.

She didn't cower behind Raven, not that I'd expected her to. While her fight training didn't rival mine or Auric's, she definitely wasn't lacking. She knew how to move and how to protect herself. Something she proved now by snatching up a fallen Nora's blade and slicing it through the air to expertly open the vein of her nearest opponent.

Beautiful, I thought, pleased. *And now I want to fuck again.*

Just as soon as I took care of the crowd around me.

I started counting each slice of my razor-tipped wings.

Six.

Eight.

Twelve.

"Enough!" the one-handed Noir shouted, his tone edged with madness and irritation, as if my killing spree was merely an inconvenience. "Capture the females!"

My eyes widened. While I'd been leaving a trail of carnage, I'd moved farther away from Layla. She held her own, just as Auric did, but a new wave of inmates had somehow separated them, shoving Auric out of range and leaving her unprotected.

Auric killed one after another, the bodies piling up all around him, but the rush from inside kept coming.

Where the hell are all these inmates coming from? I wondered. *A portal?*

Was this all meant to be a test of fate from Sayir himself? A way to make us battle all the damn Noir in existence?

And he'd hyped them up on some sort of strength-enhancing drug as well.

"Layla, move!" Auric shouted, his gaze flicking up before a group of Noir crashed into him, sending him tumbling to the ground in a tangle of ebony and porcelain feathers.

I saw it too late, a series of nets hoisted by Noir with black eyes that sparkled with silver. They dropped, trapping Layla in one contraption and Raven in another.

I ran, only to slam straight into the one-handed Noir.

What the...? How did he move that fast?

"No!" Zian shouted as a hungry group of inmates separated him from his mate, one team dragging Raven toward the mountains and the other carrying Layla toward the tree line.

I made to move after her, only to meet the massive elbow of the one-handed Noir. It stopped me dead in my tracks, his body a mass of muscle that shouldn't exist.

"Fuck!" Sorin took off running after Raven, leaving Layla to her fate.

I met Zian's gaze, begging him to help Layla, reminding him that Raven was a warrior more than capable of taking care of herself. She also already had Sorin running after her.

I tried to shove the giant away from me once more, only for him to push me backward with far more strength than one should possess. I stumbled, my eyes widening as Zian took off toward Raven.

That left Layla completely unprotected.

Unacceptable.

A growl rumbled in my throat, words almost leaving my lips, except a searing pain smarted across my jaw.

Fuck. I blinked, my eyes momentarily blackened from the agony of being clocked in the jaw by the hilt of his dagger. *What kind of drug is this guy on? The ash?*

"Kill the Nora!" my attacker shouted, throwing up his good hand with his bloodied blade. The strike could have decapitated me had his aim been any better. "I'll take care of this one."

I scoffed and swiped the blood from my jaw. I'd take care of this asshole, then protect Layla. He moved too clumsily with his blade to be a seasoned warrior, staggering on one leg as if off-balance when he lunged for me.

Easy.

I shifted with the air currents, going with the flow instead of against it. Then I ducked low to the ground, wishing I had remembered my stolen blade, but my wings would do.

I sliced, expecting him to fall in a heap of gore at my feet. Instead, my wings hit resistance, bouncing off of the Noir as he staggered from the blow.

How—

He launched himself at me, using all of his weight to throw me to the ground.

Fucking hell.

Layla screamed, causing me to twist under the crushing weight of the Noir pinning me down, only to see her tangled in the net as she struggled, her wings suffocated by the harsh wires. The Noir swarmed around her, taunting but not attacking. Her scream had been one of rage, not pain.

For now.

I shoved—hard—but the Noir didn't budge. He was like a fucking boulder.

"Don't you see? I'm not like these other idiots who've just tasted the ash of death." He leaned in, crushing his arm across my throat. "I've been feasting for weeks, which puts me at the top of the food chain. And you're just a snack to me. I'm stronger than you, Novak."

Who the fuck is this guy? Clearly, he knew me, but I didn't know him.

Wait, no. That wasn't quite true.

He'd lost his hand to Auric's blade.

And my little cherry had handed him his ass outside the cafeteria the next day.

Rather than speak, I smirked, somehow knowing it would irritate him. Except I really wanted to know what he meant about the ash of death. Did he mean the guard's wings? Because that was an interesting development.

What made them dissolve to ash?

The Noir ran his blade across my arm, a taunting motion that had me hissing in response.

"Where's the notorious beast now?" he asked, flashing me a bloodied grin. Silver dripped from his mouth, and I turned away, not wanting that shit anywhere near me.

Auric came into view, his naked chest heaving as he

swung his blade to add to his impressive kill count. But the inmates just kept coming. And I had no idea from where. It had to be a portal inside, which meant the Reformer had set all this up.

Sick fuck.

The idiot on top of me guffawed, claiming an early victory, his mind clearly garbage.

Had all these Noir forgotten who was in charge?

I almost sighed.

Boulder or not, this idiot would die.

And the rest of his buddies would fall in line.

Because the Reformer clearly wanted us to play this game. And I refused to lose.

The one-handed Noir tossed his blade to the ground— an arrogant move, but one I quickly learned was practical as he wrapped his fingers around my throat and squeezed.

I clawed at his wrists, my wings flaring upward in an attempt to slice him. But I was useless on my back. *Fucking rock,* I thought, furious at the idiot on top of me.

Only, he jolted in the next breath as Auric's blade landed between his shoulders at his back. A move that allowed me to shove the boulder off of me but left the commander defenseless. He resorted to throwing punches and kicks, moving lightning-fast, but the others had weapons.

I jumped to my feet, slicing my wing across the one-handed Noir's throat, then went after those attacking Auric. He knew when to duck and when to jump, having fought at my back for so many years. A century meant nothing. Our bodies would always know the other, and now that we were bonded to Layla, we were somehow even more in tune with one another.

A yelp dismantled my focus. My legs froze as my head swung toward the tree line to where Layla crumpled to the ground. The net was in shreds beside her. But that wasn't what stopped my heart.

She was holding her wing.

A wing that was twisted the wrong way.

Broken.

Someone had broken one of her wings.

Someone who was about to die.

Someone who would meet my *blades*.

Thunder rolled through my soul at the visual, ripping out of me with a guttural roar that turned my vision red.

I sprinted forward, grabbing the Noir beside her with both of my hands and squeezing his neck until it snapped beneath my hands. Then I sliced the other two beside him in half, their blood my trophy and reward.

Two more stepped forward, words on their lips that I never allowed to pass, their heads severed in an instant, and I turned to face the rest.

They will all die.

I embraced the darkness and rage as it consumed me from the inside out. Icy heat poured from me, running down my legs and entering the ground below with each step.

This.

I sliced through a Noir.

Is.

I stabbed another.

My.

I returned to the one-handed Noir.

Playground.

And severed his head with a brutal swipe of my wing.

Who else? I demanded with my eyes, spinning to face the few that remained. *Who else wants to dance?*

Shadows formed all around me, my wings spreading into their lethal form, and darkness eclipsed the sun.

Perhaps it was fate.

Perhaps it was the gods showing their favor.

But I stood in the center of the bloodbath, a child of the night, surveying the field and awaiting my next contender.

Silence.

Everyone bowed.

Even the lunatics high on the ashes.

Because no one wanted to fight.

Good. I looked at Layla, noted her wilted form, and stalked toward my desired queen. Auric joined me, his white feathers saturated in blood. And we stood before those who were left, daring them to tempt fate.

They didn't.

They kneeled and prayed.

The game was finished.

And the king had claimed the board.

CHAPTER THIRTY-FOUR

AURIC

"Jerin isn't among the dead." One of the many items that bothered me about this situation. "I also can't find a single portal." I held up the watch. "Either this calls for specific requirements to gain access or it's a dud." I tossed the item to Novak for his review.

He turned it around in his hand, his gaze assessing. Then, with a shake of his head, he dropped it and smashed it with his boot.

I arched a brow. "Do you think it was a plant? Like a listening device or some sort of tracker?"

He lifted a shoulder, which I took to mean, *Not taking any chances.*

Layla winced in my peripheral vision, her mangled feathers slowly healing with Raven's help. She'd used a blade to escape the netting, and one of the Noir guarding her had rewarded her by breaking her wing.

The image had me clenching my jaw all over again, my desire to murder her offender riding me hard. But Novak had already taken care of him.

Fuck, Novak had taken care of almost everyone.

It'd been a lethal dance unlike any I'd ever seen from him before. And I'd seen him fight. He'd always been a force of nature. But this was something else. He'd moved so fast that I almost hadn't been able to track his movements. Like some sort of warrior god.

Then the heavens had eclipsed the sun, only for a few minutes, to express their approval.

Or maybe this realm just did that.

But I felt the energy in the air, the kiss of power radiating off his soul.

Something had happened. Something otherworldly.

He hadn't commented on it. Maybe it'd felt normal to him.

"*Fuzz*," Layla said, cringing as Raven fixed the worst of the break.

"Fuzz?" I repeated. "Really?"

She flashed me a fiery look. "*Yes*," she hissed. "Fuzz."

My lips twitched, and I ran the back of my knuckles over her cheek. "After you're done, I'll bathe you," I promised.

Her gaze went to my blood-soaked wings and then to Novak's feathers. "Maybe you should start with yourselves."

"You just want to see me suck him off again," Novak replied, causing Raven to gasp. Although, I suspected it wasn't the crude statement that elicited her surprise so much as him speaking so casually.

"Are you offering?" I asked him. Because I could absolutely go for that right about now. I had a whole lot of pent-up rage that could use the release. And he likely did, too.

His gaze sparkled, and Layla's cheek warmed beneath my touch. I bent to brush my lips against her temple.

"Look what you've started, Princess." For once, I used the title as an endearment, not a chastisement. It felt good rolling off my lips. Her expression told me she liked it, too.

"The mountain range goes on for miles and miles," Zian

announced as he returned with Sorin. Novak had sent them off on a scouting mission from the sky. I suspected it had something to do with his disappointment in them leaving Layla undefended. But I couldn't blame them for that choice. Raven was their mate. Layla was ours to protect.

"No ocean," Zian continued. "No sign of civilization apart from a few random human huts. I'm pretty sure we're in Asia, but I don't know what mountain range or country."

"We're definitely in the human realm?" Layla asked, her voice a low whisper.

"Definitely," Sorin confirmed. "With absolutely no way out of it unless you figured out the portals."

I shook my head. "The one I saw the other day is no longer there, and whatever they were using from inside the prison to ferry in more Noir is gone as well." Because that part had been obvious.

We'd faced far more Noir than were kept in this reformatory. Some of the inmates were still piling bodies out in the field—another job Novak had assigned. It seemed his little lethal dance had crowned him king.

I didn't argue.

But I would never bow, and he knew it.

He had about two dozen inmates who now worshipped the ground he walked on. That would have to be enough.

"So what do we do now?" Raven asked as she took her hand away from Layla's wing. The dark-haired female hadn't been injured at all during the fight, but she certainly looked a bit haggard now after healing her cousin. Which meant Layla had been in a lot more pain than she'd let on.

I kissed the top of her head, my way of showing respect for her courage. She possessed a warrior's heart beneath all that fancy exterior. "You fought well today," I whispered to her as the others started talking about next steps around us. "I'm sorry about your wing."

She extended it slowly, then drew it back in. "I'm okay."

"I know," I said, holding out my hand to help her stand. "But I mean it, Lay. You fought well."

"You sound surprised."

"I am," I admitted. "The last time we sparred, you kept tripping over your feet."

"I was still training then," she returned, her eyes narrowing. "I've learned a lot in the last few years."

"Clearly." I drew my thumb along her jaw. "But there's more I can teach you." I allowed her to hear the double meaning in my words. *In the arena and in the bedroom.*

She shivered. "I would like that."

"I know," I said, grinning. "I suspect we're just getting started."

She reached out to stroke a cleaner section of my wings, her gaze darkening. "It's not going to be an easy path."

I glanced at my white feathers, then back at her. "We'll find a way forward, Layla."

"Doing what?" she asked, her brow furrowing. "Fighting for eternity?" She shook her head. "I don't want to kill or hurt others. I want to live. I want to be free. I want to... to *lead*." A fierce quality entered her gaze. "What's happening here is wrong. Those Noir were zombified by some sort of drug, turning them into violent monsters. And those wings... how did they turn to ash?"

"I don't know," I admitted. "But I intend to find out."

"How?" she asked incredulously.

"By taking it one day, or hour, at a time." I tucked a stray strand of hair behind her ear. "There are answers somewhere, Lay. Likely with the Reformer."

"So we need to find him," she said.

"I think he'll come to us," Novak interjected, having joined our conversation. "This was a game. He's not done yet."

On that, we agreed. "He'll be back."

"We should prepare a welcome party," Zian suggested, a smile in his voice.

"Or we should use this opportunity to run," Sorin muttered.

"And go where?" Zian replied. "We're in the middle of the human world, with no portals, black wings—except for Auric—and nowhere to hide."

Sorin folded his arms, the scratches up his left side suggesting he'd suffered a bit of a scuffle with one of the insane inmates. Probably when he went after Raven. "We won't know that until we try it."

"We should prepare for both," Raven said, moving to stand between Sorin and Zian. "Scout potential escape routes and expect the Reformer to return."

Novak shook his head. "This is about survival." He cocked his chin at the tree line, the mountains, and then the hole blown into the side of the prison. "A test."

"You think he's going to send us more cracked-out Noir to fight?" Sorin asked, arching a white brow.

But Raven answered before Novak could. "It's another kind of labyrinth." She looked around. "A maze to escape the mountain range."

"We can just fly over it," Zian pointed out.

Raven looked at him. "But not for hundreds of miles. We have to stop to rest, right?"

"And you think he's managed to arrange traps at every potential stop?" He sounded incredulous, and I rather agreed with that assessment.

Then Novak said, "Trackers."

I stared at him. "You think he can track us?" Then I recalled the ease with which he'd knocked everyone out in the yard of the former prison and frowned. "That's... a reasonable guess."

Novak grunted as though to say, *It's more than reasonable. It's true.*

And I supposed as someone who had been in the system as long as he had, he would know.

Which meant it might not have been an enchantment that had knocked them all out that day, but some sort of technology.

"We need a scanner," I said, palming the back of my neck. "Something to see if he's tagged us." I was fairly certain he hadn't tagged me, as I'd been aware and awake for most of my time here, but there were moments of sleep. So it was possible he'd managed to insert something into me. Maybe even via the food.

My lips twisted at the notion of such a breach in my privacy.

But given what I'd observed, I wouldn't put it past the Reformer to do such a thing.

Someone cleared their throat, causing me to glance around the group, waiting for that person to speak. But the sound came from behind me.

I turned to find an inmate shuffling on his feet. "Yes?" Hostility dripped from that single word. These savages had tried to kill me. I didn't take kindly to that.

Well, perhaps not all of them.

Novak had found a group huddled inside the prison, hiding from the chaos outside.

And this male had been part of that section.

So I lessened my stance but folded my arms to display my impatience.

"I-I was asked to g-give you this," the male stammered. He held out a small package, the bow on top a delicate ribbon of black and white.

I didn't accept the package. "From who?"

"The Re-Reformer." He swallowed, his blue eyes wide and fearful.

Not very Noir-like.

Not very warrior-like either.

"What class were you from when you Fell?" I wondered out loud. "Servant class?"

He gulped. "N-no. No class."

"No class?" I repeated. "You were never part of Nora society?"

He shook his head, then nodded, then shook his head again.

"It's a yes-or-no question," I said, my patience thinning.

"I was born... here."

"Here, as in this prison, or the human world?"

"Human world," he replied. "Among the Noir."

My eyebrows lifted. "Among the Noir?" Apparently, I'd turned into some sort of echo where all I could do was repeat words.

"There are Noir in the human world?" Layla asked, coming to my aid as she pressed her hand to my arm.

"Yes," the male said, his gaze lowering in reverence.

I shared a look with Novak, but he was more interested in the newcomer. "You never Fell." Not a question, but a statement.

Still, the newcomer replied, "No. I was born this way." He held out the package again.

This time I took it, more out of curiosity than anything. "Don't go anywhere," I said to the male, a dozen or more questions lining up on my tongue, all of them meant for him.

However, I focused on the ribbon first.It could be a bomb, but something told me that wasn't Sayir's style. So I ripped off the lacy exterior and opened the lid to find a note and a phone.

FELICITATIONS, AURIC. I'M SURE LAYLA'S PARENTS WILL BE THRILLED WITH THE NEWS OF YOUR MATING.
— SAYIR

I READ the note twice before I showed Novak and Layla.

"Oh," Layla whispered. "Oh, that's... this isn't... oh."

An inarticulate response, but I understood.

Her father would not be pleased. In fact, he might even send someone here to kill us all, thereby breaking the bonds to his daughter. It was the only way to free her from our mating.

My jaw ticked at the prospect.

Then the phone began to ring.

That action confirmed two things. First, Sayir was watching us from somewhere. And second, this phone had never been meant for me to use to call Sefid. Not that I ever believed it would be for that purpose. No, this was just a taunt.

I put the Reformer on speakerphone, saying, "Hello, Sayir."

"Ah, you are smarter than you look," he replied, his voice a low drawl. "I sent you a gift. I suggest you use it wisely."

I looked at the Noir before us, guessing that he was the

intended *gift*, not the phone in my hand. The mobile would probably self-destruct once Sayir hung up.

"A learning exercise?" I wondered out loud.

"And here I thought Novak was the master of strategy." Sayir sounded amused. No. *Triumphant.* "Enjoy the accommodations. I'll be in touch soon."

The call went dead and a beep began, counting the seconds.

I tossed the mobile into the pile of dead Noir, and not half a minute later, the thing sizzled into ash.

"Interesting technology," Zian said, staring at the phone.

"I expected it to explode," I admitted.

"But instead, it dissolved like those Nora wings," he replied, walking over to crouch beside the remains. He didn't touch anything, just observed and then stood. "What's the learning exercise you mentioned?"

I gestured to the shivering Noir before me. "Him. He has answers we need."

Zian looked him over. "Well, that shouldn't be too hard to extract."

The Noir's eyes widened, his palms going up in front of him. "I-I won't fight. I... I'll tell you whatever you want."

Layla stepped forward, her hand leaving my arm to lightly touch the other man's shoulder. "We're not going to hurt you."

"We're not?" Sorin asked, sounding dubious.

"No. We're not," she said more sternly. "He wasn't among those who attacked Auric, and I have a lot of questions. Starting with the Noir in the human world. Ending with how he arrived here."

"Or we could start with his name," Raven suggested.

"Well, that might be useful, too," Layla agreed, the two females apparently taking over. "What's your name?" Her gentle voice went straight to my gut, that tone one I hadn't heard her use in years. It held a touch of innocence and kindness, two aspects of her nature that had drowned under recent events. But seeing them now, I realized they still very much existed.

"Kyril, Your Highness," he said, not meeting her gaze and continuing to bestow upon her the reverence due of her station.

I glanced at Novak again. *This guy might be allowed to live*, I told him with my eyes.

Novak dipped his chin in acknowledgment.

"Kyril," she replied. "I'm Layla."

"I know," he whispered, his long blond hair falling forward to cover more of his cheekbones. "You're why I'm here."

"I am?" she asked, blinking. "Because the Reformer sent you?" A reasonable guess, considering Sayir had referred to the man as a gift.

He shook his head. "No. Not Sayir. Your parents."

Her eyes widened. "To help with my reform?"

Novak and I shared yet another look. Why would her father send a Noir from the human world to help with her reform? And further, *how* did he think this would help?

Kyril frowned. "Your reform, Your Highness?"

"Yes, did my father send you here to help with my reform?"

The male's brow furrowed even more. "No. No, he sent me here to help you find him when you're ready."

Now all of us blinked at the male.

"Find him?" Layla repeated. "I... I don't understand. Is he hiding?"

"Of course," Kyril replied. "He's been hiding since the plague. But he's almost ready to rise again."

"Plague?" Layla repeated, looking at us all for answers we didn't have. "I don't... I don't understand. What plague? Is it recent? Is my father okay?" She started to panic as her words continued. "What's happened? What plague?" She looked at me. "Is that why he's not come for me here? Is he ill?"

"The Stygian Plague, Your Highness," the male said, his unease apparent. "And he sent me here to help you find him."

"I don't... I don't understand." She released the male, her gaze radiating confusion as she glanced from me to Novak.

But Novak appeared to be considering the male's words, his gaze flashing with some sort of understanding. "Who's her father?"

"King Vasilios, of course," the male replied. "The last of the Noir dynasty." He finally looked at Layla, his expression one of pride. "Princess, I'm here to guide you home. To His Majesty and the queen. To your parents."

Silence followed that announcement. Sayir's note glared up at me from the box in my hand.

I'm sure Layla's parents will be thrilled...

Not her father.

But her *parents*.

Holy... Gates...

Was it true? Or was this just another game? A test? A trick of reformation?

The last of the Noir dynasty.

Layla's parents.

A plague.

Rogue Noir in the human world.

None of it made any sense. And yet, it did to an extent.

The watch on the ground near Novak's foot suddenly

beeped to life, the thing clearly not broken despite his hefty stomp.

An image floated out of it, one resembling a paper with script.

WELCOME TO THE FUTURE, PRINCESS LAYLA.
WHICH CROWN WILL YOU CHOOSE?
—SAYIR

The Story Continues with *Noir Reformatory: Second Offense...*

.

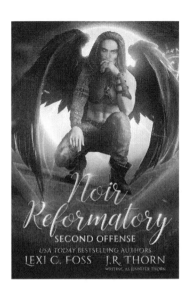

Bow or bleed.
A decision all Noir angels must make.
Because I'm their king.

It wasn't my choice. I assumed the position after the
prisoners of this nightmare reformatory went after my
mates.

Auric is my commander, even if I'm the one giving the
orders. He worships the dukedom and the princess, our
soon-to-be queen.

Layla is my crown, my purpose, the sheer essence of life.
She's the key.

The key to unlocking the darkness in my soul. There is no
reform. No restitution. Only retaliation and fear.

I'll decorate my throne with the broken wings of my enemies. Their blood will run like a river, a red carpet at my feet.

The games have just begun. The players have been cast.

And in this world of darkness and sin, all will bow to their king.

Note: Noir Reformatory is a dark fantasy ménage romance spanning six novels. There will be cliffhangers, adult situations, violence, and MM/MF/MMF content.

Curious about how Raven met Sorin and Zian? Find out in the standalone prequel, Noir Reformatory: The Beginning

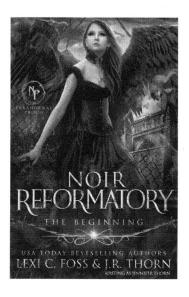

Trapped in a world of sin and sexy alpha angels.
Forever defined by my black wings.

My father, King of the Nora, sent me to Noir Reformatory to atone for crimes I didn't commit.

So what's a girl to do? Escape, obviously.

Except I need allies to accomplish that feat and no one wants anything to do with King Sefid's daughter. If anything, my claim to the throne has only made running that much harder, and worse, I'm stuck with two hot angels standing in my way.

Auric is my supposed guardian, his white wings marking him as my superior in this deadly playground. Only, I'm his princess and I refuse to bow to a warrior like him.

And Novak, the notorious *Prison King*, is hell-bent on teaching me my place. Which he seems to think is beneath him. In his bed.

This prison resembles a training camp for soldiers more than a reformatory for the Fallen. I suspect something nefarious is at play here, but of course no one believes me. I'm the guilty princess with black wings. Well, I'll prove them all wrong. I just hope it isn't too late.

My Name is Princess Layla.
I'm innocent.
And I do not accept this fate.

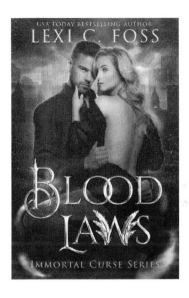

In a world where vampires and angels live in secret, one woman is prophesied to destroy them all.

Astasiya Davenport knows she's different. It's hard to miss her peculiar skillset when she can persuade everyone around her to do whatever she wants just by uttering a few words. But she's never understood where the ability came from.

Until she met him. Issac Wakefield. Billionaire extraordinaire. Vampire. A dark knight who should kill her, but offers her a deal instead.

He's full of secrets and answers and the truth about her past.

But she'll have to betray everyone she knows in order to make him talk.

A lethal game begins.
Loyalties are tested.
And a forbidden love threatens to shatter them all.

An immortal war is coming. What side will you choose?

Start the internationally bestselling series today with Blood Laws, an award winning novel guaranteed to leave you on the edge of your seat.

Author's Note: This is a series and there will be cliffhangers.

Xander

I'm used to getting anything I want.

Power. Fame. Women.

It's all mine, but boredom has set in after five hundred years as the Fae King and ruling mankind.

She's the only thing that excites me.

She's forbidden, but that won't stop me from making her mine.

Gabriella

I've trained all my life for this moment.

My ascension—to gain my wings and join the Celestial Royals.

Only, the Fae King had other plans. He ruined everything when he crashed the party and kidnapped me.

He thinks this is all a game. My life. My purity. My purpose. I have to escape him or everyone I love will die. For if I don't ascend, the world will fall into chaos, and sin will reign on earth.

Knowing the Fae King, that was his plan all along.

Captured by the Fae King is Book 1 in a new Paranormal Romance Series. This book contains sexual situations, dub-con, strong language, and violence.

USA Today Bestselling Author Lexi C. Foss loves to play in dark worlds, especially the ones that bite. She lives in Atlanta, Georgia with her husband and their furry children. When not writing, she's busy crossing items off her travel bucket list, or chasing eclipses around the globe. She's quirky, consumes way too much coffee, and loves to swim.

Want access to the most up-to-date information for all of Lexi's books? Sign-up for her newsletter here.

Lexi also likes to hang out with readers on Facebook in her exclusive readers group - Join Here.

Where To Find Lexi:
www.LexiCFoss.com

ALSO BY LEXI C. FOSS

Blood Alliance Series - Dystopian Paranormal

Chastely Bitten

Royally Bitten

Regally Bitten

Rebel Bitten

Kingly Bitten

Dark Provenance Series - Paranormal Romance

Heiress of Bael (FREE!)

Daughter of Death

Son of Chaos

Paramour of Sin

Elemental Fae Academy - Reverse Harem

Book One

Book Two

Book Three

Elemental Fae Holiday

Winter Fae Holiday

Immortal Curse Series - Paranormal Romance

Book One: Blood Laws

Book Two: Forbidden Bonds

Book Three: Blood Heart

Book Four: Blood Bonds

Book Five: Angel Bonds

Book Six: Blood Seeker

Book Seven: Wicked Bonds

Immortal Curse World - Short Stories & Bonus Fun

Elder Bonds

Blood Burden

Mershano Empire Series - Contemporary Romance

Book One: The Prince's Game

Book Two: The Charmer's Gambit

Book Three: The Rebel's Redemption

Midnight Fae Academy - Reverse Harem

Ella's Masquerade

Book One

Book Two

Book Three

Book Four

Noir Reformatory - Ménage Paranormal Romance

The Beginning

First Offense

Second Offense

Royal Fae Wars - Omegaverse Paranormal

Wicked Games

Underworld Royals Series - Dark Paranormal Romance

Happily Ever Crowned

Happily Ever Bitten

X-Clan Series - Dystopian Paranormal

Andorra Sector

X-Clan: The Experiment

Winter's Arrow

Bariloche Sector

Other Books

Scarlet Mark - Standalone Romantic Suspense

About J.R. Thorn

J.R. Thorn is a Reverse Harem Paranormal Romance Author.

Subscribe to the J.R. Thorn Mailing List to be Notified of New Releases and Deals!

Addicted to Academy? Read more RH Academy by J.R. Thorn: Fortune Academy

Welcome to Fortune Academy, a school where supernaturals can feel at home—except, I have no idea what the hell I am.

ALSO BY J.R. THORN

All Books are Standalone Series listed by their sequential order of events

Elemental Fae Universe Reading List

Elemental Fae Academy: Books 1-3 (Co-Authored)

Midnight Fae Academy (Lexi C. Foss)

Fortune Fae Academy (J.R. Thorn)

Fortune Fae M/M Steamy Episodes (J.R. Thorn)

Blood Stone Series Universe Reading List

Seven Sins: The Blood Stone Series

- *Book 1: Succubus Sins*

- *Book 2: Siren Sins*

- *Book 3: Vampire Sins*

The Vampire Curse: Royal Covens

- *Book 1: Captivated*

- *Book 2: Compelled*

- *Book 3: Consumed*

Fortune Academy (Part I)

- *Year One*

- *Year Two*
- *Year Three*

Fortune Academy Underworld (Part II)

- *Episode 1: Burn in Hell*
- *Book Four*
- *Book Five (Coming Soon)*
- *Book Six (Coming Soon)*

Non-RH Books (J.R. Thorn writing as Jennifer Thorn)

Noir Reformatory Universe Reading List

Noir Reformatory: The Beginning

Noir Reformatory: First Offense

Noir Reformatory: Second Offense

Sins of the Fae King Universe Reading List

Captured by the Fae King

Learn More at www.AuthorJRThorn.com

Printed in Great Britain
by Amazon